RE-LAUNCH

Science Fiction Stories of New Beginnings

**Edited
by
Kelly A. Harmon and
Vonnie Winslow Crist**

Pole to Pole Publishing
Baltimore

Re-Launch:
Science Fiction Stories of New Beginnings
Copyright © 2018 Pole to Pole Publishing

Published by Pole to Pole Publishing
Edited by Kelly A. Harmon and
Vonnie Winslow Crist

Cover layout copyright © 2018 Pole to Pole Publishing
www.poletopolepublishing.com
Cover Artwork Copyright © Mariusz Patrzyk
Licensed via DepostPhotos.com.

ISBN-10: 1-941559-25-5
ISBN-13: 978-1-941559-25-3

Symphony © 1999 Douglas Smith, first published in Prairie Fire magazine.
The Game © 2007 James Dorr, first published in HUB Magazine.
Ice Dogs © 2015 Kris Austen Radcliffe, first published in *Fiction River Valor*.
Shipwreck in the Sky @1954 Eando Binder, first published in Fantastic Universe Magazine.
Juliet Silver and the Seeker of the Depths © 2017 Wendy Nikel, first published in *Young Explorer's Adventure Guide*.
Behind the First Years © 2013 Stewart C. Baker, first published in Cosmos Online, May 2013.
Speedeth All © 2017 Meriah Crawford, first published in *Love, Murder, & Mayhem*.
George the Second © 2015 Gregory L. Norris, first published in the Sci Phi Journal, June 2015.
The Night of Stars © 2010 Jennifer Rachel Baumer, first published in Aoiffe's Kiss Magazine, June 2010.
Perfect Memory © 2014 Jonathan Shipley, first published in *Trust and Treachery*.
Tower Farm © 2013 Vonnie Winslow Crist, first published in *Dogs of War – Defending the Future*.
A Soul to the Stars © 2007 Lawrence Dagstine, first published in *Nova Sci Fi*.
Off Day © 2013 CB Droege, first published at TGDaily.com.
Weapons of Mass Destruction © 2007 Jude-Marie Green, first published in *Desolate Places*.
Target Practice © 1999 Steven R. Southard, first published in *Lower Than Angels*.
Lunar Epithalamion © 2014 Calie Voorhis, first published in *Trust and Treachery*.
Chasing Satellites © 2013 Anthony Cardno, first published in *Beyond the Sun*.
The Firebird © 2005 Andrew Gudgel, first published in *Writers of the Future*, Volume 21.

Library of Congress Control Number: 2016954053

RE-LAUNCH

Science Fiction Stories of New Beginnings

Beginnings are always messy.

~ John Galsworthy

Table of Contents

Perfect Memory
Jonathan Shipley

A *sudden beep in the monotonous sensor readings gave only* a moment's notice, then the shuttle was out of the Umbra. Anton gave a nod. The Umbra had seemed interminable. The lack of available jump points beyond it necessitated experiencing it at speeds reduced to light-years, not light-decades, and a Shuttle of State, for all its power, was small. The three weeks of the Umbra had been like living in a box.

A few stars winked ahead, not more than three dozen all told. The preponderance of void was telling—this was not just the edge of the sector, but the edge of the galaxy as well. He checked the radiation levels. Solar was low, but the ambient level of other background types was unusually high. With a frown, he opened a com channel to Throneworld. Nothing. Not even static. But there was an old incoming message:

"Anton—if you're receiving, I assume you're finally through the Umbra. Three weeks? Seriously? That's four diplomatic conferences and one war arbitration for me, you shirker. Com me when you can. Seaside, chair, 2317."

The Excellenza Ydaire, of course. He quirked a smile. Even after all this time, he couldn't think of her without recalling that startling first impression of her brilliant green eyes. And she'd left him an eidetic riddle composed of three experiential clues. The form was favored as a diversion among the Excellenzi who all had absolute recall, but this one would have to wait for the return trip. She was right— three weeks on a single mission was an unheard of luxury. He needed to finish this quickly and get back to his fast-paced schedule.

But at least now he understood why this mission was rated as a difficult. He was still fighting reduced functionality across all systems. Briefing reports had stated that tech irregularities were the root cause of non-interaction between Imperial worlds and this region, but he never expected the phenomenon to affect a Shuttle of State. He had navigation, but communication was severely compromised.

A less than ideal situation. But he was an Imperial Excellenz on a mission to contact the civilization on the other side of the Umbra. And Excellenzi always prevailed.

Anton identified three systems with interplanetary traffic, then he focused on the planet that seemed to have the highest concentration of traffic. He targeted the city with the densest population and prepared for the Descent.

The Descent of a Shuttle of State was not just a landing, but a statement of Imperial power. The protocols were established precisely for the most dramatic visuals. Anton had enacted hundreds of Descents and knew the subtle nuances for milking the event for maximum effect. He found a central square with an assembled crowd in the city and targeted a sufficiently open space in the midst of the throng. Then he plummeted downward.

This was the maneuver at which Shuttles of State excelled. The ultimate statement of Imperial power was dropping from the sky at insane speeds, yet managing a precisely controlled landing in defiance of all laws of physics.

But the shuttle responded sluggishly, refusing to pull out of the dive as programmed. Anton slapped his palms against the console, using physical contact to maximize the psychic pressure he was putting on the system. He forced his will on the shuttle as the ground flew up to meet him and finally anti-grav stabilizers kicked in, buoying the shuttle at the last moment.

Anton frowned. A Descent wasn't supposed to be quite that dramatic behind the scenes. But at least the visual impact on onlookers was still the intended statement of Imperial power. He rose from his seat and focused. His silver uniform glowed with a nimbus of radiance as he unsealed the door.

As he walked down the ramp, he felt the rush of data flowing into him through his implants. The ocular enhancer fed him details that it deemed important while the sounds of the crowd were absorbed into a translation matrix that would soon provide a key to the language. And even more importantly, he had the potent tool of his eidetic memory.

He looked down the broad, crowd-filled avenue with its bright banners and overwhelming sweetness of exotic wildflowers. It was late in the diurnal cycle, and the late afternoon light of the red sun cast the scene in hues of blood. This race was humanoid but divergent in an unfamiliar way. They were tall with huge, saucer-like eyes and purplish skin. It was strange that they were gathered here. This was either a pre-scheduled festival day or an organized celebratory greeting for him. He strongly suspected the latter because the crowd seemed neither surprised nor dismayed by his precipitous arrival. That raised questions. A long-range scan on their part wouldn't provide much more than trajectory of his craft, certainly not his intentions.

Dignitaries on a high, flower-draped platform rolled down the avenue toward him. "Wel-come!" shouted one exuberantly as the platform came to a halt and sprouted access steps. Anton climbed up to join the locals. "Wel-come," the same man said again.

"You speak Interstel," Anton noted, surprised. He had the basics of the native language by this point, but he kept to Interstel to follow where this was leading.

"Just learn," the man shrugged. "Need someone. Speak you."

That spawned more questions. Unlike banners and flowers, linguistic preparation took time. Three weeks would be the maximum time possible, tracking the shuttle from the moment it entered the Umbra. It might be possible for a race versed in the anomalies of this region, but it implied more technical sophistication than he'd given the local culture credit for.

"Come us," his host gushed as the platform began moving back up the avenue. "Big feast. Much honor."

"I am Anton, Excellenz by the Will of the All-Highest Emperor," he began, then wondered how much of that was actually understood.

"*Szo*, Anton," the man nodded. "Golden home."

That was one way to describe Throneworld, Anton supposed. Gold was the color of the Imperial Presence. "What is the name of your world and your people?"

The man spread his arms wide. "LaNarath." Then he pointed to himself, his silent colleagues, and the flower-waving crowd below. "LaNar."

But how would a distant culture know that the Imperial color was gold? Anton's cordial smile never wavered, but the question, once articulated, summed up the mystery of this whole reception. There had to be something else behind the scenes to produce these unexpected results. When a stranger lands a golden shuttle in your capital city, the usual reaction was surprise and fear. Not celebration.

A large, domed structure loomed at the end of the avenue. Palace, temple, government hall—his ocular implant identified all three functions inherent in the architectural design. The platform stopped and the steps emerged along the side, a clear indication to dismount and climb the broad steps to the entrance. Entrances, plural. Anton corrected as he took in the six sets of wide double doors that overlooked the avenue. The fact that the doors were designed to accommodate the comings and goings of a crowd suggested a building used by the masses.

As they entered, his hosts ushered him to the left along a side hallway, even though a wide processional way led forward. He paused at the turn just long enough to twitch his left eye and zoom in on the far end of the processional way. Definitely a large, public chamber at the end. There was misdirection in play. He had been brought to the obvious center of power—this temple was the grandest building on the visible cityscape—but not to the center of the center of power. That raised two questions: what was at the end of the processional way and why was he not being taken there?

The side hallway led to a generously proportioned room laid out with low tables and brightly colored pillows on the floor. There were no windows, but a skylight far above let in shafts of red sunlight. The unbroken wall areas were devoted to a huge mural that ran around three sides of the room. He immediately suspected more misdirection through lavish dining and entertainment.

Anton seated himself as directed at the end of one low table. He didn't like sitting on the floor as it slowed any response to a physical threat, and he didn't like being positioned with his back toward the door with only a personal proximity sensor to warn him of attack from the rear. But refusing a designated place of honor would be a petty insult that could sour the diplomatic mood. He sat and smiled as fourteen additional guests filed in, bringing the count to nineteen diners. What an odd number to plan for. Most cultures avoided that socially awkward prime number as it did not permit pairing or trioing or double-pairing, the basic units of interaction. No matter what the breakdown, one person would always remain a singleton. He was sure it was no random result, just as he was sure he was intended to be odd man out. Isolating a person by honoring him was a tried-and-true technique.

The banquet proceeded. As successive courses were placed before him, Anton sampled each dish carefully, chewing slowly to identify toxins. A few of the dishes contained akaloids at poisonous levels, but he didn't believe it was intentional poisoning, just cultural difference. The akaloid content in all the foods was higher than strictly healthy for a human. If he limited the amount of intake and ate slowly, his body could adjust and neutralize the poison. And there would be no cause for offense to those who had prepared the banquet in his honor. But odd that the same culture that seemed to know so much about his arrival had no idea of his dietary needs. The mechanism at work here had clear limits.

Because he was isolated from the other diners, he had time to study other cultural clues. The low tables and lack of chairs said this was a society without rigid hierarchy. A ruler, perhaps, but no succession of ranks between the highest and lowest. And probably not much mobility because there was no ladder of access.

He turned his attention to the murals. Definitely a depiction of praise from the masses to the rulership, represented by a pool of water. The images of adoring masses coupled with the element of water made him wonder if the governance was theocratic. This seemed to be religious or quasi-religious veneration. That could be problematic. Of all the diplomatic missions he had enacted, the most awkward were those with strong links between local religion and governance. The fact that the All-Highest was both Emperor and god to the trillions of inhabitants throughout Imperial Space both baffled and offended locals with alternative god concepts of their own. That discussion was better avoided altogether on First Contact missions.

Anton glanced over with a ready smile as his host leaned closer across the table.

"Iz acceptable?"

"Quite acceptable," Anton nodded. "I look forward to a tour of this beautiful building."

The man blinked huge, saucer-like eyes in confusion. The trapped expression on his face was telling. There was something within these walls not intended to be seen by a visitor from beyond. Anton doubted that he could force an actual tour, but once situated in quarters for the night, he knew exactly where to direct his nocturnal investigations.

His host blinked again, recovering his momentum. "Foods brought many worlds. Honor to golden visitor."

There it was again—the allusion to the color gold against all logic. The uniform of an Excellenz was silver. To be called a "silver visitor in a golden chariot" would fit the visuals, but "golden visitor" felt like an oblique reference to the All-Highest himself. Anton needed to know how this distant people had picked up that reference.

"Also to honor," the man continued, "spatial euphony. Beautiful lamentation." He clapped his hands and a trio entered, two carrying convoluted crystal devices. The three came to a halt in the middle space between the low tables and turned back to back to form a triangle facing the diners in all directions. The hands of the two device-carriers moved in unison to strike their objects, and an ethereal vibration filled the chamber. More vibrations followed.

Anton felt a corresponding sensation in his ears and nasal cavity. The whole inside of his head seemed to ring in sympathetic vibration to each stroke. It was a strange but pleasurable sensation, almost like… Ah, it *is* music, Anton decided, realizing the vibrations had pitch as well as resonance. A moment later, his observation was confirmed when the third of the trio began crooning a doleful melody: "Cometh the Cold King who bringeth the storm / He winnoweth the world as he changeth its form / All change be wrought solely with suffering and mourn / Cometh the Cold King that bringeth the storm…"

Caught up in the ringing inside his head and the darkness of the lyrics, Anton let a whole verse go by before grasping the linguistic import—this "lamentation," as his host had named it, was not being processed by his implants properly. His eidetic memory had acquired enough of the language for him to translate this formalized archaic usage on his own, but he shouldn't have needed to.

He fixed his gaze on a detail of the mural on the far wall and twitched his eye. The ocular enhancer refused to zoom in. He blinked several more times, then considered the situation from several angles.

One, either his implants had been affected by extended exposure to the Umbra, or they were being deliberately suppressed by methods yet unknown. Two, his hosts had expected reduced linguistics from him and had provided a translator. Three, the spatial resonances of this music seemed to be the causative agent and intersected neural technology in very specific ways.

At the end of the song, his host turned to him. "*Szo*, Anton. Old tale, Cold King. Change and renewal."

And that was instructive. Not only did his translator expect Anton not to understand, he was supplying a distinctly sanitized account of the lyrics. The lamentation had dwelt on the trauma of change, the pain wrought upon society by the Cold King, and the fear of the LaNar for this entity who would arise to winnow them. That was hardly "change and renewal."

There was another subtext as well. The fact that the LaNar had presented him, the visitor from beyond, with an account of traumatic change was telling. The performance was supposed to draw clear lines of comparison, not for him, but for everyone else in the room. He and his mission were being scorned in the guise of being honored.

An awkward silence had fallen on the room. Anton roused himself from his analysis to find all eyes turned to him. It seemed to be the conclusion of the banquet and something was expected—a thank you, a benediction, a dismissal. Not knowing which, he decided to present all three: "Appreciation for your hospitality and most excellent repast. Be your journeys home guided and the night restful." Then, he stood up. The other eighteen diners shakily followed suit, staring at him with huge eyes. He had spoken to them in LaNaran. His implant may have gone silent, but he had enough native vocabulary for that short speech. Perhaps that would shock them out of their foolishness. One didn't trifle with an Imperial Excellenz. But maybe overkill, he realized, recognizing true fear in their eyes along with the shock. Considering he had been modeling on the archaic lamentation, there was a good chance he had spoken to them in an elevated courtly dialect restricted to ceremonial usage. That would have overtones in itself.

As personages began hastily exiting, his very nervous host ushered him back down the side hallway and across an open courtyard to a separate building connected to the temple proper with covered walkways. Ushered and then fled. There was no mistaking the man was now terrified of him. Oddly terrified. Wariness would have been the logical response to an important guest publicly slipping his leash. But knowing their plan was off track seemed to paralyze these LaNar. Not decision makers, Anton noted. They were all answerable to a higher authority who was now a displeased higher authority.

Inside the low-slung building was a vividly colored suite of rooms with high ceilings, low furniture, and prominent murals in between. The bed was a soft mat upon the floor heaped with pillows. There was no evidence of surveillance devices that Anton could detect, but without operational scanners, it was hard to be sure. However, the culture as a whole did not seem inclined toward tech devices, though these people obviously had the capacity for interstellar travel. Odd contradictions here.

Anton sat on one of piles of cushions for a few minutes, then extinguished the central light globe with a touch. After that he waited quietly in the dark for a long while. He expected guards or watchers stationed in the courtyard and had already determined the best avenue of return to be over the rooftops. Melodramatic, perhaps, but still the path of least resistance in this instance. He was not yet ready to bump the mission up to confrontation level, though he was becoming steadily more inclined. This culture was right on the cusp of giving official insult to the Empire, a most dangerous state of affairs. Imperial fleets might be stymied by the Umbra, but the personage of the All-Highest would not be. If he took offense, there could well be a "golden visit" that would put all laments of the Cold King to shame.

The night was like a black curtain. This was a moonless world and few stars shone at the edge of the galaxy, so all nights would be unusually dark by inner world standards. Functioning ocular enhancers would have made the task easier, but Anton's well-honed night vision was equal to the challenge. He exited the suite through a high window on the back side of the building and pulled himself onto the roof. He moved like a shadow in the night, pausing when he drew near the temple itself. He had identified three watchers below in the courtyard, but they seemed oblivious to his passing.

Sliding silently to ground level, he found an unsecured door and slipped inside. He followed the side hall to its intersection with the main processional way, then followed the larger hall to a great vaulted chamber in the center of the temple. Center of the temple, center of power. And in the center of chamber was a round pool of water, just as represented in the murals. He stepped closer.

Six women, attenuated beyond the scale of other LaNar, floated in aureoles of long, fine hair. Prominent gills were another indicator of a variant of the standard genotype, but these variations must be intentional mutations for the pool to be so revered.

The white eyes of the women stared upward, seeing nothing, but instinct told him they were acutely aware. He felt a sharp pressure at the back of his head and winced at the severity of it. Then he brought it under control.

"Quooth thadta trin?" The question came from six mouths perfectly in synch. *Who touches us?*

"I am Anton, Excellenz by the Will of the All-Highest Emperor," he began formally in the same language. "Who are you and why have you deceived me?"

"Sordala," came the six-fold answer. "We saw that you would come."

Was that supposed to suffice as an answer? But interesting that blind women had "seen" his coming. He assumed precognitives, which also explained a number of smaller mysteries. At least he had finally arrived at his goal. He had no doubt that these oracles— or perhaps one oracle collectively—were the decision-makers of this society. The Highest would be most interested that a star-faring culture was organized around precognition. It could have value to the Empire.

"I bring you greetings in the name of the All-Highest," he continued. "Despite a rocky start, I see a productive interaction between your culture and mine."

"It is not what we see," they whispered back.

The pressure in his head surged suddenly, shattering his concentration. His last thought as he sagged to the stone floor was that he was under attack.

§

The morning sun rose red and bloody, casting strange shadows across the room. As Anton sat up from the mass of pillows, he realized he was back in the guest suite with no memory of returning here. A memory gap to an eidetic was like an unscratchable itch, and he cast his thoughts back again and again to the night before, trying to reclaim the missing piece of his life.

He recalled the jaunt over the rooftops and entering the temple. He recalled walking the processional way and arriving at a vaulted chamber with a pool. Then…nothing. Unconsciousness accounted for part of the void, but there was definitely a piece of memory missing as well. The texture of those two gaps was completely different.

As he rose to his feet, he tried to assess. There was no feel of an implanted false memory, nor any attempt to rearrange physical evidence. He had awakened in bed in full dress uniform with his boots on. That in itself suggested a certain insouciance on someone's part. His mind had been tampered with, and they didn't care that he knew it.

Whoever dwelt in the pool of the vaulted chamber had caused this. "How" was an important question, but he needed his memory back to know that. Consequences…openly attacking an Imperial Excellenz on a mission of state would trigger an enormous backlash. The Cadre of Excellenzi would want swift retaliation because this undercut their primary mode of diplomatic operation. The All-Highest—something more intense than displeasure from him, Anton guessed. Perhaps wrath… The train of thought faded into confusion as a strange blurring obscured the carefully delineated degrees between Imperial Disfavor, Imperial Displeasure, Imperial Wrath and Imperial…

His jaw tightened. He couldn't even remember the other degrees. Something was very wrong inside his head. This was more than a memory gap.

He looked inward. The great library of his mind, shelved with neatly indexed volumes of experiences, felt different…not so neatly indexed. As he cast his mind over the accumulated wealth of knowledge, he encountered strange gaps that had never been there before. A small surge of panic welled up within him, only to be swiftly reined in. Gaps could be filled in over time. As long as his mental processes were intact, he could still deal with the problem at hand.

But even as he settled into a mindset for moving on, he felt shaken. His mind was all-important to him. Losing bits and pieces of it was intolerable. His usual response to such a situation would be to go into full confrontation mode, flaring his shields and priming the weaponry built into his uniform. But when he thought of returning to the pool, he felt…fear.

Could those who had taken parts of his mind take even more in a second meeting? It was a strange, new fear that he had never considered, not even hypothetically. But there it was. What he needed to do was apprise Throneworld of the situation. An Excellenz never confronted danger without a backup plan in place. But because of the communication haziness, he might need to jump directly to the ultimate backup of all Excellenzi—the Anteroom. It was where they could indirectly contact the mind of the All-

Highest, leaving him messages because any direct mind-to-mind touch would be fatal.

Yes, I am to that point of emergency, Anton decided. The Anteroom was always the last recourse. He closed his eyes and focused inward. He stood there for a moment, then opened his eyes suddenly. He couldn't do it. He knew everything about the Anteroom but no longer remembered how to access it.

Looking inward to his mental library, he now saw more shelves in disorder, some completely empty. Whatever had been done to him was not a finite process. His memories were continuing to destabilize and fade. This time the surge of panic refused to be reined in. He felt his heart pounding at a much increased rate and realized he'd never he'd felt such chaotic physicality.

He had to leave now, get back to Throneworld while he still had mind enough to salvage. As he thought it, he was already in motion, heading quickly across the courtyard. Three weeks through the Umbra—that grim reality kept nagging at him. How much functionality would he have after three weeks of fading?

He crossed through the temple, ignored the processional way, and turned through the huge doorway leading to the city. A crowd of LaNar awaited him, just as before, with bright banners and wildflowers. He paused, unsure whether to raise shields or what?

Then his translator appeared. "*Szo,* Anton, you now leave us. Much honor."

Honor. Anton nearly spat the word back at the man, but instead kept going down the steps. The crowd opened before him, cheering his passage. He ignored them, walking at a brisk pace. Time, normally his friend, was now an enemy.

Down the avenue, he found his Shuttle of State exactly as he had left it. He walked up the ramp and prepared for take-off. Fortunately, the Shuttle was highly automated. It could even interpolate what needed to be done if its occupant was damaged. It would take him home.

The Ascent was shaky, not at all a statement of Imperial power. But he was free of the LaNarath and that counted for a great deal. "I need stasis through the Umbra," he told the Shuttle. "Bring me out only when communication is clear again." Then he lay back in the command chair and let the paralysis of stasis wash over him.

§

The stars winked in around him. As seeing turned into understanding, Anton realized he was awake again. And the stars he was seeing through the ocular were familiar. For a moment, he basked in the moment, feeling only relief. Then darker thoughts intruded. His mind was compromised. He looked inward for a long while, then shook his head. He couldn't tell if his mind was better or worse because he couldn't remember its last state. That probably meant worse.

"Communication with Throneworld is now viable," the Shuttle reported.

"Connect me," he ordered. "Directly to the All-Highest."

"Enter security protocols for direct access."

Anton's hand moved to the console to confirm, then froze. He couldn't remember the protocols. He blinked as that thought shifted through his being. He couldn't remember the damn security protocols! The Shuttle would be vaporized if he tried to land on Throneworld without those.

What did he remember? His fingers tapped in a familiar com sequence. "Whose access is that?" he asked.

"The Excellenza Ydaire," the Shuttle responded. "Do you wish to open a channel?"

"Yes—high priority."

A long minute passed before the Shuttle said, "The Excellenza Ydaire is in conference and cannot be disturbed. Shall I try later?"

"Yes, yes," Anton snapped irritably. Then he looked around, confused. Who was he talking to? There was no one here except him. He slumped in his seat, feeling very alone and vulnerable.

"Do you wish to contact the Excellenza Ydaire again," a metallic voice asked after a while.

The name brought up a mental image of a woman with striking green eyes…or were they blue? "Yes," he answered because that sounded right. But he was no longer sure what he wanted to say to her.

"Enter her access code."

He tried and failed a few times. He no longer remembered. Bits of his brain spoke to him in urgent whispers that he couldn't quite hear. One voice finally came through, just barely audible: "Land immediately—anywhere! Initiate a Priority Alpha distress beacon."

That sounded right. Anton repeated the words and the Shuttle dropped out of hyperlight to search for a landing spot.

"Asteroid belt ahead. Asteroid with viable gravity and atmosphere acquired."

Anton placed his hands on the controls, knowing he had done a thousand landings and it was easy. But he didn't remember exactly how. The asteroid filled the forward ocular.

Psychic attack. That thought rose sluggishly into his awareness. But it couldn't look like an attack on an Excellenz or the Imperial Wrath would be on their doorstep. Then, that thought, too, faded.

As the asteroid rushed up to meet the Shuttle, a last image flashed in Anton's head. Purple women in a pool of water, floating so close to each other that they seemed one great mass of green-brown hair.

They looked at him with blind eyes and smiled.

Juliet Silver and the Seeker of the Depths
Wendy Nikel

*J*uliet Silver raised the doorknocker—a gilded image of a tentacled monster—and let it fall, sending a metallic *clang* up and down the deserted city street. Sunlight streamed over her, peeking out from the horizon with golden tendrils that seemed to tap her on the shoulder, to question what she was doing on the ground when the skies were so crisp and clear, so perfect for sailing.

As she waited, Juliet's fingers twitched at the hilt of her sword. It'd been months since she'd seen the sunrise from land, and she ached to rise above the dingy scraps of garbage and the hungry rats of the city's alleys. But Stenson, a rival captain of the airship *The Bearer of Bad News*, was insistent that she meet him today, this morning, at this particular shop.

Whatever the old codger wanted, it had better be worth her time.

When the bolt finally slid across, the iron door opened with a groan of its massive hinges. The door was large enough for a steam carriage to power through, and likely many did over the course of a week. Upon entering, however, Juliet's attention was drawn not to the carriages, nor even to the new-fangled bits and baskets, snares and rudders that she might have used to upgrade her own ship, the *Realm of Impossibility.*

Instead, she was drawn to an item sitting solidly in the center of the workshop, stout and bulbous and crouching like a frog. Its outer shell gleamed so that within its curves and panels, her reflection stared back at her. The metal was cold to her touch.

"Meets your approval, captain?"

Juliet caught Stenson's reflection as he stepped beside her. She didn't turn but proceeded to walk about the contraption, examining every inch of it.

"For exploring underseas, I take it?" She knocked upon its side. "I have to wonder how well it would hold up to the water pressure."

"Just as well as it's sitting here before you. The iron-welder who built it is one of the city's finest."

"I'd much like to meet him."

"He's a solitary type. Doesn't care much for pleasantries or small talk."

Curious that he would make Stenson's acquaintance then. The old man was quite the gossipmonger. Juliet wisely kept this opinion to herself.

"And the headlights?" She cast a skeptical glace at the blue domed lights. They hardly looked as though they'd cut through fog, much less a murky sea.

"Mostly for show. This craft has something even better, Miss Silver." The older captain reached forward and sprung the door open. Its pneumatic hinges hissed. Inside, a flat screen blinked to life. "Sonar. Even if the windows are filled with grime, you'll be able to see any obstacles before you as clear as a pretty spring day."

"And what do you intend to do with this little fish?"

"I intend to give her to you."

Ah, now the real bargaining would begin. Stenson wasn't the generous type; Juliet wondered what the real price would be. "And what do you want from me?"

"I want the treasure of the *Argonaut*—the largest haul of stolen gold and gems anyone has ever seen, lost beneath the Sea of Prosperity. And I want you to fetch it for me."

"I'm not a dog." Juliet brushed past him, making her way for the door.

"No, you're not. You're a shrewd captain, one who's daring enough to go where none has before."

Juliet hesitated, her hand upon the door. Well, he wasn't *wrong*.

"And wise enough to know that this little fish," Stenson said, tapping the hull of the underwater vehicle, "could make you rich beyond your dreams. We both know that the *Argonaut* wasn't the first airship to plummet from the sky into troubled waves, though its treasure is the only one I wish to stake a claim upon. After delivering it to me and receiving your share—"

"Sixty percent."

"Thirty, and don't interrupt. After receiving your share, this little *Seeker of the Depths* will be yours to do with as you wish. It won't take a daring young lass such as yourself to make a fine fortune in underwater salvaging. I'd do it myself if I were a few decades younger."

Juliet considered this as she resumed her perusal of the machine. The interior was small, intended only for one diver. The rest of her crew would have to wait above the surface; she didn't trust anyone else to the task. She'd be lying if she said that the coffers of wealth in the belly of the *Argonaut* didn't tempt her.

"Are you daring enough?"

It was Stenson's voice that spoke aloud, an echo of the question already swirling about her heart and mind. A question to which she already knew the answer.

"Yes."

§

The Seeker was strapped to the *Realm of Impossibility* with great lengths of chain that clanked and rattled like bones. All along the dock, crews neglected their own ships to watch the activity about Juliet's. She stood before the gangplank, arms crossed over her chest and feet planted, daring them with her scowl to come forth and stake their claim. *The Argonaut's* treasure was, after all, pirate's booty, and there were plenty among the airpilots who'd fallen victim to it.

Geoffries, her first mate, was the only one who approached. "You know they won't raise arms against you today. They'll wait until you've returned with the prize…if you return at all."

"Do you doubt me, Geoffries?"

"Not I, Captain. But they don't know you as I do. Undoubtedly, most expect that your little bronze fish will sink to the depths with you in its belly and neither of you will be seen again."

"Fools."

"The ship's prepared, Captain," a crewmember called out.

Juliet took a final, defiant glance about her and—with firm footfalls upon the grated gangplank—took her place on the *Realm of Impossibility.*

§

The Sea of Prosperity was a misnomer at best—a putrid soup of grease at worst. Even the skies above it were a swamp of foul-smelling brown. Not a single bird traversed the clouds, and neither did Juliet expect to find anything living beneath the water's stagnant surface.

Geoffries looked on as Juliet strapped herself into the *Seeker's* chamber. It was some sort of recklessness, perhaps, that would lead a woman to crawl into that round, iron coffin and allow herself to be lowered into the sea. But she'd tested the equipment herself, and if all went well, she'd return in just a few hours. In the meantime, she'd simply crawl along the seabed, picking through who-knows-what-she'd-find-there until she uncovered the wreckage of the *Argonaut* and the treasure hidden within it.

"All set, Captain?"

"Aye, aye!"

The door hissed shut and sealed, leaving Juliet in such an absolute silence that—had it not been for the movement seen through the window—she'd have thought the outside world had ceased to exist. With an abrupt, jarring motion and the faraway clanking of iron chains, the *Seeker of the Depths* descended.

Murky water closed over the window. Glistening particles floated in the rays of sun that somehow cut through the layers of silt and sediment. These bright specks of light grew sparser as the vessel descended and the darkness deepened. Finally, the *Seeker* settled on the ocean floor. Outside the window, all was black and still, save for the occasional flick of a phosphorescent tail fin.

Juliet flicked on the sonar. She pulled handles and turned levers to operate the vessel's spidery legs, dragging it meter by meter across the sea floor. The sonar flickered with outlines of flat expanses, jagged cliffs, and crevices that seemed to descend into the center of the earth.

Juliet had hardly begun her search when the *Seeker* became stuck. She wrenched at levers and pressed dials, but though the iron mechanisms rattled, the *Seeker* refused to move. Cursing Stenson, Juliet pressed the distress signal.

She sat in the never-changing stillness of the depths, waiting for the chattering of the chain and the lightening of the murk that would indicate the *Realm of Impossibility* was lifting her to the surface, but it never came. Was she too deep for the *Realm* to receive her signal? Had the chain broken somehow? Juliet was just debating her next course of action when the *Seeker* jerked into motion.

She fumbled with the controls. The vessel was moving, but the comforting rattle of its spider legs was missing. Had some sea creature swooped in and gobbled her up? Considering the blackness around her, it seemed possible. Except…the sonar still showed the landscape of the deeps.

Had something crept up and snagged her from behind? If so, there was little she could do about it now, besides to be ready when it stopped. She gripped her knife and studied the sonar.

Finally, the *Seeker* reached a cliff wall. Instead of going around it, however, the vessel proceeded through what appeared to be a narrow tunnel. It opened out into a vast cavern—a cavern filled with light.

Juliet blinked against the sudden brilliance. The cavern ceiling arched high overhead, glowing with light from thousands, millions, perhaps billions of phosphorescent creatures swimming about. Some were the size of whales, while others were so small that their lights seemed like those of fireflies buzzing about.

Beneath this sea of magnificent creatures was an even more magnificent sight—a city, constructed of glass panes, crisscrossed and held up by frames of shining gold. As the *Seeker* drew nearer, Juliet could see the people wandering about inside, people with golden skin coming out of golden houses and walking down golden roads, conversing and carrying on about their lives as if nothing was more natural than living leagues beneath the surface.

A panel opened in the side of the city, and the *Seeker* was carried inside a narrow tunnel—an airlock, in fact—where all the water rushed out around it. Juliet pressed the release button on her craft and jumped out, wielding her knife.

The *Seeker* had, indeed, been captured from behind by a craft not too unlike it. They shared the same bulbous shape and the same thin, spidery legs, but this one also had front appendages that now held the *Seeker* in place.

"Stenson," Juliet seethed. He must have known about this place, about these people and their craft. How else could his design be so strikingly similar? Had he stolen their ship, or merely the design? Her breath came hot and furious, but she didn't fight as two armed guards grabbed her from behind.

The hatch of the larger craft sprung open and a man with golden skin and close-cropped hair leaned out. "Take her to the Queen."

"Yes," Juliet said between clenched teeth. "I'd very much like to speak with her."

§

None of the other structures came near the opulence of the palace's shimmering walls. Every inch of it was composed of pearls stacked into bricks, each one perfectly polished and luminescent. Its sprawling courtyard contained innumerous metal sculptures of all types of sea life. These creatures ran by clockwork, rattling and chattering as they stretched and dove and swam through the air.

As the guards led Juliet through the entrance, she took note of the squid whose head made up the capstone and whose tentacles cascaded down either side of the doorway, a skillful piece of metalwork. From there, they entered a cavernous throne room. At the far end, separated by a carpet of tiny, polished shells, sat the Queen. She wore a sparkling robe of fish scales and a crown composed of dozens of tiny fish ribs that rose in intricate whorls to a peak high above her brow. Her face was long and golden and unlined, though her eyes looked old and wise. She was flanked on either side by a pair of ladies in lavish gowns and bright, bejeweled headdresses.

Juliet shook free from the guards' grasp and dipped her head in a reverent bow.

"What have you brought me?" The Queen's voice was clear and crisp as glass, though in it, also, was the sharp edge of the same.

"Please, your majesty," Juliet said before the guards could speak. "I am Juliet Silver, captain of the airship *The Realm of Impossibility,* explorer of the skies."

"What purpose would an airship captain have in the dominion of the water-dwellers? Surely you know of the truce and punishment due to those who break it."

Juliet seethed silently at Stenson. "I knew of no such truce, nor— truly—of your glorious city's existence."

"How is it possible you've never heard of the great and powerful city of Prosperia? Has it been so long since we closed our gates that all have forgotten our existence?"

Juliet stood silently. Certainly, she'd heard of the undersea city of Prosperia, but it was a myth, a legend, a bedtime story to amuse small children. To find that it was true was akin to discovering the mythical Bandybell's lair.

"Liska." The Queen turned to one of her ladies-in-waiting. "How many years have passed since our isolation?"

"Five hundred twenty-two, your Highness."

"Hardly a bat of the eye...yet perhaps for you short-lived folk with your warring and wandering that would be long enough to forget.

Still, I find it hard to believe this warning would not have been passed down from the older, more experienced captains to the younger ones."

"Indeed." It would certainly explain why Stenson—superstitious man that he was—had no desire to dive beneath the waves himself. He'd certainly have heard the stories, though Juliet—a newcomer to the skies and without a mentor to guide her—had not. Had he hoped Juliet might slip past the Propserians and recover the *Argonaut's* treasure? Or was this all a ruse to get rid of her? "Well, now that we've established my innocence, if you could return me to my vessel—"

"My dear girl." The Queen rose to her feet and cast her deep shadow upon Juliet. "Ignorance is not akin to innocence. In order to preserve our isolation, we are quite unable to allow your return."

"I see." Juliet narrowed her eyes. "And what is my punishment to be?"

"It just so happens that this is a year of sacrifice to the kraken. I trust you'll make him a fine morsel at festival time. Until then…" She turned to one of the ladies on her right. "Sofia, please bind her. Then, the guards shall take her to her cell."

The lady she spoke to rose, dipped her hand in a pocket, and pulled out a length of delicate chain. She bound Juliet's hands with nimble fingers, and from another pocket procured a tiny lock, with which she secured the restraints. She pulled upon them to test their strength and—as she did so—a small sliver of metal dropped into Juliet's palms.

Any thought that this slip might have been inadvertent left Juliet's mind when the woman met her eyes. Then she turned and announced to the Queen, "The prisoner is bound."

The Queen nodded, and with that, the guards led Juliet away.

§

The cell beneath the ocean floor was spongy and smelled of rotting fish. Juliet stood in the dark, turning over in her hands the tiny lock pick—for that's what the lady Sofia had slipped to her—as she waited. For what, she wasn't certain. On the surface, it'd have been for the darkest part of night, but here the hours stretched on without a single variance of the phosphorescent glow that bled in streaks through the grated window high above her, nor to the pacing of the guard beyond her door.

She'd just resigned herself to try to get a small bit of sleep when the sound of a commotion in the hall outside her door sent a rush of adrenaline through her, dulling any thought of slumber.

Immediately, she took out the sliver of metal to pick the lock on the door. Gears within it turned and the bolt retracted. The corridor beyond was empty, save for a slim figure in a long gown, heels, and a massive, jeweled headdress, carrying a small jar with one of the phosphorescent creatures swimming about in it.

Lady Sofia.

"Quickly!" Sofia said. "The guard will return any moment."

Juliet followed her through winding pathways, their feet squishing on the soggy dungeon floor. When the lady paused in a quiet corner to catch her breath, Juliet's tongue loosened.

"Who are you? And why are you helping me?"

"Sofia—the royal tinker. And I'm not helping you; you're helping me…to escape."

"Escape? Why?"

"You think we enjoy being trapped down here with no contact to the outside world? Our isolation was based on the Queen's own emotional pride alone, not any logical rationale. She only cut us off to punish him for leaving." She set off again down the dark corridor, and Juliet followed on her heels.

"Who? Who left?"

"Her son, the heir. When her search for him proved futile, she flew into a rage and commanded Prosperia be cut off from the world above. Now hush, or someone will hear."

"Do you have a weapon?" Juliet whispered. Without her sword or knife, she felt positively helpless, completely at the mercy of this overdressed aristocrat. Sofia reached up to her headdress and pulled out a hat pin the length of her hand and passed it to Juliet, who took it with some skepticism. It was no dagger, for certain, but it was better than nothing.

They turned a corner and Sofia screeched, nearly backing up directly into Juliet. The guard had returned by another route and was blocking their path, his sword at the ready.

Juliet stepped in front of Sofia, brandishing the hairpin. The guard smirked, obviously unimpressed. Juliet lunged. With a quick, well-placed jab, she pierced the gap between his chest plate and helmet, causing him to cry out and giving her the element of surprise needed to knock his sword from his hand. Finally, a proper weapon!

"Lie down on the ground," she instructed him, "and count to three hundred. If we meet again, I will not be so merciful."

Juliet urged Sofia on, and the bewildered woman took off down the corridor once again. Juliet paused now and again to glance behind her and see that the guard was still lying prone, as Sofia rushed further ahead. She climbed a flight of stairs, and Juliet rushed to follow, blinking as her eyes adjusted to the brilliance of the phosphorescent light.

At the top of the steps, Juliet stopped short.

Sofia stood before her with a guard's blade pressed to her throat. On either side of her stood a dozen other guards, their swords drawn. Juliet hesitated, her mind racing to devise a strategy that would leave Sofia unharmed. She was just about to step forward when the guards shifted, parting in the center to admit the Queen herself.

"I see that I've a traitor in my midst. Dear Sofia, I do hope the kraken doesn't mind if his feast begins early. I could hardly hope to keep you contained in the locks and chains you designed yourself."

"If you lay a hand on her—" Juliet began, holding her weapon steady.

The Queen raised her eyebrows and placed a hand upon her chin, as if amused. On the third finger, she bore a dark ring with a design Juliet recognized from the palace's curved arch—the kraken. "Go on. What shall you do?"

Juliet lowered her sword, her eyes transfixed on the ring. The palace entrance wasn't the first place she'd seen that design.

"You will allow Sofia and me to return to the surface unhindered, and I, in turn, will tell you where to find your son."

§

Juliet stood on the deserted city street once again and raised the ten-legged doorknocker—the gilded kraken. Beside her stood two women, dressed in long cloaks and hoods to protect their golden skin from the rays of the early morning sun.

The Realm of Impossibility's crew had been surprised at Juliet's return after they believed they'd lost her, and even more surprised at the two strange women she'd brought with her. Juliet had held off on answering their questions, promising she'd explain all once she'd held up her deal of the bargain.

The bolt slid across and the door opened with a *creak*. This time, it was not Stenson who opened it, but a lean man donned in a smock, long gloves, and an iron-welder's mask over his face. Upon seeing the three in the doorway, the iron-welder slowly raised his mask, exposing his golden skin.

"Mother?"

The Queen rushed forward to embrace him. Juliet and Sofia hung back, though Juliet could see how the tinkerer's eyes danced about the workroom, taking in all the tools and metalwork there. *The Realm,* too, had fascinated the Queen's lady-in-waiting, and Juliet had spent much of their journey back to the city explaining the airship's inner workings to her.

"Let's leave them to their reunion," she whispered to Sofia.

They waited beside the iron door, watching the carriages bustling past and people walking to the market as the city awakened to a new day.

"I'm sorry you lost your vessel," Sofia said.

"It wasn't mine. Not yet anyway."

"Will its owner hold you accountable for its loss, then?"

"Perhaps." If Stenson wanted the *Seeker* back, he'd have to retrieve it from the Queen himself. As for the *Argonaut* and its treasure, when Juliet had questioned her earlier, Sofia verified that the wreck had already been picked apart by Prosperian scavengers. They'd used every bit of metal for repairs of their underwater city.

"What are your plans now, as a free woman?" Juliet asked, breaking the silence.

"I…I don't know." Sofia fiddled with the buttons and levers on her belt. The metal jangled like a song and glimmered in the sun. "I hadn't dared to hope for anything beyond escape."

"I've a proposition for you, then." Juliet spied an airship on the horizon and shielded her eyes against the sun. "*The Realm of Impossibility* could use a good tinkerer on board, someone to help out when the mechanical parts require repairs. Tell me, how do you feel about the skies?"

Sofia looked up from her belt, startled. Then, she, too, raised her eyes to the blue sky and slowly, a smile spread across her golden face.

Chasing Satellites

Anthony R. Cardno

*H**ow the hell did this happen!"*
 Zimmerman was ranting at Werder, the new kid, when Milne reported for his shift in the communications hub. One of the tallest humans on Orpheus, Zimmerman would tower over the shorter, stockier Werder even if the kid hadn't been sitting rigidly at his console.

"How the hell did what happen?" Milne asked, around a yawn born of too little sleep. Parenting a tween-age child on Orpheus was no easier than it would have been back on Earth.

"We've lost contact with Earth," both men replied, the anger in Zimmerman's voice in rough counterpoint to the timidity in Werder's.

"How long ago?" Stifling his second yawn, Milne crossed to the beverage station for some coffee. Wu, his shift partner, was already there looking equally exhausted. Milne cocked an eyebrow at him, silently asking *another heavy drinking night?* Wu's strained smile was answer enough.

"Six hours." Werder's answer went a long way to shaking Milne's lethargy. Wu's eyes widened a bit, too.

"Six hours! You didn't call me. Who did you call?"

"Zimmerman." Werder shot a sideways look at his trainer. Zimm puffed his cheeks out like he was going to interrupt, then thought better of it. "He said it was probably just solar interference on their end, like the last time, and that I should log and monitor it. So, I did."

"Okay, but for six hours? You didn't think to call it in again after, say, hour two? The last time this happened, it only lasted an hour and a half."

"I…uh." Werder turned slightly red, making the freckles on his face stand out even more, and mumbled something Milne had no problem understanding.

"You. Fell. Asleep." He put the half-made coffee down with a bit more force than he'd intended and stalked to his own console, bringing it online with a series of swift, sure finger movements. "Kid, transfer me the data, so I can figure out how much of a problem we have."

Werder grimaced, hunched his broad shoulders, and started tapping at his own console haltingly. Milne tried not to roll his eyes; the kid knew the layout and presets of the console but was clearly flustered by Zimmerman's reaction. He cast a quick look at Zimmerman and Wu. "And what have you two been doing since you got here? Why is Werder's the only console up and running?"

"Trying to figure out what the hell the kid was thinking, falling asleep…"

"Give it a rest, Zimm." Wu's voice barely made it out of the beverage station, every word tinged with hangover. "We've all done it. Even you."

"Not for six hours!"

"Let it go!" Milne had no patience for Zimmerman's posturing. Of course, Zimm's reaction was over the top. He was the one who had proclaimed Werder ready for solo-shifts. Part of the problem was rushing kids out of school and into training. A necessary downside to where they were as a colony. "We need to figure out what to do, not waste another hour berating the new kid."

"No, I'll take care of that while you're fixing this."

Milne sprang from his seat and snapped to attention at the new voice, mirrored by Werder. Zimmerman was a second slower, and Wu came to attention with only a slight wobble and without spilling his coffee.

Commander Foley stood in the hub's doorway, arms crossed and an unusual—but not uncalled for—scowl on her face. Werder went pale and blushed at the same time, something Milne thought a physical impossibility. Foley walked in and pulled the door shut behind her.

"Situation."

"Commander, the kid here dropped the ball," Zimmerman began.

"Not you." Foley interrupted, and Zimmerman's mouth stopped moving. She turned to Werder. "You."

Werder's mouth worked soundlessly for a moment. He cleared his throat and started again. To his credit, the kid didn't stammer once he got going.

"Sir! At 0100 hours, the communications channel with Earth read normal: not much chatter but coming through clear. Thirty minutes later, there was no chatter at all and a staticy background. Per protocol, I logged the interference. At 0200 hours, the static had increased, so I called Lieutenant Zimmerman. He reminded me of the previous comm-break's cause and ordered me to continue monitoring and logging."

"Why didn't you call Lieutenant Commander Milne?"

"Sir, as you know, Lieutenant Zimmerman is my trainer and immediate superior. As he was not overly concerned about the break, I thought it inappropriate to interrupt Lieutenant Commander Milne's night with his husband and daughter. Family First, sir!"

"Respecting the Prime Rule." Foley had a slight smile. "Very good, as far as it goes, but six hours is an unrealistically long time to monitor a comm-break without a follow-up report."

"Sir, Lieutenant Zimmerman is correct that I shirked my duty. By 0300, I had fallen asleep at my console. I have no good excuse for—"

"We'll discuss that later." Foley turned to Milne. Behind her back, Werder visibly deflated. "Status?"

Milne sat back down and reviewed the data streaming in from Werder's console. A scan of just the first hour's worth of data showed something Werder should have noticed and that the others certainly would have.

"The problem's not with Earth or solar activity. The freakin' transponder satellite isn't where it's supposed to be." He slapped both hands on his console in frustration. "I can't pinpoint where it is, but I can tell it's moving erratically. We could lose it, but even if we don't, it's too far out of position to do us any good when Earth is in proper alignment again."

"Solutions?"

"None that are optimal. If we try to course-correct it from down here without knowing exactly where it is, we're as likely to send it spiraling into the void as crashing into the surface of Orpheus."

"And if we don't resume communications," Foley shook her head, "Earth will assume we finally succumbed to the more hostile elements of this planet and write us off."

"As if they haven't done that much already," Wu grumbled. "Ten years, not a single supply ship. Just encouragement to thrive until they can spare resources. Thanks for nothing, homeworld."

Milne knew that Wu was not a negative person except when nursing a killer hangover. Foley knew it, too, and she rounded on him.

"Stow the fatalism, Lieutenant. It's unbecoming of an officer in front of the ranks."

"Is that true?" Werder's eyes were wide. "I've grown up here because Earth refuses to send help?"

"It's complicated, kid." Despite being best friends, there were times Milne would like to smack Wu upside the head with a blunt object. "Look, you're military now. You're going to hear things the civilians may not know yet. Discretion is key. Think about how that news would affect the colony. Family First, right?"

"Yeah, Family First." Werder didn't sound as enthusiastic about the Prime Rule at this moment.

"Suggestions." Foley brought the conversation back on track.

"Only one I can think of." Milne took a deep breath. "We go up."

§

"Zimmerman to hub, we have achieved orbit."

The shuttle had been equipped with enough tracking sensors and automatic relays for the hub to know exactly where they were, but verbal verification made the crew feel better and assured the folks on the ground that they were still alive.

"Locking trackers onto the transponder satellite," Wu reported. Zimmerman was piloting, Wu was locating. Milne would make repairs, if necessary, before they repositioned the satellite to the optimal position.

Zimmerman refused to move the shuttle until they had a set destination.

"Got it!" Wu sent the satellite's new coordinates to Zimm's console. From the data, Milne could see the satellite was moving slowly away from them.

"The shortest route is in the opposite direction," Zimmerman grumbled.

"Better than circling the entire planet," Foley said from the hub. "Turn around."

They moved in a controlled stationary rotation and then on minimal thruster power based on Wu's input. Milne watched his console and waited for the forward external cameras to pick up the satellite so he could begin damage assessment.

"We have camera-visual," he announced moments later, manipulating and transferring images from the cameras to the hub before the shuttle was in range for actual line-of-sight confirmation. The quicker they analyzed the situation, the better.

"Damage?" Foley asked over his headset.

"Checking now..." Milne kept his focus on the visuals streaming across his console. "One distended antenna for sure, hard to tell, but I think it can be corrected." He zoomed in for a close-up, cleaned up the image as much as possible, and transmitted it. "Several dents all in the same basic area surrounding the antennas. No other surface damage visible from this angle."

"Eye-visual confirmation," Zimmerman interrupted.

Milne had not noticed the slight increase in speed Zimmerman had applied to close the distance faster without overshooting.

"We will have close contact for extra-vehicular activity in three minutes."

Milne bit back a comment about how easy it was for Zimmerman to say that, since it would be Milne going out there.

"Dents and broken antenna," Foley cut back in. "More escaping ring debris?"

"Looks like it," Milne confirmed. "We'll know in a moment if what we're seeing is the worst of it."

"Does everyone realize today is the tenth anniversary of the crash?"

Werder's voice caught them all by surprise. They'd almost forgotten he was in the hub with Foley. In the morning's commotion, the anniversary had slipped Milne's mind, but how he didn't know.

"And your point is?" Zimmerman barked into his headset. "We're kinda on a time limit up here, kid."

"Debris escaping the ring brought the *Poitevin* down. We haven't paid much attention to the ring since, resources being limited, so how do we know this isn't an annual event, like meteor dispersal?"

"It's worth looking into, Ensign." Milne was impressed that Werder had made the connection before the rest of them. Maybe the kid did have a future in this line of work. "Think you can analyze the stored transponder records from the past decade and find a pattern? Might help in repositioning this thing if it's still working."

"On it!" There was a slight click as the kid muted his headset so he could work his console without interrupting communications between shuttle and hub.

A private message popped up on Milne's console. NICE JOB. Effusive praise from Foley. Milne typed back: SOMEONE DID THE SAME FOR ME ONCE, and then, with a small nod, set himself to figuring out what tools he was going to need to salvage the antenna.

§

The antenna was in worse shape than it had appeared from a distance, and Milne sweated some of the repair work. In the EVA suit, with all the tools attached to him via leads, he didn't need to worry about sweaty palms or things flying out of reach. Sweat dripping in his eyes was the problem.

He rewired the antenna and bent the metal back straight again. If anyone was annoyed by his occasional grunts or sighs, they wisely kept it to themselves, and left him to his work. Still, it was taking too long.

When it was time to screw the antenna rod back into the base, it took three tries to get it to thread correctly. Each time it stuck, Milne bit back a curse and took a breath before unscrewing and trying again. If he jammed it and couldn't get it loose, the mission was a bust.

On the third try, it stuck for a moment, and then slipped past like he had stripped the threads. That time, he did shout an expletive, louder than he'd intended. Four alarmed voices asked if he was okay.

"Fine, fine," he answered. "I thought I screwed up, but the antenna is reattached and okay." He paused, and then uttered a sad laugh. "Heh, get it? Screwed up? While screwing the antenna in?"

"Lieutenant Commander, how much more work do you have to do out there?" Foley's voice was measured, but Milne knew she was concerned when she addressed him by rank.

"Let's run the diagnostic on the antenna," he answered, "before I start looking for other problems. If it's not working, there's no sense checking for other damage. Wu, ping a signal to the antenna."

Milne waited in silence. Without visual displays, he had no way of knowing if the satellite received the signal.

"Pinged and pinged back," Wu said moments later with noticeable relief. "I sent the usual connection protocol, and the satellite responded appropriately."

"Hub, are you reading anything from the satellite?"

"Affirmative," Werder answered. "Reading static, but much less than last night."

"So, the patch job isn't perfect, but at least the antenna is working." Milne took a moment to collect his thoughts. "Commander, I have a suggestion."

"Go ahead."

"We should start broadcasting the message we recorded now. We know the transponder's not malfunctioning, we know the antenna is at least temporarily fixed. By waiting 'til we bring the satellite back into optimal position, we're taking a chance. Based on the remaining static Werder is hearing, let's not risk it. Even if it's not beamed directly at Earth, at least it'll be there for ships to hear."

"Ensign Werder," Foley ordered, "Begin transmitting the message. Shuttle, check to be sure it's going out."

Milne pushed back from the satellite, extending his tether so that he was in the path of the outgoing signal. The problem with these tight-beam transponders was that the recipient had to be in virtually direct line with the source, no matter how far away, to receive the signal. Within a moment, Commander Foley's prerecorded voice came over Milne's headset.

"THIS IS COMMANDER FOLEY OF ORPHEUS COLONY, FORMERLY OF THE *ESS POITEVIN*. IF YOU HEAR THIS, OUR TRANSPONDER SATELLITE IS FAILING AND WE'VE LOST COMMUNICATIONS WITH EARTH. PLEASE RELAY THIS SIGNAL. OUR COLONY IS NOT IMPAIRED OR FAILING, BUT WE NEED HELP REESTABLISHING COMMUNICATIONS WITH—"

There was more to the message, but it cut out suddenly.

"Milne! Get out of there!" Werder's voice cracked mid-shout, and Milne had the urge to slap his hands over his ears at the kid's volume. "Shuttle! Reel him in!"

"What the hell are you on, Werder?" Zimmerman interrupted.

"Satellite sensors are picking up a debris storm in the ring, headed out-bound! Coming your way, now!"

So much for the statistical analysis. Milne finger-toggled the suit thrusters and pushed towards the satellite, even as he felt the tug of the tether line pulling him in.

"Milne, what are you doing?" Wu's words came over in a rush.

"Grabbing the satellite! If we can pull it out of the way, we can take it with us, circle around, and reposition it!"

"Screw that!" Zimmerman replied. "We're getting out of here now! Wu, pull him in double-time!"

Milne laid his hands on the satellite shell and felt for a good grip before Zimmerman hit the thrusters and pulled him away. The tether and the satellite pulled against each other. His grip held and the satellite started to follow him.

And then, all hell broke loose. Small bits of debris zinged past his face-plate. He pulled his head back, closed his eyes and held his breath, waiting for an impact that didn't come. He opened his eyes again and watched more pebbles pass, imagining he could hear the whistle the way someone who narrowly avoids being shot hears the whine of the bullet as it misses. The sweat on his forehead poured faster as his heart-rate soared. He blinked rapidly to clear the sweat and stop the sting. But his grip still held, and the satellite moved with him as the tether brought him closer to the shuttle.

The amount of debris passing him increased in frequency, speed and size. Debris ricocheted off of the satellite shell and dispersed in every direction, although the shell itself protected him from the rebounds. It wouldn't take much to puncture both layers of his suit. He whispered goodbyes to his family. The others were putting out so much chatter he doubted they heard.

The satellite vibrated as larger debris struck and Milne tightened his grip. How much further to the shuttle? They'd been reeling him in forever. A sharp pull from behind jerked him sideways and one hand slipped off the satellite. "What the—?"

"Milne!" Wu sounded panicked. "Debris tore your tether! Let go of the satellite so we can haul you in before it rips through!"

Milne bit back another curse. The choice was taken out of his hands as a large piece of debris caromed off of the shell, straight "up" from Milne's position, while the satellite pulled to his right, away from Orpheus. Once his hands were loose, the tether yanked Milne towards the shuttle. More debris hit the satellite dead on, pushing it farther out of reach and out of orbit.

As he was pulled backwards, more debris impacted his suit, surely creating minute tears in the outer layer. Thankfully, nothing punctured the inner layer. Yet. He twisted so he could see the shuttle.

"Stay still!" Wu yelled. "You've got about two strands holding you to us and a couple of feet to go! On my mark, curl into a ball and you'll slide right into the airlock!" The pause was the longest of Milne's life outside of waiting for Aleksander to accept his proposal. *There aren't enough stars in the sky to swear by,* Alek had responded. There were more than enough stars around Milne now.

"MARK!"

Milne pulled himself into a ball, gripping his knees with his hands. He sped up slightly and forced his eyes to stay open so he could see the upper edge of the airlock gliding past him. He untucked as the door slid shut. Several pieces of debris ricocheted off the closing door and into the room, one pinging off his visor and starting a spider-web effect. Milne held his breath and waited for the door to be shut and the tell-tale hiss of oxygen filling the airlock chamber before he released it. The visor hadn't completely cracked, but the suit would never be usable again.

He was out of the suit and barging through to the bridge in seconds, leaving the suit crumpled up on the floor. Zimmerman swore under his breath, fingers flying across his console to determine the fastest, safest landing vector.

Wu turned from his console long enough to punch Milne hard on the arm. "You deserve a punch in the face, but we don't have time to set any broken bones. Not that it'll matter, since there's a good chance we're crashing."

Milne slid into his seat, buckled up, and accessed his own console. He was still getting data streamed from the satellite as it slid further and further out of range, still broadcasting.

"Zimmerman, what are you seeing that we're not?" Werder was all calm and professional now. "We've lost the satellite data-stream."

"Yeah, well, we've lost the satellite, so that makes sense." Zimmerman barked. "There's a ton of debris headed our way, and the pieces are getting larger. We've got a problem if we don't get down fa—"

The shuttle shook with the impact of something large. All three men grabbed their consoles. No alarms sounded to indicate a hull breach. The shaking stopped after a moment, and Zimmerman resumed a course to take them home in one piece. The shuttle continued forward and down towards the atmosphere.

There was another impact, a stronger one. Milne gave a sideways glance to Wu's console, catching the bright red of the impact on a schematic of the shuttle, surrounded by yellow markings for smaller impacts they were not feeling. The number of yellow markers worried him. Enough smaller impacts could be as troublesome as a few larger impacts. Smaller debris could also settle into the engines through the exhaust panels.

Milne returned his attention to his own panel. The signal from the satellite continued to diminish in strength as the distance between them widened. He boosted the gains as much as he could, and the signal flared for a moment. The satellite was moving off at a different direction from the majority of the debris exiting the ring. That could be a blessing, in that the satellite would not suffer any further immediate damage, but also a curse, as the new trajectory was pushing it farther out of line with Earth. As the signal weakened, he tried to think of other ways to boost the connection. At least they'd started broadcasting. Other colony ships might drop out of warp in a location to pick up that signal and relay it back to Earth.

The cabin lights went red. Claxons sounded warning of an imminent breach of the outer hull.

"Personal protective equipment NOW!" Zimmerman shouted over the alarms, just as Foley's voice came over the radio.

"Shuttle! Scuttle mission and bring yourselves down immediately!"

"As if we had a choice." Wu grumbled before toggling his mic open to the planetary frequency. "Werder, give me a beacon to lock onto, outside the colony. Screw looking for a soft landing; we're gonna be lucky to land at all."

All three pulled on protective suits and then continued working their consoles: Zimmerman trying to pilot away from the larger pieces of debris heading their way, Wu laying in coordinates for a landing that would keep them well away from the colony itself if they came down explosively, and Milne collecting and relaying the diminishing data from the satellite.

Zimmerman cut off the alarms and the chamber, still washed in red light, was eerily quiet.

"We know we're in trouble. We need to hear each other better," he said to no-one in particular.

With the alarms off, the number of direct hits and partial glances the shuttle was taking from the debris became more noticeable. Milne had hoped they were heading away from the storm, but it seemed like they were now in the middle of it. Every reverberation through the shuttle shook them in their seats and made them tense up expecting the breach alarm and their suits to seal.

The breach alarm never came, but the shuttle took its most violent hit yet, and a different alarm sounded.

"Engine rupture!" Zimmerman shouted.

Milne could feel the shuttle swinging around as forward momentum ceased. Another piece of debris hit the rear end of the craft. "Thrusters?"

"Firing," Wu answered. "Werder, forget that beacon. We can't control our descent beyond what the thrusters are capable of." He paused, swore. "And we're leaking what little fuel we have left. There's a good chance once we hit the atmosphere, we'll be leaving a flaming trail for you to find us by."

"Get yourself to the ground," Foley responded instead of the kid. "We'll be waiting."

Hands worked consoles feverishly. Wu tracked the fuel. Zimmerman fired the thrusters, pushing them down into the atmosphere. Milne gave up tracking the satellite data and tracked the debris storm, which they passed out of as they moved closer to the planet.

They could feel increased resistance on the shuttle as they entered the atmosphere. The shuttle became harder for Zimmerman to control even before the fuel reserves ran out.

Milne switched his sensors over to positioning data, to figure where the shuttle would come down. "We'll come down outside the colony by several miles."

"But not on anything soft," Wu added.

"Not in that location, no." Zimmerman concurred.

"Foley is on her way out to your projected landing site," Werder's voice came over the line. "We've mustered every crewmember we can."

"Hey, kid," Zimmerman interrupted.

"Yeah?"

"Sorry I was so hard on you. And so easy, too. Shoulda spent more time teaching, less time blaming."

"You'll have plenty of time to make that up, Zimm." The fact that Werder addressed him by his nickname wasn't lost on Milne. "And the rest of you, too."

"Still, just in case." Milne chose his next words carefully. "Tell our families we love them, and you do everything you can to keep comms running in case Earth ever does get in touch. Got that, Werder?"

"Yeah." Werder sounded resigned. "Yeah, I do."

"Good. Now stop talking to us, and let us try to set this thing down without a big explosion, okay?"

"Yes, sirs."

And then there wasn't time to think, just react, as the ground drew closer.

Zimmerman pulled the nose up and they landed on the shuttle's belly. But the shuttle had been built for controlled vertical landings with landing gear deployed, not for landing like an old Earth aircraft.

Milne passed out as the shuttle began an uncontrolled skid across the flat plateau in front of them.

§

He came to in a hospital bed, wrapped in bandages. His blurry right eye opened after several blinks; the left forced closed with something heavy and unmoving. Something immobilized his neck, but he tried to look to his right anyway. A headache spiked behind his eye in response to the movement, and he gasped.

"Welcome back. It's been a rough few days." Werder moved into his line of sight.

"Faa..." Milne tried to speak, but his mouth was too dry.

"Your family's right outside. Doc had a feeling you'd be waking up soon. You and Wu have been recovering at about the same rate and he came to an hour ago."

"Zzz..." Milne tried to speak again.

"I'm sorry. We got you and Wu out before the fire got to you, but Zimm...he was crushed by his console. I—I'd rather let Foley give you all the details. I'm gonna get your family."

Milne grabbed Werder's arm as he turned away. The kid spun to look at him.

"Sss..." Milne tried again.

"Satellite's gone, man. But we got a ton of extra data from it thanks to the boost you gave the signal before it slipped out of range. It was still broadcasting. Maybe someone'll hear it and chase it down. Meantime, our days of chasing satellites are over. Can't afford to risk any more lives up there. We're here, this is home now. Let me get Aleksander and Renee. Family First, right?"

Milne nodded, and let Werder leave. Family First, he thought. Orpheus Colony would survive, thrive, or fail, on its own. This had always been true. But now it would be a known reality. At least the planet was hospitable, the colony strong and secure. With the comm satellite gone, they could put their energy and resources into exploring the world they were trapped on.

Milne's daughter pushed through the door and rushed the bed before Aleksander, trailing behind her, could rein her in. Milne grunted with the impact, and his good eye blurred with tears. It hurt, but it was a good hurt.

The Firebird
Andrew Gudgel

Do you have it?" asked Tomasz, Baron Windebank, setting down his menu and leaning over the table.

"Yes," sighed Marek. "I have it. Next time, though, you go deal with those damned, dumb-matter loving Turks yourself."

Baron Windebank wagged a finger at his younger dinner companion. "Now, now, Marek. Just because the Caliphate chose not to host a Consensus in Istanbul doesn't make them damned."

Marek snorted. "Might as well be. The place was a pit. Gray. Dirty. Nothing changes there. Nothing *can* change there." He shook his head in disgust.

Tomasz shrugged. "It's their choice not to allow Programmable Matter. Just like it's ours to be part of the Prague Consensus." He tugged at his lace cuffs and ran a hand over his wig, patting the curls into place. "Well? You have it; are you going to give it to me?"

Marek reached down and produced a blue cloth-wrapped bundle, which he handed across the table with a disgusted sniff. "Here."

Tomasz opened the bundle to reveal a leather-bound book with antique, gold fleur-de-lis I/O connectors along the spine. "Any problems in getting it?"

"Let me see. Other than having to get on a decrepit, old *airplane*, fly a couple of hours to spend four days in a hellhole of a city, deal with that grimy antiques dealer you sent me to—who by the way, muttered prayers at me like I was unclean or something—*and* missing all of this year's Changeover parties...no."

Tomasz raised an eyebrow but said nothing. He flipped open the book, glanced at the displayed text, then icon-tapped his way through the first dozen pages. Satisfied, he snapped the cover shut. "You could have said you didn't want to go."

"You twisted my arm with fifty kilos of PM. You know I can't afford to turn something like that down this early in my career." Marek shrugged. "Plus, you're the one who sponsored me to join the Consensus." He took a sip of his coffee, then gestured with the cup. "Why didn't you go yourself, Tom? You love far-retro stuff; Istanbul would have been right up your alley."

Tomasz wagged his finger. "We're in a new year and season. You're talking now to a peer of the realm. The proper title of address is 'milord.' Now, I didn't go because I want to keep a low profile. I'm still recovering from last year's little...problem."

During the Jazz Age, the Consensus had proposed tearing down Tyn Church, as well as the medieval clock in the old town square, and replacing them with PM structures. Tomasz, whose hobbies were dumb-matter machines and re-creating antique nanotech, had been a strong and vocal supporter of the minority in opposition. It had cost him a lot of the reputation he had built up over the years among his patrons in the upper echelon of the Consensus. And was probably the reason why he'd only been elected to the rank of baron at this year's Changeover.

"I see," said Marek. "So, the damage to my reputation doesn't mean anything to you."

Tomasz laughed. "My dear Marek, this early in your career you don't even *have* a reputation to damage."

Marek looked hurt. After a moment, he pointed across the table. "What book is that, anyway, that I hurt my supposedly nonexistent reputation to get?"

"This," said Tomasz, tapping a finger on the leather, "is the private lab book of Andreas Karlo."

"Who?"

"Andreas Karlo. One of the earliest nanotech pioneers. Lived a century or so ago. His work paved the way for PM. If it weren't for him, there wouldn't be a Consensus in Prague—or London, or Rome, or anywhere else."

Marek nodded politely, uninterested, then picked up his menu, scanned it, and set it back down. "Wish this year's theme wasn't the Restoration. I can't make any sense of this far-retro stuff. If we were still in the Jazz Age, I could at least read the menu. Look at this stuff! What the hell is a syllabub, anyway?"

"A kind of dessert." Tomasz smiled. "Tell you what. Here's a copy of my historical research packet, gratis." He held out his hand, and Marek took it. After a moment, Marek's signet ring beeped. "Read it," said Tomasz, "it'll get you up to speed on this year's theme."

Marek stared at the gold band on his finger, reading the text projected directly onto his retina by a million nanoscale lasers.

"Wow! That's quite a detailed packet, Tom...I mean, milord. How'd you get so much info? The changeover was just a couple of days ago." Marek looked up.

Baron Windebank smiled and shrugged. "I got advance notice of this year's theme from a ...connection."

Marek raised an eyebrow. "You still have them after last year?"

Tomasz shrugged. "A few. If my info packets keep selling like they have been, I should make enough to earn back some of the respectability I lost last year."

"What you need to do is to suck up to your connections. Give one of them a big present, so you can then..."

"The king," said Tomasz.

Marek blinked in confusion. "The king?"

"Yeah," nodded Tomasz. "The king. Go straight to the top."

"You *are* ambitious, milord. But how then do you impress the king?"

"The same as anybody else—a gift. But it'd have to be something really spectacular." Tomasz smiled. "That's why I sent you to get Karlo's lab book." He picked it up off the table. "He was famous for the little knickknacks he crafted in his spare time. There's bound to be something in his notebook that I can use."

"But his stuff is all pre-PM."

Tomasz shrugged. "So? He was so far ahead of his time that they're *still* not sure how some of his creations worked. Besides, what better way to impress the leader of a far-retro year, *and* turn my hobby from a liability to an asset, than to give him a retro gift?" He set the book back down. "I'm hungry. Shall we eat?"

Marek nodded. "Go ahead and order, since *you* can read the damned menu."

"I'll have the venison pasty with a sallet," said Tomasz to the tabletop. "Syllabub for dessert. And a glass of Rhenish wine."

"I'll have the same," said Marek.

"Talk about sucking up," joked Tomasz, tucking a napkin under his chin and fingering the silverware the tabletop had just extruded. "Speaking of that, I need a toady. You want the job?"

"A what?" asked Marek.

"A companion. A hanger-on. Anybody who was anybody in the Restoration period had one. Somebody who's always around to talk, or play cards, run errands, things like that. Think Johnson and Boswell."

"Who?"

Tomasz chuckled. "Never mind. Think of it as friend and errand boy."

"Salary?" asked Marek hopefully.

"None right now, but when I sell a few more info packets, we can talk. But I *will* cover your expenses until then."

Marek smiled. "Then I'm your man."

§

The Baron's beetle-black carriage rolled slowly through the town square. In the harness labored a bronze equinoid, like a statue off its marble base and come to life. Tomasz patted the horse's rump appreciatively. They passed members of the Consensus promenading across the square in their still-new-enough-to-be-uncomfortable Restoration fashions. Tomasz doffed his hat and smiled as the carriage rolled out of the square.

A few blocks later, they turned onto Tomasz's street. All along it, houses were still reshaping themselves, their programmable matter flowing like warm wax. One still sported striped awnings left over from the last season's Jazz Age. At the end of the street sat a perfect red-brick, Restoration-period house. Tall windows reflected the light of the setting sun.

"Just need the roof to grow a few more shingles, and the house'll be finished," said Tomasz as he stepped down from the carriage.

"And the inside, of course," said Marek.

Six hundred kilos of pseudo-oak swung open when Tomasz approached the entrance. "No, that's already done."

A homunculus in Baron Windebank's livery met them at the door and took their coats. Dying sunlight reflected off the android's golden skin as it crossed the black and white, polished marble floor.

Marek looked around and whistled, and the sound echoed around the foyer. "I like it. The twin staircases are a nice touch. They must have taken a while to form."

Tomasz smiled and shrugged. "I got a bit of a head start, remember?" He tucked the book under his arm and walked deeper into the house. "Come on. The lab's in back."

The Baron stopped at a small door and touched his signet ring to it. The blurred edge of the pseudowood sharpened as the molecules unbound from the frame, unlocking the door. He pushed it open and entered, Marek a few steps behind him.

Inside the small room sat a workbench and a stool. And a single couch-sized object under a sheet. Tomasz commanded the windows to opaque, then called for a couch, a table, and a decanter of brandy. He dropped down on the couch even before it had finished growing from the wall. He unstoppered the brandy and poured two fingers.

"Thank you, milord," said Marek, taking the glass held out to him.

Tomasz poured another for himself. "To a good year."

"To a good year."

"Now," said Tomasz, "let's see what if we can find something fit for a king." He lifted the book from his lap, crossed his legs, and opened the cover.

He icon-tapped his way through the first few pages. "Ah, here's a neat one. How about a monocle that can see through solid objects?"

"Variable depth? Could you see just under people's clothes?"

Tomasz consulted the book, then looked up. "Nope. Doesn't look like it."

"No good. The king won't want to spend all day looking at his courtier's guts."

Tomasz nodded and returned to the book. After a while, he heard a snore and looked up.

Marek had sat down at the other end of the couch and fallen asleep, his head resting on the arm. Tomasz got up and moved over to the stool. He set the book on the workbench, tapped through another page or two, then stopped.

"Perfect," he said under his breath. He hopped off the stool and removed the sheet covering his antique nano-assembler. He ran his hand along its graceful metallic curves, then checked the feed hopper, and laid his finger over the On switch. A green light flashed on the control panel as the machine powered up.

Tomasz went back to the workbench and examined the book's I/O connectors, then asked the bench to create an appropriate patch cable. He used the cable to connect the book and the assembler, then highlighted a section of the book's text and tapped the "transmit" icon in the margin. The ancient symbol of a tumbling hourglass appeared over the highlighted text. While the data uploaded, Tomasz poured himself another drink.

When the upload finished, he set the assembler to work. Tomasz watched through the chamber's diamond window. A carpet of powdery gray mold spread into the chamber, thickening toward the center.

Marek padded over, yawning and stretching. "What are you doing, milord?"

"I've got the perfect present for the King," said Tomasz, turning away from the tiny window. "A firebird."

"A what?"

"A firebird. It's an egg that opens, and a bird made of fire appears inside. The bird slowly turns the egg to ash, and then the ashes consolidate back into an egg."

Marek shrugged. "Doesn't sound all that interesting to me."

Tomasz raised an eyebrow. "Well, I think it'd be pretty impressive. We'll see once I get it all together and working."

The assembler chimed twice. Tomasz went over and pushed a button on the control panel. Air hissed back into the chamber. He opened the door and retrieved a fist-sized metal egg. The surface was covered with a tangled-silk pattern, like a chunk of acid-etched meteorite. The large end flattened out into a natural base. He set the egg on the workbench.

"Doesn't look like much, so far," said Marek.

Tomasz looked over at him. "It's just a lump of micro-circuits and nano-machines. You have to have programming fluid to make it work." He highlighted the appropriate text in the book and tapped the "transmit" icon a second time.

The programming liquid took a long time to assemble—whole minutes longer than Tomasz thought. When it was done, he removed a vial from the assembler and poured a few drops of the pearly liquid into a match-head-sized hollow in the base of the egg. When the liquid had been absorbed, he set both egg and vial back down on the table.

The egg began to vibrate. Suddenly, it cracked into four petal-like sections, which opened like a flower and laid flat. In the center, a tiny blue flame appeared. It flared, becoming thumb-sized, then swelled into a ball the size of an orange.

Within the ball of flame appeared a golden peacock. Tiny gold sparks hissed down onto the tabletop as the bird spread its tail, and let out a trilling, musical call. Layers of shimmering blue and orange flames formed its feathers and tail.

"I was wrong. That *is* impressive," said Marek, not taking his eyes off the firebird.

Tomasz and Marek watched the bird open its beak, peck at each of the egg sections in turn, then preen its tail.

The cycle of open tail/call/preen/peck repeated itself. But after only a few repetitions, the firebird vanished. The egg had been reduced to a vaguely cross-shaped smear of ash.

"How long will it take for it to re-form?" asked Marek.

Tomasz checked the lab book and sighed. "Longer than I thought. About four hours."

"That's not going to work for a present for the King."

"No," said Tomasz. "It's not." He grunted. "We'll worry about that in the morning. Let's call it a night."

§

Tomasz tugged at his lace collar with a finger. The salon just outside the throne room was too warm, and he'd been waiting for over an hour to be presented. A trickle of sweat rolled down over his temple. He swore under his breath and mopped his head with an ornate handkerchief.

After what seemed like an eternity, the door opened and his patron, the Earl of Portland, appeared. Tomasz stood and bowed low.

"My lord."

"Good to see you, Tom."

"You too, sir."

The Earl cocked his head. "You have your gift all ready, I assume? I'd like to have a look at this present of yours before you take it in."

Tomasz stuffed the damp handkerchief into his coat and dug into the opposite pocket. He removed a small, purple velvet pouch and extracted the firebird egg.

"Very nice," said the Earl, taking it from him. Flashes of spectral red, blue, and green shone from the gems Tomasz had added onto the surface of the gold-plated egg. "Very nice indeed. This must have taken some work."

The past week had been a nightmare. He'd gotten ahead of himself and foolishly called the earl to ask for an audience with the King. Only then did he discover just how complex a creation the egg really was. He'd wasted days trying to every trick he could think of to shorten the regeneration cycle. Nothing worked.

He finally had to admit defeat and abandon the idea of using dumb matter altogether. The thing to do was replace the original egg hardware with a chunk of programmable matter, and re-work the programming fluid. While the idea seemed simple on Wednesday night, reworking the fluid had caused a whole new set of problems with the fire-suppression algorithms built into all PM. He found a work-around, but only after a thirty-six-hour-marathon hack session, and with only hours to go until his audience with the king. The new firebird egg would need to be "fed" periodically with small pieces of PM to check the mass loss of combustion, but by that point, Tomasz didn't have time to take care of that little hitch, let alone take notes on all the changes he'd made to the milky fluid. Worse, he'd almost had a disaster when, exhausted from the hack session, he'd knocked the diamond vial of re-worked programming fluid over as he set it on his workbench.

Fortunately, he had the presence of mind to have the bench catch the fluid in a dimple in its top. He'd had only enough time to calve off a gold, bejeweled egg from a chunk of PM, inoculate it, get dressed, and make it to the palace with minutes to spare.

Tomasz smiled and waved his hand dismissively. "Not much."

The earl handed the egg back. "Well, shall we go in and see His Majesty?"

Tomasz replaced the egg, tucked the pouch into his pocket, and followed the earl in.

King Charles II, leader of the Consensus for this year of the Restoration, sat on a red-silk-and-gilt throne, surrounded by his advisers.

"Your Majesty, I present to you Tomasz, Baron Windebank, a personal friend. He has a most curious and unusual gift for you."

Tomasz bowed low. "Your Majesty. May your reign be a happy one."

"We thank you, Baron Windebank. Please rise."

Tomasz stood. He recognized the face of the king, who had been Prague's most popular saxophone player during last year's Jazz Age.

"Your Majesty," said Tomasz, removing the pouch from his pocket. "I have a curiosity I'd like to present as a small token of my esteem." He removed the egg and held it out. "May I approach?"

"You may, Baron Windebank."

Tomasz set the egg on a small table beside the throne. "This is a firebird egg, adapted from an ancient recipe I discovered in a most curious book. I am a lover of antique..."

The king cut him off. "Your, *ahem*, proclivities are already known to me through other means, Baron Windebank. Please just show me this marvel of yours."

Tomasz paused a long moment before speaking again. "It's really quite simple, Your Majesty. It opens and closes like so."

The King raised his eyebrows when the egg opened and the firebird appeared. He remained silent as it cycled through its routines. When it was done, Tomasz stepped back. "It requires only that you feed the egg with a pea of programmable matter every few operations, Majesty, to keep it in perfect working order."

The King pursed his lips, then broke into a grin. "Baron Windebank, your little firebird is quite remarkable. We thank you for this curious gift."

Tomasz bowed low. "I'm honored, Your Majesty." Sensing the audience was over, he backed away from the throne, then moved towards the door, followed by the Earl of Portland.

"Well done, Tom!" said the earl after the door had closed. "I think the king really likes your present. I wish I had gotten a chance to see it in action earlier."

Tomasz had a sudden inspiration. "Well my lord, your personal egg will be ready shortly. Then you can watch your own firebird as much as you'd like. Shall I send eggs—plainer looking than yours and the king's, of course, but still of excellent quality—to those you feel deserve them?"

A sly smile spread across the Earl's face. "Well done again, Tom! That's an excellent idea. I'll send a list of names later, but I think there would be about twenty in all."

Tomasz nodded. "No problem, my lord. I can have them delivered by the day after tomorrow."

"Excellent!" The earl looked back towards the throne room door. "Now, Baron Windebank, if you'll excuse me."

Tomasz bowed as the earl left. A liveried footman saw him out of the palace. Once his equinoid and carriage had trotted out the gates, he chuckled to himself. With luck, the egg would not only restore his reputation, but put him on the short list for a membership in the upper echelon.

§

"An excellent dinner, milord," said Marek, patting his lips with a linen napkin.

"Thank you. More wine?"

Marek shook his head. "No thanks, I've had plenty."

Tomasz poured himself another glass and sat the decanter on the table.

Just then the house homunculus glided in. "Milord, the Earl of Portland's house just informed me that you're about to receive a call."

Tomasz's signet ring beeped, and he looked down. The face of the earl appeared in the center of his vision.

Tomasz smiled. "Good evening, my lord."

"Hello, Tom. Celebrating?"

"A little, my lord."

"Well, you have every right to. The king absolutely adores your gift. He played with it all day, and even took it back to his private chamber for the night."

Tomasz smiled. "Really?"

"Yes. Tom, I've attached the list of names. Please send them out as soon as possible."

"Certainly, my lord."

"Oh, and if you're free tomorrow, come have lunch with me at my house. There are some gentlemen I'd like you to meet."

Tomasz's smile broadened. "Of course I'm free, my lord."

The earl nodded. "Good. See you tomorrow at noon, then."

The call ended and Tomasz puffed out a breath. He looked over at Marek. "He wants me to come for lunch tomorrow."

Marek smiled. "Congratulations. Sounds like you're back on your way up."

"One can only hope." Tomasz took a sip of wine. "House!"

"Yes, milord?" replied the homunculus.

"How many names on the Earl's list?"

"Seventeen."

"Read them to me."

The homunculus recited the names in clear, crisp tones—princes, privy council members—all men of influence.

"That'll be all for now."

The homunculus left. Tomasz stood and picked up his glass of wine.

"Let's go to the lab. I want to get these other eggs out tonight."

In the lab, he opaqued the windows and set his wineglass on the workbench, while Marek called up a new couch to sit on. He reached for the vial of programming fluid and felt a lump as his arm slid across the top of the bench. When he looked, the smooth plain of the surface was marred by a small dome-shaped mound. He clucked his tongue. The bench must have continued working even after he'd told it to get rid of the fluid-catching depression.

Tomasz commanded the workbench re-level its surface, then went to the far side of the lab and returned with a standard ten-kilo block of programmable matter. Using an interface grown from the table-top, Tomasz calved off a jewel-encrusted golden egg, then set it to work forming the other, plainer eggs.

When all the eggs were ready, Tomasz inoculated them with the new programming fluid. As a final touch, he used the left-over PM to grow red velvet bags embroidered with the coat of arms of the various recipients. Then he called for the homunculus and sent it off to deliver the firebird eggs.

§

Tomasz woke to an unfamiliar smell and the homunculus keening in his ear. It took him a moment to recognize the smell as smoke. He threw the covers back and leapt out of bed.

"What's going on?"

"There's a fire in the laboratory," replied the homunculus. "I'm unable to control it. I suggest evacuation."

Tomasz pulled a cloak from his wardrobe and threw it over his bedclothes. "A fire? That's impossible."

"The temperature in the laboratory now exceeds three-hundred and eighty degrees Celsius."

Smoke tickled his nose. "Go wake Marek. Get him out of the house."

Tomasz hurried downstairs. The smoke grew thicker as he descended.

He went to the lab and threw open the door. The room was a sheet of flame. His workbench was gone. In its place stood a meter-high egg and a firebird taller than a man. The walls and ceiling sprayed water as fast as they could extract it from the surrounding air, but the firebird's heat was overwhelming. His antique nano-assembler began to smoke, then with a dull *whump*, flames shot out the top.

The firebird gave a deafening, trilling, musical shriek. Tomasz turned to run but fell sprawling in the hallway.

Sparks of fire burned his skin as he scrambled to his hands and knees. The floor was littered with dozens of firebird eggs. As he stared, one rose up from the pseudomarble in front of his face. The firebird shrieked again.

He scooped up one of the loose eggs and crawled through the thickening smoke out of the house.

On the curb, Tomasz stood beside Marek and watched as the first tongues of flame appeared in the ground floor windows. Over the crackle of the fire, he heard a continuous stream of musical, trilling calls.

"What the hell happened?" asked Marek.

Tomasz looked down at the ovoid still clutched in his hand. "My workbench turned into a giant egg that set the house on fire. I had to subvert the fire-prevention algorithms to get the program to work with

PM. The bench must have been contaminated when I spilled the fluid across the top."

"Yeah, but then where did the other ones come from?"

Tomasz shrugged. "Maybe sparks from the larger firebird. If they contained traces of the program, that could be enough to contaminate... Oh my God!" His eyes went wide. "The king! His egg will have contaminated the table by the throne, as well as his bedchamber..."

The homunculus glided up beside him. "The city mainframe just reported a large fire at the palace," it said.

"I'm ruined!" cried Tomasz.

"Maybe worse," said Marek. "If the Consensus decides to adopt Restoration-period laws to try you..."

Tomasz dropped to his knees on the cobblestones. "I'll be hung as an attempted regicide." He pulled his arm back to toss the firebird egg into the now-blazing house, then stopped. He stood and turned to the homunculus. "Bring me my carriage."

The carriage emerged from the stable entrance down the street. Flames glinted off the bronze body of the equinoid as it approached. Tomasz leapt in and motioned for the homunculus to follow.

Marek stepped up and put his hand on the carriage door. "What are you doing?! You can't just leave!"

Tomasz looked down at him. "There's nothing left for me here now. I'll be kicked out of the Consensus for sure." He glanced at his burning house, then held up the firebird egg. "But this just might get me started back up the ladder again. What better defense against PM than a program that makes it self-destruct? They'll love me!"

"Love you?" Marek pointed to the inferno that had been Tomasz's house. "Where would they love you for something like that, Tom?"

"Istanbul," said Tomasz, former Baron Windebank, and rode off into the night.

A Soul to the Stars

Lawrence Dagstine

Darren Spickler crouched blindly in the control chair as the soul climbed slowly. He heard John Walcott speaking with the warmth of a man who had put himself in another's place. "It's a beautiful sky," he said. "Another body, another day. Crystal clear."

"Roger that. Hitching a ride with the heart attack victim, too, huh?" Of course, if the body down in the clinic had had a stroke, then the ghost might have flown the men to the moon in record time.

"Best flight fuel in the whole universe," Walcott replied simply.

At the tip of the atmosphere, when John contacted the first sphere pilot for the male soul, Darren was lost again in the strange fog of fear he had felt throughout the morning. He even glanced at the familiar instruments and the panel of warning lights, hoping for a red one that would cause the flight to abort. But there was none. He heard Ike Shepherd over the sphere's transcendental communicator. "Two-minute warning, Darren. The doc couldn't save him, so buckle up. This time's for real."

Automatically, he punched the stopwatch in the titanium cockpit. As if in a dream, he went through the randomized space flight routine, feeling the tense knot in his neck and shoulders draw tighter, hearing the wispy sound of his breath fighting the pressure of the oxygen in the system. Now the time was racing, and he heard Ike's voice, counting coldly at first, and then with excitement as he reached the end: "Ten seconds, boys. Nine, eight, seven…"

He flicked on the data transfer switch that would send his own sphere's telemetering information to the ground, that would enable the paranormal engineers to learn all from the flight of the dead man's soul whether he himself lived or died.

"This is a huge step for the aerospace industry," someone said from the launchpad.

"We still need to take precautions when using a spirit's essence for space travel," the other, more opinionated scientists remarked. "The soul is still a fairly new kind of energy source."

"Six seconds, five, four..."

Darren had the moment of uncertainty that he always had just before the fixed rising point (or the *ascension*): What had he forgotten? And this time, with startling clarity, he saw his son catching up with him at the elevator to the launchpad, holding out his hands. "Daddy, why don't you just once before leaving this place, wait and ask yourself: 'Have I forgotten anything?'" The boy was smart for his years, having known his father too well.

"Three seconds, two, one..."

At the last moment he had a mad desire to cancel himself out of the flight and let the soul continue on its way—to heaven, hell, wherever. Cancel and claim a red light, maybe even sickness.

"Take-off!"

There was a final *"vrooshhh!"* and he was climbing up the molecular shaft of light at three thousand miles per minute. For a moment he sat frozen in the glaring shock of the predawn sunlight. Then he heard Shepherd's voice crackling through his communicator. "Good job, Darren. You rose fast and clear. Drifting free."

Automatically Darren reached for the sphere's booster rocket switches, and with the others in wait. Where he started in the spirit's heart, traveling to the neck and head, the others were situated in the arms or legs, working their way up to the hips and shoulders. He flicked the green switch labeled Number One, flinching as the giant downward shoves from G-Force began pummeling.

It was that hectic test-flight seventeen all over again, but on this ascension, with the rocket engines from each and every sphere finally blasting full throttle for the first time, he was to undergo accelerations that would cram him back into his seat with roughly five times the force of gravity. When booster number seven lit off—which would have left the sphere on the soul's upper left side trapped inside the elbow joint—he couldn't see how sustaining the added force with booster number three and four would help. Since he had already flicked its firing stud, setting off a reaction to the other spheres, he could only sit and wait. Booster three and four burst into life with a throbbing surge that disabled part of the ascension drive and practically immobilized him. Through roaring static he heard Shepherd. "They're all lit, buddy. Give it all you got...."

He stared at the switches and dials, the panels and miniature computer banks before him, hypnotized, while his speed, along with the soul's speed, increased. Male souls were always faster for some reason than female ones, especially if the male had been strong or athletic in his lifetime. And when his sphere's speed increased, little by little, so did most of the others; Walcott, controlling the right side, was already in the forearm.

He sliced through the sound barrier in an upward angle almost instantly, part of the soul's ascension methods being the route cause, and, as the Mach and G-Force numbers slid swiftly up, he heard his sphere's air pressurizer whine like metal contorting, as if in a fierce battle with air friction at a thermal phase. The outer shell was pushing a thousand degrees, minimal, but not too far from the limit. Seen through the tiny-slitted, nine-inch thick windows above his panel, the titanium skin on the outer windowsill was glowing an orange and red melody, and closest to the cockpit. Cherry-red was the color covering the base of the sphere. He finally eased up the sphere's ascent in its present vertical course. The glow became less bright, and the numbers gradually fell. He tore his eyes back to the dials before him and heard himself chanting his speeds to Ground Control. "All spheres' G-Force levels falling properly. Mach speed still rising. 10,000...now at 20,000... now at 40,000... reaching peak levels and ascent soon."

"That sounds about right," engineers and scientists concurred. "Don't level off or up too fast. We only just called him a few minutes ago. The clinic hasn't even conducted an autopsy yet to be sure it *was* a coronary. We don't want to waste any of the soul's energy either. All spheres need to share the fuel, share of the essence before you break."

When he'd heard that, he questioned them on it. "Are you sure this is ethical? Or the soul I'm using even powerful enough?"

"Don't worry," they assured him. "You'll be among the stars in no time. You're the lead astronaut this time around, and with your qualifications, that says a lot."

Shepherd and Walcott had overheard. "Hey, it's okay, buddy. Remember, there's no slingshot necessary when we do this. Once we're over the planet, we'll follow up to where your sphere is and begin disengaging, begin letting the spirit follow its own course. Then, we'll make sure every last bit of molecular fuel is dry before it *too* withers out, connect up in the cerebral cortex area, stabilize airlocks, and have ourselves a drink to celebrate."

He was still uncertain; better, yet slightly nervous. "Yeah, I…I guess I'll be seeing you guys soon enough," he said.

The grinding force of acceleration seemed to build again, as if a powerful being—no, *supernatural* being—had taken over and wildly decided that he would roar even faster, forever and into the afterlife, with Darren and the others hopping along for the ride, through the trackless sky. Darren felt that if one more iota, one more ounce of thrust were added on to the cumulative push, his guts would burst through his back. Disregarding the mask by his side, he concentrated on pressure breathing and fought the oxygen cramming firmly but violently into his lungs. And still the downward shove increased.

Startlingly, he heard an engineer's voice, fading momentarily but clear: "Paranormal Consistency from Ground Control. Readings?"

Readings, my ass, he wanted to say. *I can hardly breathe; something's not right.* "I have a Mach Ascent reading of 200,000 and rising." His voice was a strained grunt. "It's now almost 250." With the soul guiding his sphere, he was traveling faster than man had ever flown. "We're over 250 now. Left the cloud masses a long time ago."

"Good," the engineer said. "Remember your simulated runs on the people who were dying in the clinic those other times, and you should be just fine."

Through the mental cloudiness that was enveloping him came a warning flash. The soul was at 275,000 feet. In an instant he would be in the controllability phase, prepping to disengage the spirit and join his comrades. He had a decision to make. The arms and legs… He had to decide. Should he try it? His mind cleared. If he did, and the soul threw off his control, what of his son? His wife had died five years ago, and the boy really didn't have any other family but him. One little tap of pressurization, and they'll most certainly know one thing: whether, as an astronaut, you're the real thing, or a phony in a flight suit.

The shimmering waves of vibration starting again, Darren's sphere was beginning to describe areas of black infinity. Just a tap, and they'd know. *He'd* know himself.…

"Are you in the controllability phase?" Shepherd asked.

"Entering it now." Darren tensed his legs.

"Do you intend to check your pressurizers?"

The question lay heavily on the airwaves. The indecision was over for Darren. *You think it's that simple,* he thought. *Why not on reentry, if at all?* A strange, exultant kind of freedom suddenly possessed him. "Negative," he said clearly. "I'm taking my hands off the piloting controls." He slid his feet to the steel floor, smiling as the waves of oscillation shimmied across the sphere, secure in an almost religious faith that, if he gave the spirit's mass some head, they'd all teeter through the atmosphere at a critical altitude.

And the soul did. With a final shiver he abandoned the support of its ascension and accepted the metamorphosis into a speeding projectile in space. Moments later, after the burn-out, his *own* sphere became a silent ballistic missile hurtling toward that very black infinity, immutably guided in its soaring circular arc by the laws of motion. It would only be controllable temporarily, he figured, for the spheres would disengage again upon final reentry into the atmosphere, the gravity conditions leveled as if he'd never even left the launchpad.

At the moment of burn-out, he became weightless, and so did the equipment around him that wasn't bolted down. It was as if an immensely powerful behemoth had lifted an incredibly strong hand from his chest. The contrast dazed him, and far more than it had on previous flights. He heard himself automatically announce, "Burn-out. We're in free flight, guys."

The instruments swam before his eyes. Floating gently against his chair, he crossed his legs in midair and peered at the panel before him. When his vision cleared, he stared at the gravity meter. It was incredible. So carefully had his flight path been planned, and so predictable were the celestial laws of scientific force concerning the male soul, that he had almost exactly hit his point. The needle of his gravity meter was creeping downward now, as it would until he reached the top point of his journey.

"We'll be joining you soon," Walcott said. "On the minute."

"Roger," he heard Shepherd say. There would be no more reports other than one at the peak of his flight and one for the flight engineers who started out in the soul's ankles. And just before his weightless ride would end, on his *own* sphere's condition.

So now he could slip into it—the fantastic realm of space flight, the ecstatic universe of motion beyond normal motion, of complete surrender to the law that swung the stars and planets. For ten minutes he would be weightless, detached from his environment of normal gravity. For much shorter times, on previous missions, and even simulations, he had known this ultimate privilege of man, this visceral freedom, but there was somehow today a new flavor to it. He knew all at once what it was and how it felt. He had lost his fear. He had emerged from a scorched and padded grassland into clear and magnificent terrain. Floating weightless against his harness, the view of a blue and green world many miles below him, he almost shouted in relief.

The immense blackness, which he had hardly glimpsed before, had turned a thought or two about the possibilities of *this* kind of space travel. The early sun in its majesty had shone white-hot from their orbital range. He was one with the sphere in a soundless and infinite and unmoving void. Only his own breath, rasping tightly against the pressure of his oxygen, broke the reverie of silence.

He began to search the blackness for areas with the most stars. And there they were, steady and in place, in a habitat unfiltered by air. His course seemed northeasterly, and the orbit of his sphere pointed sharply at Venus, the star unwinking in the void. Seconds later he glanced at the rate of his own sphere's altitude above the Earth. With the soul's ascension complete, he would eventually slow to zero soon and decrease, and at around five hundred feet per second for each second of his flight. The same would happen when the others caught up. Still, he was proud—proud because he was the first to get there and enjoy a few moments of solace with the galactic spectacle outside his window.

The sun slashed across half his instrument panel, painting its switches and screens a glaring white. The other half, in shadow, was completely black and unreadable. And all through his sphere's cockpit this phenomenon had settled; that which was encapsulated in sunlight was in bright, harsh color, all else black. It was a black and white world, some of it incredible and of almost startling clarity.

His mind fought against its acceptance, as he floated here in a reign of absolutes, the stark onslaught of some chilling force binding; as if, naked in the limitless void, far from his environment, he was being assailed by a course of thought too cutting for the human mind to sheathe.

The other spheres soon joined him, docked, and the airlocks were given the okay. In minutes, the five steel orbs formed a docking station, where one astronaut could travel or commute between the other, and hovering just within reach of their home planet.

Walcott was the first to board his sphere, champagne bottle in hand. "Good job with the gravitational stabilization, Darren," he said, popping the cork. "Time to celebrate."

Shepherd followed him. "Hey, don't start the party without me. After all, we've only got a few hours up here until that leftover fuel from that dead guy's essence dissipates on us. We need those reserves like *any* soul for reentry, the molecular body makeup of any who have passed on from *this* life into the *next*."

Walcott laughed and started pouring, and soon the engineers joined them. "Now you know I wouldn't start a shindig without you, Ike, only things are going to be different this time upon reentry."

Darren took a seat and sipped his drink and asked, "Like how?"

"Well, this isn't a test run yet it *is*…" Walcott started off by saying, "and the scientists down at Ground Control want us to try another method. Something new they discovered about the dying soul and the living soul. Hey, I don't know much about the paranormal side to this particular flight or even the simulated liftoffs when a dude's about to kick the bucket, but I do know this: ascension and descent—what goes up one way must certainly come down the same way, or in a similar fashion. Since the living soul supposedly won't have enough proper thrust when we head back, the fuel reserves of that guy will support us like food for nurturing."

"Food for nurturing? Are you serious?" Darren was confused, but he'd learn that the experimental reentry stages he'd gone through prior to this flight would be put to good use soon enough, and when the *next* kind of soul approached from beyond the stars.

Walcott shrugged his shoulders. "I'm only a pilot." He could only explain so much.

Shepherd threw them both a conforming glance. "Ditto that." Then he picked up his champagne glass and said, "Amazing the tech we operate today. We've come a long way since Apollo or Voyager. Anyway, what should we toast to?"

Walcott stood up and said, "Let's toast to man's future in space," and with this they raised their glasses, "and *supernatural* science."

§

Reentry would be a tough animal to tackle. When the spheres disengaged again and positioned themselves below Darren's, he was told by Ground Control that he had to wait for something. He'd know what it is right away, so just trust us and *wait*. But what?

From out of the blackness came a soul, smaller and shaped like a giant apple seed, in a trajectory that made it seem very much like a speeding asteroid on a collision course. It was an embryonic soul of sorts, reminiscent of the other man's essence, vibrant and full of life.

"Here comes the egg," Walcott communicated up to him. "Get ready to hitch a ride."

"The living soul approaching in three minutes," Shepherd calculated. "Align yourself with its path and we'll stabilize ourselves to your coordinates."

"Fuel outtake on," he said, switching to standby. "I'm about to enter the fetus's heart and secure gravity upon reentry, just so the newborn doesn't turn premature and so we don't burn up at the same time."

Through the booster rocket controls beneath the sphere he had eased the motion arc perpendicularly, then felt the cockpit shiver as the fetus encapsulated him and the others within its molecular light. He disengaged and injected the spare fuel from the male soul, whatever was left, and saw the first thin line of atmosphere begin to work on his control's surfaces. He had regained his speed in the weightless fall and was hurtling downward at about Mach seven when the tiniest hint of infantile resistance pulsed to his arm from the joystick. He knew that he had only moments before he truly reentered the atmosphere, and through the controllability barrier, the fetus entering some lucky mother's womb.

He called Ground Control and said, "250,000 feet. I'm in, over."

"Damage assessment," they called back up.

"No apparent physical damage. Reentry successful."

"Roger that," Walcott's voice came back. "He carried us nice and well, Ground."

Shepherd said as if he were in the same cockpit, "You mean those rays haven't made you scared, Darren?"

Darren smiled. "Negative, Ike."

The fetus carried them to 200,000 before it went its own way. When he saw the light of the newborn streaking off, he thought about his *own* son. How life and death could be the means to man succeeding in their plight for new frontiers. Life *itself*. For an instant he fought the massive certainty of it, tense and straining, but happy nonetheless.

Soon, in the ultimate moment, he knew that he had had it all—even, finally, of being an outstanding astronaut. Impassively he watched the last, horizon-swinging mountains roll and the Space Center's runways rush toward him.

And in that last second, he had forgot nothing because he felt his son beside him.

Weapons of Mass Destruction
Jude-Marie Green

The first emissary blew herself up.
The observatory contained the damage well; no window blow-outs and no loss of pressure. Those of us in the observatory's window room with her were coated with sappy gunk and bits of cellulose plant matter, the blood and flesh of this particular species of alien. Plus needles. Her stem was covered with bristly needles, just like an Earth-home cactus, and those needles penetrated our unprotected skin.

"Wait!" I said, as my coworkers started plucking the needles out of their skin. "Jeez… Medical Officer, we need blood scans and chemistry analysis, now!" I jiggled one needle that stuck out of my cheek. "Who knows if there's a poison or soporific on the needle? Maybe the needles have the same explosive she brought on board and they'll explode if you touch them. Stop!" I said again as Captain Johnson rolled his eyes and swept a handful of gunk and needles off his chest.

"Maggie Flowers, you're always too excitable. This isn't a terrorist action. Maybe the air pressure got to her." His calmness reassured my other coworkers, and they ignored my warnings and wiped themselves down. "Let's get to the showers, boys," he said.

The four of them, captain and three explorers, filed out of the window room, trailing bits of gunk.

Diego Rivera, the medical officer, arrived with a full kit. I stood in a puddle of gunk, bristling needles, and dripping alien goo. I suppose I should have expected him to laugh.

"What happened to you?" he said when he could speak again. "You look like the bad end of an Irish pub crawl. Hold on," he said as I reached for the sample kit, "let me do it. What are we looking for?"

"Explosives. Soporifics. Plant-based poison. And heck, let's sequence the DNA... she should have DNA, right? But for right now, I'd like you to tell me I'm not gonna die."

He inserted a sample into the synthesizer and waited for the hum to Doppler from slow to fast to slow again. The green light flashed, the machine beeped and a result printed on the screen. I tried to read over his shoulder, but he blocked me.

"Well, the bad news is, you're gonna die," he said. "Good news is, not today, not from this stuff. Go ahead and wipe down." He handed me some paper towels and a water mister.

"What the heck happened, Magdalena? One of your experiments go terribly wrong?"

Ah, he didn't know about our visitor.

"We had an emissary from the sentient aliens of this world, Diego. She just knocked on our door and we just let her in. And then, she blew herself up. She didn't try to communicate or anything."

I sounded depressed. I wanted an open communication channel between us and the native aliens. We all did. But sometimes the natives don't want to bother with talks, they just wanted to blow shit up. That was okay, we had established methods for dealing with such hostilities, but I didn't want to see yet another battlefield.

Diego frowned. "Are you sure it wasn't a pressure gradient issue? Or a temperature thing?"

I shook my head. "No, we lowered the pressure in the observatory just so she could enter. Not that we had to lower it much. We've made a big deal about the pressure difference, but there's just not that much. Not enough of a difference to cause explosive decompression!" I sighed. "It must have been a deliberate explosion."

§

The observatory dripped plant gunk from all its surfaces, and I spent an hour collecting samples before I let the clean-up team set things to order. I tried not to look out the window, but that was difficult since the window encompassed the entire outer hub wall from the ceiling curve twelve feet up to a six-inch threshold at ground level. I didn't like the view at all. Heck, I didn't much like this planet.

Sand stretched out to the horizon, barren gritty sand, the desolate emptiness only stopped by the sharp red mountains on the horizon. Red, brighter than the horrifying Sangre de Cristo range on Earth-home, not purple or green or gray like any decent range. These cactus-aliens lived on the mountains, according to our survey satellite, and avoided the desert. We set our observatory down here, smack in the middle of the desert, for just that reason. We hoped the aliens of this world would not mind us squatting in their desert.

Apparently, they did.

Before we arrived, the planet was desert-sand, barren mountains, plenty of underground water but small, shallow oceans, a desert botanist's dream. We didn't have a desert botanist on board. I was the closest thing, a general lab scientist. My job was to ride herd on any terraforming project. If the planet contained sentient indigenous aliens we'd have to get their permission before starting.

Of course, there were indigenous aliens. We found evidence of sentience easily enough, settled cities full of buildings. In truth they were only collections of sheds and glassine shacks spread out in a root-system along the gray coastlines and the dirty, red mountaintops, and covered a tiny percentage of the planet. Most of the land was utter sere landscape, dry and desolate.

Our observatory circled this little planet and we spent some orbits making our survey before settling on the middle of the great northern desert as a good neutral landing spot.

Great neutral spot, I thought as I juggled my sample bags. Deserts and exploding cacti. At least there weren't any spiders, like in one of those nasty urban legends about cacti and tarantulas. Nope, just gunk and needles. And maybe a little chemical something?

I tested the gunk in the synthesizer, the DNA sequencer, the acid tests. I put some under a microscope and looked at cell structures. I had, ultimately, no idea what I was finding, but the computer would hold onto the results. Perhaps someday a trained biologist would read them and figure out what happened. I found some nitrogen crystals, little golden cubes like contaminated salt, mixed in the gunk. All plants…all living things had nitrates, but not in these concentrations. Since the computer did not come up with an answer, I blue-skyed an idea with the sim.

"What if," I said, "the cactus grew a load of nitrate crystals in her skin? And then she'd only need some pressure to set off the explosion; she could have, I dunno, hugged herself. Would that have done it?"

The sim replied, "Yes, with enough nitrogen and enough pressure. Is that the probable cause of the explosion?"

"The computer isn't saying." I rubbed my temples with my fingers. "All I know is that there aren't any traces of conventional explosive. No traces of any chemical that would react like a poison or drug with human biology. Mostly just some mineral-saturated water and the nitrate crystals."

I sat down and put my feet up. "I don't get it. Why did she attack?"

Diego sauntered into the lab. "Maybe they don't want us here," he said as he settled into the chair across from me. He put my feet on his lap. "Maybe if we know there are sentient species on a planet, we should find the next one down the road." He rubbed my calf, so gently.

I smiled. "Why are you even on an exploration vessel, my love? You just want to go somewhere peaceful and paint." I squirmed a bit under the pressure of his fingers.

"Yes, I want to paint beautiful women and gorgeous sunsets," he said. "There's a gorgeous sunset outside right now. Would you like to join me?"

I swung my feet off his lap. "Yes, let's." I could not care less about another sunset, especially on this dry desert, but time with Diego was precious. I hooked my arm around his waist and we went outside.

§

We greeted the second emissary with as much friendliness as the first, but this time we wore body armor and face shields. She stood still on the threshold while Captain Johnson spieled the welcome-and-thank-you speech. We waited for her reply when he finished, waited until I felt the need to move my legs and my body armor clanked just a bit. The alien turned around—spun, really—and we realized we'd been addressing her backside. The captain smiled through clenched teeth. He was waiting for her to explode. I know I was.

Instead, she flowed over the threshold and moved directly to Captain Johnson. She wrapped him in her thorny arms and hugged him.

He yelled. Not an anguished sound, but the outrage of an upset child.

"Hey! That hurts! Damn it!" He pulled away from her (or she released him, it was hard to tell). He was covered mask to boot with needle flechettes she'd squeezed into him.

She approached me for a hug and I backstepped so fast I fell over. She waved an arm at me and flechettes discharged into my suit armor. They penetrated far enough for me to feel the sharp points.

"Jeez, don't let her touch you!" I yelled. "Get the captain some help! Medical officer, report to the observatory! And security, don't just stand there, get her out of here!"

I'd volunteered Josef and Bob to be security. They carried tasers, which they pointed at the alien, but they weren't sure if the electrical jolts would even faze her, I could tell from their expressions. They were seconds from bolting out of the window room.

"Shoot her, shoot her now!" I yelled. "Do it quick!"

They both shot her at the same time.

"Just like microwaving a potato," Josef screamed.

Indeed, it was like microwaving a moist fleshy vegetable. She screamed, a nasty high noise like an off-pitch flute. Steam rose from her skin and her arms waved involuntarily; then she fell over.

Diego helped Captain Johnson remove his body armor. The captain's skin was pierced and puffed and slightly bloody, like he'd been attacked by a million angry bees. He caught my eye.

"It's war."

§

The problem he and his officers couldn't quite resolve was how to battle sentient plants. We established a perimeter around the observatory with electrical wire, but that was breached the first night by suicidal cacti.

Sim woke us with a piercing alarm when the first cactus touched the wire. We all rushed to the window room and watched the pyrotechnics. The cacti did not try to escape the wire; they just threw themselves on it. The sparks flew into the sky, blue and yellow, but not a fire hazard as there was nothing to burn except the cacti.

Later, we counted twenty burned husks on the wire.

"How did they get here?" Captain Johnson said. He paced back and forth in the common room, fifteen steps north, a quick turn, fifteen steps south, a quick turn, and again more steps. "There were no cacti on the desert plain when we went to sleep. They didn't drop from the heavens."

"It's their planet," I said. "They know how to get around. Maybe underground tunnels?"

The captain got that stubborn set to his jaw. "Sim, do a sounding of the perimeter ground to a ten-foot depth. Find the tunnels."

Diego said, "What does it matter how they got here? They obviously want us gone. We should go."

Captain Johnson stared Diego down. "We're not leaving. We won't be run off by plants."

"No tunnels, Captain Johnson," the sim reported.

"Fire," Josef said. "Fire cures most ills. Can we flame-fry the populated areas, you know, the mountain region? That'd get rid of the cacti, anyway."

The captain smiled. "Excellent! There's some thinking! Sim, feasibility on a burn-out of the populated areas."

A minute later the sim reported, "The area is too large for effective fire control; and we do not have enough fuel for full coverage, so the plants will be able to just walk away without any hazard."

The captain said, "Okay, then. Basic military preparedness. We're gonna dig a perimeter trench."

We dug that trench the next day. Four hundred yards, three feet deep. Even with all five of us digging, that was not fun. We wore our body armor, masks, boots, in that heat. We finished that same day, mostly because Diego fed us stimulants and I kept us hydrated.

Josef and Bob had flame-throwers, and they took turns keeping us covered. I felt safer having an armed guard.

The trench was no more protection than the electrified wire had been.

When the cactus erupted behind Bob and grabbed him, he barely had time to squeak, much less aim and fire his flame-thrower, before falling to the ground, dead. Josef turned on the flames and barbequed the cactus, but somehow I don't think it cared. We knew from the previous night, the electrical fence suicides, that the cacti were willing to sacrifice themselves.

Captain Johnson glared at the burned ground. We stood around in silence.

Finally, he said, "Maggie Flowers, you got any of those terraforming seeds?"

"Yes," I said slowly, "but it's illegal to start without indigenous permission. Once the process starts, we can't stop it."

Captain Johnson glared at me. "We aren't losing any more people. Start the process."

§

The seeds were the heart of any terraforming project. Originally, they were developed in 20th Century Earth-home battlefields to detect landmines; they'd grow on any kind of substrate and flower at the merest detection of minerals. Scientists tweaked the sturdy plants, a kind of morning glory with multi-colored blossoms, until they'd grow under any condition and utilize any kind of material for food. They'd eat whatever was in their way and leave behind compostable vegetative matter and cubic tons of oxygen.

I'd used them successfully on several dirtball worlds; they always found a toehold, always worked.

I hydrated half my supply and filled the sprayer canister. Not too heavy, lighter than a scuba air tank.

"You don't have to do this, you know," Diego said from the lab's doorway.

"You always show up like that, you bad penny you," I said, trying a light tone to hide my nervousness.

"You keep speaking of them as 'aliens,' but you know what? We're the aliens here. They have every right to want us gone."

I swallowed. "The captain wants this. And, and— Bob was a friend of mine." I didn't want to look at Diego.

"You're violating the rules, you're using terraforming as a weapon, you're being punitive against the sentient natives of this world. What you're doing is wrong." He said this with the most serious tone of voice.

"Maggie Flowers," the sim said. "Time to go, Maggie Flowers."

I clenched my teeth. "Tell your damned sim to back off, Captain," I said. "I know my duty. I'm ready."

Diego walked out of the lab.

I got into my body armor without assistance. The clunky outfit didn't help much with my mobility, but I wasn't going outside the observatory without it. I had the canister of activated seeds strapped to my back, the spray nozzle ready in my right hand. I walked to the trench we'd dug around the observatory and stared down into it. Someone had called it Arroyo Seco and the name stuck.

It looked like a desert flash-flood channel, cracked and dusty, steep crumbly walls and no plant growth at all. Lots of rocks, some in desert-pale colors of tan, aqua, lime, lavender, some just stone-gray. I pointed the nozzle at the far wall and opened up the spray.

This did not require a thick coat. I walked slowly around the perimeter of the trench, trying not to stumble in the ground cracks as I aimed the sprayer and kept a thin painting of seeds and nutrient matrix flowing onto this horrid desert. I smiled. Given a bit of time, not too long, the seeds would metabolize the sand and grow, roots, vines, flowers. We'd know it was a successful terraforming when the flowers bloomed, and we'd know mineral content of the land from the color of the blossoms.

The observatory wasn't a huge vehicle and the trench was only about a quarter mile diameter, maybe 440 yards, but I was sweating by the time I returned to the beginning. The body armor, the heat of the day, the nimble hopping over the cracks at the bottom of Arroyo Seco, and I hadn't had a moment to look up. The flowers draping down the arroyo wall finally caught my attention.

"What the hell?" I goggled at the blossom-laden vines. They looked like morning glories on steroids, thick and furry and green. "Are these my...?" I knew better than to touch the vines; they'd wrap around me and try to digest me, I had a much higher nutrient content than sand.

Apparently, the sand here had a much higher nutrient content than I expected. But I'd tested the sand.

I stared at the arroyo wall behind the vines. What was feeding my plants?

Pits studded the wall. I backed up a bit and looked at an area I'd just sprayed. The seeds were burrowing into a soft mass of what I'd thought was stone. The seeds sprouted before my eyes.

The stones were not stones.

I climbed up the opposite wall as fast as I could manage in the bulky body armor. I stood up inside the perimeter and looked out at the desert.

The vines were spreading like wildfire. Flowers blossomed with miraculous speed. The dusty gray sand was turning green with dots of color.

"Oh, no, no, no, no, no," I mumbled. The only way they could spread so fast was if the sand contained huge amounts of food for my seeds. And it did. The sand contained vast amounts of plant life. The sand contained the immature forms of the alien life.

I don't know how long I stood there in the sunshine, watching my seeds take over the desert. I came back to myself when Captain Johnson shoved me.

"What the hell is happening, Maggie Flowers?" He couldn't have been all that angry or he wouldn't have used my nickname.

"Speciation," I said. Then, I started again. "Immature forms of a plant can look like any number of things before the final form." He still looked blank. "This desert," I pointed out toward the rapidly greening land, "is a nursery. We landed in the nursery. No wonder they've been attacking us. All those stones? Baby sentient cacti. Is that clear enough for you?"

He didn't say anything. One more effort, I thought. I'll try one more time.

"We're committing genocide," I said. "We're killing all the babies. And there's no way to stop it."

He tore his gaze off the horizon.

"Well, then, they won't be able to attack us any more, huh?"

§

The vines spread in gangrenous stripes across the desert to the very foot of the red mountains. I assumed the cacti had found a chemical method to slow down the vines' pace. I doubted the method would hold. The vines spread underground, like mint, as well as with runners like strawberry. But perhaps they'd bought themselves enough time to escape.

"How long do we have to wait, Maggie?" The captain was impatient.

"I dunno," I said. "The flowers will die off as soon as the surface nutrients are consumed. The oxygen concentration around here is already at reasonable levels. They'll start to brown soon. We'll just have to wait."

The captain wasn't too happy with that idea.

"I'd like to send an exploratory mission out towards the coast," he said. "Who wants to go?"

No one spoke up, not even the security dudes. I was surprised; I thought they'd do anything the captain wanted. Perhaps they were growing brains.

"I think we're all a little worn out," Diego said. "None of us are used to fighting like this. It's hard enough keeping our perimeter clear." The others nodded.

Captain Johnson was not pleased.

"I'll go alone, then," he said. "I can't stay cooped up in this damned ship a minute longer!" He must have hoped his friends would chime in, change their minds, want to join him, but they remained silent.

"Fine," he said.

The sim said, "This is a bad idea, Captain, and it's against regulations. You are required to stay with the ship while it is under attack."

The captain snorted. "Under attack? Why, Maggie Flowers here has settled this war for us. We're not under attack, we're the ones attacking!" With that he left our common room.

"Sim, keep an eye on him, okay?" I said.

Diego stood and stretched. "Captain's not the only one going a little stir-crazy," he said. "We should just leave."

I shook my head. "You know we can't do that until the vines are resolved. It would be extremely irresponsible." I stopped.

Diego didn't say anything, but then he didn't have to. He stomped out.

"Aw, damnit, Diego!" I said. He would probably go outside to watch the sunset. Outside was so dangerous now, but I'd go out there to be with him.

I saw them outside the observatory, arguing. Diego and the captain were nose to nose and their mouths were wide open, yelling. I was glad I could not hear them.

The ground erupted under their feet and suddenly I was screaming. Barrel shaped green plants shot up from the ground, then exploded, covering both men in sticky gunk.

I screamed for the security dudes. "Perimeter, quick! The captain and Diego have been attacked!" I ran for the door and tugged on it. It wouldn't budge.

The sim said, "I cannot let you outside right now, Magdalena. There are three unexploded cacti out there. You will be harmed."

I screamed. "I'll be harmed? I'll show you harm, you damned computer simulation of a mentally-deficient idiot, if you don't open this door right now! Diego!"

The security dudes showed up then, both white-faced and panicked. Their flame-throwers were out and aimed but neither wanted to open the door.

"Open the door, sim, we need to get out there!" I kicked at the door. "No."

"Oh you bastard…Josef, you have a flame-thrower? Give it here," I said. Josef gave me his flame-thrower and I turned it over and opened the bottom end. A magnet nestled there, part of the trigger assembly, and I knocked it out. It was small, but it worked to unlock the door. I ran out, not looking to see if the security dudes were behind me.

They were. As I reached Diego, who lay moaning on the ground with red blisters rising wherever the gunk had touched, the barrel cactus beside me burst into flames. A moment later the other two were similarly turned into candles, before any of them could explode.

Josef threw the captain over his shoulder in a fireman's carry, and I grabbed Diego the same way. I staggered to the door, which was again locked.

"Sim! Let us in, you bastard!"

The door snicked open.

Moments later we had both men in the med dorm. I washed Diego's skin clear of the gunk; he was still alive, but in shock and unconscious, according to the sim.

The captain wasn't so lucky. Josef wiped the captain's body then pulled a sheet over his head.

Josef had a white shocky face. I gave him pills and some water and sent him to his bunk. Then, I sat with Diego and waited.

§

A third emissary knocked on the observatory door. When the sim announced this, I dropped the Petri dish I'd been prepping.

"Let her into the window room," I said, "and make sure she doesn't go away. And watch her for sign language! Maybe if you figure it out we can communicate finally."

I ran back to my room for my body armor and face mask and boots. Who knew what this one would do? I grabbed my diving knife, too, just in case.

The willowy creature, taller than the previous two, stooped in the observatory, leaning against the window. She rustled her limbs, a delicate fan dance.

"Sim, can you translate her sign language yet?" I said.

"The data is not perfect yet. However, I can tell you that she is distressed."

Thanks a lot, I thought. I already knew that! I took a deep breath.

"We can offer you all a safe haven," I said, "a place to wait until the flowers finish processing. But you'll have to decide soon. The flowers are encroaching on the settled portions of the planet, the mountains and coastlines, not just this battlefield."

The alien spun, and the Sim voiced some kind of warning, but I was wary this time, and prepared. I raised my right hand and switched on the nozzle and sprayed her with seeds.

The flowers sprouted from one of her arms…no, several of her arms, and her torso also. I saw the flowers sprout in a cleft on her chest, the cleft of the bosom on a human female. Her decorated arms flailed delicately.

She wailed. A giant cactus writhing and wailing. Surveillance cameras swerved to observe her. "Don't just stand there!" I yelled. "Get some nitrogen, quick, and a bag of soil! She needs food, she's starving!"

The sim caught what I wanted and treated it like an imperative order. Moments later, bags of rich composted soil were dumped on the observatory floor next to the emissary. I split one open with my knife and she sank into the loamy dark soil.

The combination stink of desert cactus ozone and fertile active soil assaulted my nostrils. I held a hand to my face, sneezing. With all the nutrient surrounding her I thought she'd be consumed by the flowers, but she wasn't. I watched her for some time, an hour perhaps, with the surveillance cameras recording every moment. The flowers covered her in a blanket of vines but failed to consume her. She moved again, wiping some of the vines away, and stood up from the bed of soil.

She indicated the loam. Encapsulated bits of her body, her fingers and toes, in effect, were in the loam and growing. She'd reproduced right there.

Her arms writhed in a dance that might have been sign language or might have been some kind of thanks. The flowers on her body continued to bloom, and the vines circled her like dark green chains against her gray-green skin.

The sim spoke up. "My analysis of her language is complete," it said. "She says we must leave."

I nodded. "Of course," I said. I didn't look at her but at the buds in the loam. I reached for one.

A spindly arm, bristling with needles, stopped my hand. Her other arms waved.

The sim translated, "'If you touch them I will kill you.' I suggest you leave them alone."

The buds traveled up her limbs and attached themselves to her body.

A ghost of the captain's voice echoed in my head. "Kill her before she escapes, Maggie Flowers. She's integrated the vines into her DNA, they can't kill her now; and she'll spread that immunity to all the rest of them. Kill her!"

Diego's voice in my conscience sounded so calm next to that. "Let her go, Magdalena. It is time for us to leave." Calm and quiet. And gentle.

I ordered the sim to open the barrier door. The cactus writhed and danced as she flowed over the threshold back onto her planet's soil. The surveillance cameras followed her as she crossed the arroyo and disappeared into the field of flowering vines.

"Diego's right, Sim, it's time for us to leave. Get us outta here," I said, as calmly as I could manage.

I went to the med dorm and sat next to Diego's bed. He held my hand and I held his swollen paw, gently, gently. Together we watched on the digital screens as we lifted off the planet.

When we arrived, the planet was desert-sand, barren mountains. We left a field of flowers, soon to be an entire planet of flowers. But the beauty was a mirage. Like the photograph of a past love, we could never return.

Shipwreck in the Sky
Eando Binder

*T*he flight was listed at GHQ as Project Songbird. It was sponsored by the Space Medicine Labs of the U.S. Air Force. And its pilot was Captain Dan Barstow.

A hand-picked man, Dan Barstow, chosen for the AF's most important project of the year because he and his VX-3 had already broken all previous records set by hordes of V-2s, Navy Aerobees, and anything else that flew the skyways.

Dan Barstow, first man to cross the sea of air and sight open, unlimited space. Pioneer flight to infinity. He grinned and hummed to himself as he settled down for the long jaunt. Too busy to be either thrilled or scared he considered the thirty-seven instruments he'd have to read, the twice that many records to keep, and the miles of camera film to run. He had been hand-picked and thoroughly conditioned to take it all without more than a ten percent increase in his pulse rate. So, he worked as matter-of-factly as if he were down in the Gs Centrifuge of the Space Medicine Labs where he had been schooled for this trip for months.

He kept up a running fire of oral reports through his helmet radio, down to Rough Rock and his CO. "All Roger, sir ... temperature falling fast but this rubberoid space suit keeps me cozy, no chills ... Doc Blaine will be happy to hear that! Weightless sensations pretty queer and I feel upside-down as much as rightside-up, but no bad effects....

Taking shots of the sun's corona now with color film ... huh? Oh, yes, sir, it's beautiful all right, now that you mention it. But, hell, sir, who's got the time for aesthetics now?... Oops, *that* was a close one! Tenth meteor whizzing past. Makes me think of flak back on those Berlin bombing runs."

Dan couldn't help wincing when the meteors peppered down past. The "flak" of space. Below he could see the meteors flare up brightly as they hit the atmosphere. Most of those near his position were small, none bigger than a baseball, and Dan took comfort in the fact that his rocket was small, too, in the immensity around him. A direct hit would be sheer bad luck, but the good old law of averages was on his side.

"Yes, Colonel, this tin can I'm riding is holding together okay," Dan continued to Rough Rock. If he paused even a second in his reports, a top-sergeant's yell from the Colonel's throat came back for him to keep talking. Every bit of information he could transmit to them was a vital revelation in this USAF-Alpha exploration of open space beyond Earth's air cushion, with ceiling unlimited to infinity.

"Cosmic rays, sir? Sure, the reading shot up double on the Geiger ... huh? Naw, I don't feel a thing ... like Doc Baird suspected, we invented a lot of Old Wives' Tales in *advance*, before going into space. I feel fine, so you can put down cosmic ray intensity as a Boogey Man.... What's that? Yeah, yeah, sir, the stars shine without winking up here. What else?... Space is inky black—no deep purples or queer more-than-blacks like some jetted-up writers dreamed up—just plain old ordinary dead black. Earth, sir?... Well, it does look dish-shaped from up here, concave.... Sure, I can see all the way to Europe and—say! Here's something unexpected. I can see that hurricane off the coast of Florida.... You said it, sir! Once we install permanent space stations up here it will be easy to spot typhoons, volcano eruptions, tidal waves, earthquakes— what have you—the moment they start. If you ask me, with a good telescope you could even spot forest fires the minute they broke out, not to mention a sneak bombing on a target city—uh, sorry, sir, I forgot."

Dan broke off and almost retched as his stomach turned a flip-flop to end all flip-flops. The VX-3 had reached the peak of its trajectory at over 1000 miles altitude and now turned down, lazily at first. He gulped oxygen from the emergency tube at his lips and felt better.

"Turning back on schedule, Rough Rock. Peak altitude 1,037 miles. Everything fine, no danger. This was all a cinch.... HEY! Wait.... Something not in the books has popped up ... stand by!"

Dan had felt the rocket swing a bit, strangely, as if gripped by a strong force. Instead of falling directly down toward Earth with a slight pitch, it slanted sideways and spun on its long axis. And then Dan saw what it was....

Beneath, intercepting his trajectory, coming around fast over the curvature of Earth, was a tiny black worldlet, 998 miles above Earth. It might be an enormous meteor, but Dan felt he was right the first time. For it wasn't falling like a meteor but swinging parallel to Earth's surface on even keel.

He stared at the unexpected discovery, as amazed as if it were a fire-breathing dragon out of legend. For it was, actually, he realized in swift, stunned comprehension, more amazing than any legend.

Dan kept his voice calm. "Hello, Rough Rock.... Listen ... nobody expected *this*...hold your hat, sir, and sit down. I've discovered a *second moon* of Earth!... Uh-huh, you heard me right! A second moon! Tie that, will you?... Sure, it's tiny, less than a mile in diameter I'd say. Dead black in color. Guess that's why telescopes never spotted it. Tiny and black, blends into the black backdrop of space. It has terrific speed. And that little maverick's gravitational field caught my rocket.... Of course it can't yank me away from Earth gravity, but the trouble is—yipe! my rocket and that moonlet may be in for a mutual *collision* course...."

Dan's trained eye suddenly saw that grim possibility. Barreling around Earth in a narrow orbit with a speed of something near or over 12,000 miles an hour the tiny new moon had, since his ascent, charged directly into his downward free fall. It was a chance in a thousand for a direct hit, except for one added factor—the moonlet exerted enough gravity pull out of its many-million-ton bulk to warp the rocket into its path. And the thousand-to-one odds were thus wiped out, becoming even money.

"Nip and tuck," reported Dan, answering the excited pleadings and questions from Rough Rock. "It won't be a head-on crash. I may even miss entirely.... Oh, Lord! Not with that spire of rock sticking up from it.... I'm going to hit that ..."

Dan had heard an atomic bomb blast once and it sounded like a string of them set off at once as the rocket smashed into the rocky prominence. The rock splintered. The rocket splintered. But Dan was not there to be splintered likewise. He had jammed down a button, at the critical moment, and the rocket's emergency escape-hatch had ejected him a split-second before the violent impact.

But Dan blacked out, receiving some of the concussion of the exploding rocket. When his eyes snapped open he was floating like a feather in open, airless space. His rubberoid space suit, living up to its rigid tests, had inflated to its elastic limit. But it held and within its automatic units began feeding him oxygen, heat and radio-power. He had a chance, now, because he had been ejected cleanly from the rocket, without damage to the protective suit.

The stars wheeled dizzily around him. Dan finally saw the reason why. He was not just floating as a free agent in space. He was circling the black moonlet, at perhaps a thousand yards from its pitted surface.

"Hello, Rough Rock," he called. "Still alive and kicking, sir. Only now, of all crazy-mad things, *I'm* a moon of *this* moon! The collision must have knocked me clear out of my down-to-Earth orbit... I must have been ejected in the same direction as the moonlet's course, in its gravity field.... I don't know. Let an electronic brain figure it out some time.... Anyway, now I'm being dragged along in the orbit of the moonlet—how about *that*? Yes, sir, I'm circling down closer and closer to the moonlet.... No, don't worry, sir. It was a weak gravity pull, only a fraction of an Earth-g. So I'm drifting down gently as a cloud.... Stand by for my landing on Earth's second moon!"

The bloated figure in the bulging space suit circled the black stony surface several more times, in a narrowing spiral, and finally landed with a soft skidding bump that didn't even jar Dan's teeth. He bounced several times from a diminishing height of fifty-odd feet in grotesque slow-motion before he finally came to a stop.

He sat still for a moment, adjusting to the fantastic fact of being shipwrecked on an uncharted moonlet, crowding down his pulse rate which might be over ten percent normal now.

"Okay, Rough Rock, I hear you.... You're telling me, sir?... Obviously, I'm *marooned* here. No rocket to leave with. No way to get back to terra firma ... what? If you'll pardon my saying so, sir, that's a silly question.... Of course I'm scared! Scared green. Sorry about the rocket, sir, losing it for you.... Me, sir? Thank you, sir. But stop apologizing, will you? I know you haven't got any duplicates of the VX-3 ready, no rescue rocket...."

Dan listened a moment longer then broke in roughly. "Oh, for Pete's sake, will you stop crying over me, sir? So, I get mine here. I might have gotten it over Berlin, too. Forget it—sir."

Dan grinned suddenly. "Look, what have I got to kick about? I'll go out in a flash of glory—at least one headline will put it that way—and I'll get credit in the history books as the man who discovered that Earth has *two* moons! What more could I ask, really?"

Dan blushed at the reply from Rough Rock. "Will you lay off please, Colonel? How else should a man take it? I'm still scared silly inside. But, look, I've really got something to report now. This little runt moon makes tracks around Earth in probably two hours minus. If I remember my Spacenautics right I'm already looking down over the Grand Canyon, heading west. I'm going to get a pretty terrific bird's-eye view of the whole world in two more hours, which is just about how much oxygen I've got left.... Lucky, eh?"

Dan looked down, watching in fascination the majestic wheeling of the Earth below him. His little moonlet did not rotate, or rather it rotated once for each revolution around Earth, as the Moon did, keeping one face earthward, giving him an uninterrupted view. The Sierras on Earth hove into clear view and the broad Pacific. There would follow Hawaii, then Japan, Asia, Europe.... No, he saw he was slanting southwest. It would be across the equator, past Australia, perhaps near the South Pole, then up around over the top of the world past Greenland, following that great circle around the globe. In any case, his was the speediest trip around the world ever made by man!

"Before we're out of mutual range, Rough Rock, I'm going to explore this new moon. Me and Columbus! Stand by for reports."

Dan did his walking in huge leaps that propelled him fifty feet at a step with slight effort, due to the extremely feeble gravity of the tiny body. What did he weigh here? Probably no more than an ounce or two.

"Nothing much to report, Colonel. It's a dead, airless pip-squeak planetoid, just a big mile-thick rock, probably. No life, no vegetation, no people, no nothing. Guess you might call me the Man in the Second Moon—and the joke's on me! Well, one and three-quarter hours of oxygen left, by the gauge, or 105 minutes—sounds like more that way.... What's that, sir? Your voice is getting faint. Any last requests from me? Well, one favor maybe. Pick up my body some day with another rocket.... Yeah, it'll stay preserved up here in this deep-freeze of space.... Thanks, sir.... Can't hear you much now. Going out of range. Give Betty my fondest. You know, the blonde.... Well, sir—goodbye now."

Dan was glad that Rough Rock's radio voice faded to a whispery nothingness. It wasn't easy to stay casual now. There was nothing more to say, really, and he didn't want to hear any more crying from the CO. The Old Man had sounded almost hysterical. He wanted just to be alone with his thoughts now, making his final peace with the universe....

He checked the gauge with his watch—ninety minutes of oxygen to zero. Or, he thought with a grin, eternity minus ninety minutes.

He was beginning to have trouble breathing. But it was awesomely grand, watching the sweep of Earth beneath him, the procession of dots that were islands strung across the Pacific South Seas like a necklace of green beads. He was still within radio range of ships below at sea. Yet he didn't contact them. He had nothing to say, like a ghost in the sky.

Idly, he kept pitching loose stones, watching their rifle-like speed away from him. Again, a phenomenon of the weak gravity of the moonlet. Actually, he was able to pick up a boulder ten-feet across and heave it away with ease. *We who are about to die amuse ourselves,* he thought. Then, because a thread of stubborn hope still clung in a corner of his mind, he got an idea. It had lurked just beyond his mental grasp for some time now. Something significant....

Abruptly, face alight, Dan switched on his radio and contacted a ship below, asking them to relay him to Rough Rock with their more powerful transmitter.

"Ahoy, Rough Rock! Stop adding up my insurance, Colonel! I'm coming back.... No, sir, I haven't gone out of my head, sir. It's so simple it's a laugh, sir.... See you in a few hours, sir!"

And he did.

Dan grinned when they hauled his dripping form from the sea. Aboard the search plane they cut him out of the space suit to which was still attached his emergency twin parachute. But his helmet was gone, ripped loose, for Dan had been breathing fresh Earth air during the long parachute descent.

They stared at him as at a dead man come alive.

"Impossible to escape?" He chuckled, repeating their babble. "That's what *I* thought too, until I remembered those data tables on gravity and Escape Velocity and such—how, on the Moon, the Escape Velocity is much less than on Earth. And on that tiny second moon—well, my clue was when I threw a stone into the air *and it never came back.*"

Dan gulped hot coffee.

"I got off the moonlet myself then, got up to more than a mile above it where I was free of its feeble gravity. But I was still in the same orbit circling Earth. I'd have continued revolving as a human satellite forever, of course, but for this emergency gadget hooked to my belt."

Dan held up the metal gun with its empty tank and needle-nose half burned away.

"Reaction pistol. Fires hydrazine and oxidizer, ordinary jet-rocket principle. Aiming it toward the stars, opposite earth, its reactive blasts shoved me Earthward, thanks to Newton. I needed a speed of about one-half mile a second. The powerful little jet gun had only my small mass to shove in free space, without gravity or friction. That broke me from free-fall *around* Earth to gravity-fall *toward* Earth.

"Then I spiraled down under gravity pull. I reached lung-filling air density just in time, before my oxygen gave out. One more danger was that I began heating up like a meteor due to air friction. I flung out a prayer first, followed by my twin parachutes, designed for extreme initial shock. They held. Slowed me to a paratrooper's drift the rest of the way down."

"Wait," a puzzled pilot objected. "Your story doesn't hang together. *How* did you get off that moonlet? How did you get up there, a mile above it, away from its gravity? There was nobody to throw *you,* like a stone."

"I threw myself," said Dan. "First, I ran as fast as I could, maybe halfway around that moonlet, to get a good running start. And then—"

Dan Barstow's grin then was undoubtedly the biggest grin in history...

"Well, then, since the feeble gravity couldn't pull me back again, what I really did was to *jump clear off that moon.*"

Symphony
Douglas Smith

FAST FORWARD: Third Movement, Danse Macabre (Staccato)

*T*hey *had named the planet Aurora, for the beauty that danced* above them in its ever-dark skies. At least, it had seemed beautiful at the time. Now, Gar Franck wasn't so sure.

Gar huddled on the floor, shielding his two-year-old son, Anton, from the panicked colonists stampeding past them in the newly-constructed pod link.

"Damn you, Franck! When will you make it stop?" a man cried from across the corridor. A woman lay in the man's arms, convulsing as her seizure peaked. She was dying, but to Gar's numbed mind her moans harmonized with the screams of the mob into a musical score for his private nightmare.

Anton sat on the floor, a broken comm-unit held before his blank face. The child let it drop to strike the metal surface with a dissonant clang. More people fled by. The child ignored them. With morbid fascination, Gar watched Anton repeat the scene. Pick up the comm-unit, let it drop. Pick it up, drop it. Again. Each clang as it struck the floor was more chilling to Gar than any cry from the dying.

This attack had blown the colony power grid. The only light now came through the crysteel roof. Gar looked up. The aurora blazed and writhed in the night sky, a parody of the chaos below. Greens, reds and purples shimmered strobe-like over the corridor, turning each person's frenzied flight into a macabre dance.

"God, no!" the man cried. The woman stiffened, then fell limp. "No!" The man pulled her to him, sobbing.

The rainbow lights of the aurora dimmed and the flickering slowed. The screaming died. Gar stood and looked around, dazed. People were shaking their heads, helping up ones who had fallen, poking at bodies. The man still sat holding the dead woman, his eyes hard on Gar. Other colonists stared at Gar, too. Gar swallowed. Picking up Anton, he walked past accusing faces toward their dorm pod. Anton squirmed in his arms. The child didn't like to be touched, let alone held.

Someone whispered as he passed. "How will he talk to this *thing* when he can't even talk with his own son?" Gar pulled Anton closer, smothering his sobbing in the child's sleeve.

REWIND: *First Movement, Prelude (Agitato)*

Six months ago. Anton was eighteen months old. Their ship, the *Last Chance,* had just dropped out of the worm-hole, leaving a poisoned Earth and the plague behind. Earlier probes through this hole had identified a G2 star with planets within range.

The plague had forced the *Last Chance* to launch before completion of its biosphere. The ship was only partly self-sustaining. They had only a year left to find a new home. It wasn't called the *Last Chance* for nothing.

Gar lay exhausted on the wall bed of the small ship cabin that he, Clara, and Anton shared. Clara's latest holographic sculpture spun suspended before him—shifting geometric shapes in greens, reds and purples. Vivaldi filled the room, wiping words from his head like rain washing graffiti from a wall. Gar lived with words all day. He'd had enough of words.

The jump had flooded MedCon with hyper-space shock cases. Gar was logging eighteen-hour days translating between colonists and doctors. Fluency in ten languages and a name in computerized speech translation had won him his berth as Communications Officer.

With over six thousand refugees from all over Earth, both human and automated translators were invaluable.

Gar rubbed his eyes. Overtime was at least an escape from the routine of translating the captain's messages to the crew and passengers. And from the growing tensions of his family life.

He checked the time. Clara worked as a laser and photonics specialist in TechLab. Her shift should be over by now.

Anton sat on the plastek floor, flapping his hands, staring. At what Gar could not say, and a fear grew in him each day that Anton did not know either. Gar got down in front of the child. "Hey, big guy. What're you doing?" Anton looked right past him.

"He stared like that for twenty minutes today." Gar turned. Clara stood at the door, her lip trembling. "I measured it."

"Clara..." Gar felt himself tighten up.

"These spells just seem to blend together now."

"Maybe it's the jump," he said, not believing it himself.

"He was like this *before* the jump, Gar."

"He's just slow developing. How was your shift?"

"Most children are speaking by a year," she said.

"He walked on time, right?" Gar turned up the music a bit, not looking at her. "I just did a translation. They've found the system. We'll be there in four months."

"He never looks up when we speak, Gar."

"We'll have his hearing tested again."

"He won't let me hold him." Her voice broke and Gar turned back to her. She was leaning against the wall, her arms wrapped around herself, sobbing. "I can't hold my own child, Gar."

Gar swallowed. He walked over and took her in his arms.

Clara pushed away from him. "I want Ky to look at him."

Ky Jasper was MedCon Leader. "He's too busy," Gar mumbled.

"He owes you for all the overtime. Talk to him."

Gar looked at Anton. The child sat with his hands over his ears, rocking back and forth. The Vivaldi, calm and soothing in the background, gave the scene a surreal feeling.

"He's disappearing, Gar. Disappearing into his own world."

Gar closed his eyes to shut out both the scene and his tears. He nodded. "I'll ask him tomorrow."

First Movement, Finale (Largo)

In the ship's darkened MedLab, a hologram of Anton's brain spun glowing and green, areas of red flashing within it. Gar stood stunned beside Ky Jasper and Clara. The imaging unit beeped musical tones as Ky outlined a red area in purple.

"...repetitive mannerisms and actions. Autistics are neurologically over-connected, as in this area of the cortex that handles hearing. Their senses are so acute they can overload. A touch is painful. Speech scrambles. Soft sounds are like explosions. One overloaded sense can shutdown the other four."

"So he covers his ears. And won't let us hold him." Clara spoke in a monotone, face blank. "Why won't he talk?"

Gar shook his head. This wasn't happening.

Ky sighed. "Autistics are blind to other minds. Anton doesn't know we're fellow beings with thoughts and feelings. To him, we're just things, moving through his world at random."

"Is there a cure?" Gar asked. Clara's sobs and the beeping of the imaging unit played like a discordant sound-track to the scene. Ky turned to him, his face half in darkness, half in green from the hologram. He shook his head.

Second Movement, Main Theme (Accelerando)

They were lucky, the captain had said on reaching the system and finding a habitable planet. Breathable atmosphere, 0.95 Earth gravity. Hotter than Earth, but a polar temperate zone held a suitable land mass. The axial tilt meant they'd be in night for the first 2.4 Earth years, but that was a small issue. Besides, the polar zones offered spectacular auroral activity.

Lucky, the captain had said. Still reeling from the news of Anton, Gar hadn't felt very lucky at the time. Now, no one did.

On first seeing the aurora on orbital displays, Gar had felt a dread he couldn't reconcile with its beauty. He had assumed he was subconsciously linking its colors to those of Anton's MedLab hologram. Now, he wasn't sure. Now, people were dying.

Walking through the main colony dome, Gar noted without surprise that all ceiling panels had been opaqued to block any view of the sky. He cranked up Mozart in his translation headset and tried to relax as he neared the newly-built dorm pod.

The construction of the colony on the planet had gone well in the beginning. Gar had made planet-fall with the first group. To translate between engineers and work crews, he had said. Both he and Clara knew he was avoiding the situation with Anton.

Clara had accepted the diagnosis quickly. During the trip to the planet, she had buried herself in researching autism and working with Anton. Gar just couldn't. So he hid in his work.

At their dorm unit, Gar hesitated then stepped inside. Clara sat with Anton, one of her light sculptures hovering before them. Anton rocked back and forth, eyes on the floor.

"Is that a new sculpture?" he said, forcing a smile.

She looked at him and his smile died. "Old one. New colors." Gar noted the absence of greens, reds and purples. "Autistics think visually. Words are too abstract," she said. "I hoped the shapes and colors might prompt a reaction."

Gar noticed she wasn't in uniform. "Did your shift change?"

"The captain needs to see you about an announcement. He asked me to brief you." She spoke a command. The hologram disappeared and a MedLab report appeared on a wall screen.

Clara led a photonics team analyzing the aurora. Gar had no idea how her work had been going. They didn't talk much lately. He scanned the report. "...high amplitude gamma waves in the brain, resulting in massive and prolonged epileptic seizures. Most victims are adult females. Attacks match peaks in aurora activity. Shielding attempts have failed."

"So it *is* the aurora," he said, as he finished.

"This thing isn't an aurora." She didn't look at him.

"What do you mean?"

"This planet's magnetosphere is too weak." She stared at Anton. "So are the solar flare levels. Besides, the timing of the attacks doesn't even match the solar wind cycle."

"Then what's causing the aurora? Or whatever it is?"

Clara reached out and stroked Anton's hair. The child began shaking his head violently and she stopped. "We think we are."

Gar felt a chill. "What?"

"The aurora was stable until our planet-fall. It's grown steadily since. We think our arrival prompted the attacks and our continued presence is causing their escalation."

"Attacks?" He wished she'd look at him.

"It's not a natural phenomenon. The electron flow doesn't even follow the planet's magnetic field. It appears to go where it wants to, and it seems to want to be over our settlement."

"But why?"

Clara finally looked at him. "We believe we're dealing with a sentience, Gar. An alien intelligence. The Captain wants to try to communicate. He's asking you to lead that team."

FAST FORWARD: *Fourth Movement, Nocturne (Allegro)*

Gar leaned against the wall of the main colony dome, staring at the fire raging above. Out here he was at least alone in his misery. No one else could stand the sight of the sky any more. Gar preferred it to the accusing stares of his fellow colonists.

All their attempts to communicate had failed. His team had used ideas from the ancient SETI project, transmitting universal mathematical concepts. For six Earth weeks, they had broadcast over the full range of EM frequencies detected in the aurora.

If any message had been received, it created no visible effect. The deaths continued. The aurora still burned the heavens, and he could no more tell what message it held than what was in his own son's head. Standing, he started to walk.

She sat slumped against a boulder crying, Anton in front of her. The child had his back to her, rocking gently. Gar sat down and pulled her to him before she realized he was there. She pushed away at first but then collapsed against him. Her sobs stopped, and they held each other for a long while.

"Do you know why I came out here?" she asked finally.

He paused. "You hoped the aurora might reach Anton."

"In a way," she said. Gar had never seen her face so sad.

"Well, it's quite the light sculpture," he said.

"Gar, I came here... so this thing would kill our son."

The words ran around his head as he tried to pull some meaning from them. "Clara..."

"Practically every victim's been a woman," she said.

"That doesn't..." He stopped. He understood.

"What will happen to him then? You won't..." She turned away, not finishing. He sat there, his face burning, realizing what she had been living with, and living with alone.

"I'm sorry," he whispered.

"Promise me you'd take care of him, that you'd love him."

"I promise," he said. They made love then, there on the ground, Anton as oblivious to their passion as he was to the monster rampaging above. After, they lay gazing at the aurora.

"I realize now how Anton must feel," Gar said.

"What do you mean?"

"Blind to other minds. We've been blind to this thing. Now, we're shouting, 'Hey look, we're alive' and it doesn't hear us."

She looked at Anton. "Maybe he's shouting too." Clara stared at the sky. "Words, mathematical symbols are too concrete, too cerebral for this thing. We need something more abstract. Something with emotion. I can feel it."

"'Music is born of emotion.'"

"That sounds like a quotation."

"Confucius. Music can express ideas, subtleties, and emotions that words can't. The language areas in the brain show activity when we listen to music. Too bad the sky has no ears."

Clara smiled. "You and your music. That's what first attracted me to you, when we met after the launch."

"Really?"

She nodded. "The first crew briefing. You had Bach playing in the room. I remember the colors—all golds and reds."

"Music helps to...wait a minute. Colors?"

She looked embarrassed. "I'm a synesthete. Sounds make me see colors. That's why I always have music playing when I work on my light sculptures. Inspiration."

"Synesthesia. You've never told me about this."

"I once worked in a laser lab with another synesthete. With her, light prompted sounds, even tastes and smells. It was so distracting for her that she had to quit her career. So when I applied for a berth on the ship, I kept quiet about it."

"No need to be ashamed. Lots of creative types have been synesthetes. Scriabin even built a 'color organ' for *Prometheus: Poems of Fire...*" He stopped and stared at the sky.

"Too bad my synesthesia isn't like that. I could tell you what kind of music the sky is playing..." She stopped, too.

They looked at each other.

"We could use colors for different pitches," he said.

"You mean, correlate the spectrum of EM frequencies displayed by the aurora with sound frequencies of the music."

"That's what I said."

"Rhythm can just stay the same. Brightness for volume."

"What about orchestration? The timbre of each instrument?"

"Holographic images. Different shapes for each instrument."

"Your sculptures! We could adjust sizes too."

"Small shapes for high notes, larger for the bass range."

"And add more shapes for more volume as well," he said.

"What about harmony? Melody?"

"Tough one. Don't know what colors or shapes go together."

"You'll figure it out." She stood and picked up a wriggling Anton, giving him a hug. "Come on. We've got work to do."

Fourth Movement, Finale (Crescendo)

Gathered under the sea of swirling light, the entire colony seemed to hold its breath as Gar spoke the command. Lasers flared into life, and Schubert's *8th Symphony* danced in cubes and stars and dodecahedrons of rainbow colors across the sky. Gar had always thought the *Unfinished* was music for the end of the world. A fitting epitaph for the colony if they failed.

A computer controlled the shapes, colors and other aspects of the display, monitoring the aurora and repeating patterns that prompted lower EMR levels. "Audience feedback," Clara called it.

The music of the lights played. The colors and shapes of the music kept changing and the colony kept waiting. Ten minutes. Fifteen.

The aurora seemed to slow, to drop in intensity. A murmur swept through the crowd, and Gar's heartbeat quickened.

Someone screamed.

Gar spun around. A woman trembled on the ground. Another fell. Then a man. More dropped. Gar's ears buzzed and his head throbbed. "Gar!" Clara fell to the ground, hands stretched toward him, twitching. Anton still just sat, staring at the sky.

Gar moved to help Clara. Pain flamed in his head and he fell. The air seemed thicker, misty. Then he understood.

The aurora had dropped from the sky. It enveloped them, a swirling cloud of colored sparks and flashes. Electric shocks stung his skin. Saliva trickled from Clara's mouth. The comm-unit to control the display lay before him. He forced his hand forward. The screaming grew louder as he clawed the unit to him.

His lips began to form the command to kill the light music when he saw Anton. The child still sat but his eyes...

Gar felt a thrill of joy as for the first time Anton's eyes focused on something in this world. Clara's sculptures danced in the sky to Gar's music and their child followed every pirouette.

Twisting his head, he saw that Clara was watching too, the happiness in her face shining through the pain.

Whether it was the sculptures or the music or the aurora, Gar neither knew nor cared. He let the comm-unit slip from his fingers. This scene would play itself out.

He reached out to clasp Clara's hand, wondering with a strange calm if they would survive. Together they lay in the dirt of that alien world and watched their son turn to look at them—and smile.

Speedeth All
Meriah L. Crawford

KEPLER-443b
27 March 2318, UTC 14:27

*I*t was shortly after dawn on their thirteenth day on the Bee, as they'd all started calling it. Not just as an abbreviation of the planet's designation, but because it was annoying—and painful, if you didn't watch what you were doing. Long days, vicious heat, nasty bugs, and hidden tunnel systems where the lizards hid. Add to that the lack of water or food, and almost complete absence of cover, and, for a "simple recon mission," it was about as bad as it could get. About the only positive aspect of the place was that the atmosphere was breathable, though no one quite knew why.

Squad Leader Vetter leaned against a red boulder in a small impact crater watching Trine cleaning and repairing their comms unit. The box had taken a hit from a pulsed laser weapon, and it was dead.

Trine had assured Vetter there was nothing that could be done to fix it, short of replacing "almost every single bishtup part," including a lot of parts he didn't have spares for. He'd been removing, cleaning, and repairing parts for the last two hours of his watch, anyway. Vetter didn't need to ask why. She'd have killed for a task, however pointless—but there was little she could do but wait.

Macksin was snoring. Bastard could sleep through anything—was probably the best-rested biped on the dirt—but he seemed to have the mental capacity of a rutabaga. He'd follow orders if you explained them slow enough, but in a firefight, he was next to useless. And most of the time when he *was* awake, he just sat and read through technical specs and manuals, like he'd never set sight on the insides of the machines he'd been trained to maintain. Damn shame, too, because he was an exceptionally well-constructed soldier, and command didn't much mind fraternizing if they didn't see it happening—not during off-world missions. They'd gotten along well, too, at first—until things started to go wrong, and Macksin proved himself to be the least competent mechanic she'd ever seen.

Vetter shook her head. How she'd found herself left with these two—alone in their sector, as far as she could tell—was a mystery. Macksin, at least, should have been the first to go. Some of the squad started calling him a good luck charm after the third time he narrowly missed being killed or maimed. They were dead now. Every last one.

When the war with the lizards started just nine months ago, Vetter's squad and almost two thousand other soldiers—a rough mix of lifers and draftees—were sent to the Bee. The planet supposedly had some very useful minerals but minimal tactical value, though the orders to constantly scan the surface and relay the data to orbit each watch suggested it was far more important than they'd been told. Beyond that, she had little idea what was going on. None of them even knew what had started the war—they only knew it was happening. The better their tech got, the less information command shared. Smart, she supposed, but annoying. Frustrating. And this time, maybe lethal.

It took them almost six months to arrive on the Bee. When they arrived, the soldiers had been deployed on the surface in squads of twelve. The annies had done all kinds of math to select that number for this arena: three watches of ten hours each, accounting for someone to focus on comms, someone to manage nav, one on scout, and a low-level mechanic for the hugos. In the field, of course, it was bullshit. They were all so turned around by the planet's thirty-hour days, massive temp swings, and the aggressive insect life, that they could barely piss straight, let alone function like a trained squad.

Their last transpo was dead, too, as of that morning. All three of their five-ton tracked hugos had been blasted into pieces that were mostly too small to play tag-o with, let alone try to piece back together. Macksin was supposed to be the squad's senior mechanic, but he couldn't change a tire without a manual, a video, and a helper, so there was no chance. Not a single damn chance that they'd reach their evac coordinates on schedule.

Assuming they ever could have.

Vetter re-seated her goggles, and sprayed the two men with more of the fancy new bug spray they'd been issued, finishing the can on herself. It helped with the flyers and the crawlers, though not so much with the jumpers. *They* wouldn't be out for another few hours, thank god. Not until the temperature reached 43C, or so. Damn near hot enough to fry your brains.

Macksin opened his eyes for a moment as she sprayed, and resettled his goggles, but otherwise neither man reacted. They'd all had their senses dulled by the constant onslaught. The pounding heat.

Next, she deployed the sun screens, knowing they would do little to blunt the force of the heat stabbing down at them from the eternally navy-blue skies. But, it was better than nothing.

There'd been no way to be truly prepared for this planet, since they hadn't known more than the basics about surface conditions until they arrived. The probe they sent ahead was low- tech, and it hadn't reached the Bee until after they'd already left the solar system. But the transit time had at least given the engineers and med ops enough lag to cobble together a kit to keep them alive. She had to give them some credit for that.

She realized she'd been staring at Macksin again. The muscles of his back, straining at his shirt…

She shook her head and reminded herself how long it had taken him to recalibrate the nav con on their last hugo—and how much of a tick she'd been about it. She winced. Macksin surely hadn't forgotten about that.

She shifted the sun screens slightly, and focused her attention back on the mission. Thoughts kept poking at her from the dark corners. She pulled up satellite imagery on her pad again and studied it. The orders she'd been given were simple: Go to these coordinates, eliminate any resistance; travel to the next set of coordinates, scanning as you go; set up camp, eliminate any resistance; wait for the order to evac. Minimal hostile presence, they said. Just identify key features, look for traps and weapons caches, upload the data, and get out.

That was before they discovered the tunnel systems. Before they realized there was water underground. And before they learned that the tunnels were filled with booby traps, mines, and a hell of a lot of lizards. And as they'd discovered on their second day on the rock, some of the massive two-plus meter tall lizards were mined themselves, so they exploded after their hearts stopped. None of her squad had gone anywhere near their kills since then. That lesson had cost them Jesson, Paik, and Amaechi.

Vetter overlaid the images with terrain data and started doing the math, again. And then, she heard a click and whine, ducking before she realized it came from the comm box.

She gaped at Trine, eyes wide.

Then, there was a snap and a pop, and the whine was gone. "Trine?"

He shook his head. "Residual charge," he said, shrugging. "Dying gasp."

"Is it possible—?"

But he was shaking his head more firmly. "It's chicken sticks," he said.

"Chicken sticks?"

"Battered and fried." He smiled awkwardly. "Sorry, I…"

"From the country?" Vetter asked.

"No," he said. "Just used to watch a lot of movies. I like slang. It's…" he smirked at her. "It's pretty frazz."

Frazz was slang from her town—her time. He must know, but how? She smiled at him, wishing for a moment that she knew more about him—but glad she didn't know more about the others. The less she knew, the less there was to mourn over.

In the brief pause, Trine focused back on the comm unit. After a moment, Vetter tipped up her pad again, aligning the map with the imagery, calculating distances and movement rates.

Vetter shifted quickly to the right to scratch at something that might or might not be slithering up her back, and the top of the boulder she'd been leaning on exploded. The cramped, semi-protected circle of rocks they'd been sheltering in was suddenly filled with laser blasts, and the *whumps* of EDs landing nearby.

The only bits of tech they had left, aside from her pad and a scanner, were three kick-ass, high-velocity rifles, and about a thousand rounds of explosive ammo that were far too heavy to carry any significant distance. She rolled to her weapon, hauled it into place, and aimed.

The sights located the targets quickly—five lizards, three hundred meters away. They had a slight advantage of elevation, but not enough to make a difference. Rock fragments were kicking up around her as Vetter fired, pausing after each shot to acquire a new target. The rounds had just enough smarts in them to fly true if the targets moved within about a ten-meter range, so diving for cover wasn't much help. Running flat-out could work, but that generally just flushed the lizards into the open so someone else could take them out. She and her squad had decided that was why they saw so few of the lizards: they knew by now that they had little to gain by coming out of the tunnels, and a lot to risk. All they really had to do was wait for the planet to kill the humans, and pop out occasionally to take out the stragglers.

Vetter watched through the sights and confirmed four kills, with one target running. Her magazine was empty, so she looked to her right to see if Trine was sighting on the target. Trine was hunched over the comm unit as if he was ducking—except the top half of his head was gone. Vetter gasped and felt a powerful ache, but she pushed it away. There was no time.

She turned back to her rifle to reload—jumping when a shot was fired from her left and just behind.

Vetter twisted sharply. Macksin? She gaped at him and he looked back at her, scared, as if he'd done something wrong. Vetter turned back and checked her sights, confirming it: the last lizard was down. Dead.

She turned back to Macksin. "Good job. That was fast."

He blushed and looked at Trine. "Could have been faster." Vetter shook her head, but before she could speak, Macksin said, "Could have been awake, standing guard."

"You were off watch," Vetter said, and ran the scanner across the territory around their position. "You were supposed to be sleeping."

"We're supposed to keep each other safe."

"*I'm* supposed to keep *you* safe."

Macksin shook his head and looked up at the sky, but didn't say anything. He didn't have to. Anyone on this bishtup rock knew whose fault it really was.

And how many of them were left on the ground? Over one hundred and eighty squads had been dropped on the Bee. How many had been retrieved? How many troops still breathed?

Even if they'd had comms, it wasn't a question she could ever ask; it wasn't a question that would ever be answered.

Macksin started opening up a med kit.

Vetter waved him off. "We need to move. Our position is compromised."

Macksin gestured at her head. "You're bleeding."

Vetter swore, with feeling. They'd been warned to dress wounds promptly—both because of foreign bacteria and because the lizards could track blood trails like supercharged bloodhounds. So Vetter let him bandage the wound. At least he was good at that. Better than at repairing hugos, anyway.

"Macksin, why did you put in for mechanic?"

He smiled, just barely. "I put in for medic. Used to be a trauma med tech back home." After a moment, he added, "Only thing I've ever been good at."

"But, why…?"

"My dad is a mechanic. Wanted me to be one, too. Figured the war would train me, somewhere safe, and I'd come home and work for him. He bought the head of the draft board a couple of drinks and slipped him some cash, and here I am."

Vetter sat in silence while Macksin smoothly, gently plucked rock chips from her forehead. "I'm sorry," she said, wincing at the sheer idiocy of it. "Really sorry."

It was heartbreaking, to waste good medic skills. There were always more mechanics—and more kids who loved cars and trucks and shuttles, and who took to the training like fish to batter. But good medics? Rare as hell, and took forever to train.

Macksin shrugged. "At least I can do this. Nice to finally contribute."

Vetter thought she could hear bitterness in his voice, and she felt even worse. *If only I'd known,* Vetter thought. But, what if she had? Would it have mattered? He would still have been their mechanic. At least...at least I could have been less of an arkot about his mechanical skills.

She winced, and Macksin said, "Sorry, did that hurt?"

"No, no," she said. "Just...thinking."

He nodded. "I try not to do that. I guess that's why I sleep so much."

Vetter winced again. "For what it's worth, I'm sorry."

He looked at her and touched the side of her face, gently. "Do over?" he asked, with a slight quirk of his lips.

"Do over," she said, and wished like hell that they could do all of it over. When Macksin was done, Vetter scanned quickly for any new signs of activity. Nothing. Not surprising: the lizards usually traveled in small groups. But, they could have called for help. She and Macksin had to move.

After they'd packed what they could carry, including all of the water and food they could find in the others' packs, and about fifty rounds of ammo each, Vetter scanned Trine's ident chip with her pad, recording the time and location of his death. She also needed a photo—it was SOP—but she hesitated. All you could see from this angle was his head wound, and the photos were accessible to the next of kin.

She looked at Macksin. "Technically, we're not supposed to move him..."

Macksin understood immediately, and stepped forward. "Let me."

"I can…"

"No, it's OK. In my work, back home…I'm used to stuff like this."

Macksin gently shifted Trine's body and lay him down on the ground, while Vetter scanned the area for movement.

"OK," he said.

When Vetter turned back, Trine's face was visible, and his head wound less so. It was a huge improvement, though still horrible. Still dead.

Vetter snapped the picture and said, "Right, let's get moving. And…thanks." Their eyes met for a moment and they nodded to each other, then started pulling on their gear.

When they were ready to move out, Vetter touched Macksin's hand, and he slid his into hers.

"Think we'll make it?" he asked.

Vetter smiled. "I guarantee it. In fact, I'll buy the beer in the next bar we get to, if we don't."

"Deal," he said, squeezing her hand tightly.

Vetter's previous plan had been to wait until a shuttle was nearby and signal. It had seemed like the safest, smartest option, given that they had some rare good cover, and non-transportable ammo. But their position was blown, and she'd seen precisely zero signs of shuttle traffic within the atmo. So, now that they were set, she gestured to Macksin to take point, and they started walking.

She scanned incessantly. The lizards had better stealth tech than any of their equipment could really handle, so they just had to hope for movement. The scanner alarm chirped faintly as she put it on audible, and Macksin's shoulders relaxed just a bit. They might have no more than a split second of warning, but at least she could give him a chance.

If all went well, they'd reach their evac site three days and a couple hours after they were supposed to arrive. Would the squad shuttle wait? No. Not a chance. But, what choice did they have? They just had to keep looking for signs of a shuttle. And they had to keep moving, or the bugs or the lizards, or who knows what else, would get them.

§

They'd been walking for almost nine hours—trudging, really—trading positions every hour or so to help keep them alert, when they heard the beeping. It was faint but rhythmic—a signal calling for evac. Where was it coming from?

"Shee," Vetter said. "My sense of direction is the worst. Can you locate it?"

Macksin turned his head slowly, finally pointing off to the right. "There."

Vetter led the way, both of them moving more slowly, scanning for an ambush or explosives of some kind. They hadn't found anything like that on the Bee, but that didn't prove anything.

There was no kind of shelter except where they were headed. Was there a squad there? A clutch of lizards?

"Wait," she said. "You wait here." She pointed at a cluster of low rocks. "Hunker down there and provide cover."

"No."

Vetter turned and stared at him. "What?"

"There's no point. If it's lizards, we're dead. Let's…let's just go. We need to keep moving, anyway."

"But…" Vetter couldn't think of what to say, and that's when she realized how hot and exhausted she was. The stims hid it so well, until all of a sudden you were dragging. And the drugs were mixed in with the food, so you couldn't avoid them. The hardest thing was remembering to sleep, and she'd been due to rest a good eight hours ago.

While they stood, unmoving, a pair of jumpers landed on her chest. She swatted the three-inch-long brown bastards off with just the edge of panic, stomping on them when they hit the ground. The jumpers bit hard, if they had a second on your skin, and they released a toxin that caused swelling and itching that was a good ten times worse than any mosquito she'd ever met.

"Shee. Fine. Come on." At least while they were moving, the jumpers stayed away.

§

All their caution turned out to be pointless. When they ducked their heads around the boulders into the small, protected site, they found no threat. Just a very big mess.

Macksin groaned softly, and Vetter spun and vomited. Macksin said, "You want me to…Can I…?"

"What?" she said, her voice rough.

"You should rinse your mouth out and drink some water. And I can grab the, uh…"

After she rinsed her mouth out, Vetter forced herself to turn and look. Her stomach lurched again when she saw it. The beeping comm box was still clutched in the hands of a woman who had half her torso blown off. It looked like she'd ducked forward to protect the box, but an ED had killed everyone.

Vetter closed her eyes and tried to steady herself. She wasn't exactly a seasoned veteran, but she should have been able to deal with this. It was probably the stims, the exhaustion, the desperation. Still, she couldn't ask Macksin to do it. She shouldn't.

She heard movement and looked, and he was already halfway there, walking through a waking nightmare. Macksin paused and slid the data chip from a broken scanner that lay beside a large headless man. The navigator's dark brown fingers still cradled the scanner, and Vetter shuddered when she saw the distinct pattern of callouses that marked him as a lifer. He had to have been in the force a lot longer than most of the poor bastards who'd been sent to the Bee. Who had he pissed off to get assigned to this damned rock?

Macksin continued forward, toward the woman with the comm box. He groaned again when the woman wouldn't release the box without force. He stepped quickly away once he had it, pressing it and the chip into Vetter's hands as he passed her.

His wake pulled the stench of decomp with it, and she stumbled away, joining him at a safe distance. Both of them took deep breaths and stared at the shimmering rock in the distance.

The comm box buzzed three times, and then: "All squads still on the surface: report, report, report. Last call. Report now."

Vetter fumbled with the box, pressing her code and keying a response. They were supposed to avoid voice transmissions whenever possible, and to be ruthlessly brief in their text messages. Still, she found herself aching to call out to them, tell them what had happened, and summon a rescue. She thought of her mother and how calm and cool she always was, even in the midst of a crisis. It settled her—though she'd found herself wondering, more and more, if her mother had ever had to face anything like *this* while she was in uniform.

A message scrolled onto the screen: "Squad 6689, report. What is your status?"

Vetter keyed in a response, adding a request for evac.

"Squad 6689, upload your data."

She handed the box to Macksin and pulled their data chip out, removing it from its case and wiping the contacts clean. She reached out to insert it into the data slot on the comm box, but Macksin grabbed her hand.

She looked up, surprised, and saw a look of wide-eyed fear on his face.

"No," he said. "You can't. They're not—they aren't coming to get us. If you upload the data, there'll be no need to."

"They wouldn't do that," Vetter said, without even thinking. "They wouldn't just leave us here."

Macksin raised his eyebrows at her.

Vetter opened her mouth to argue, when doubt and fear took old. "Oh, gods," she said. "Oh, bish."

She put the chip away and keyed in another response: "Chip reader damaged. Chip won't read."

"Is chip damaged?" the screen read.

"No. Can read on pad. Also possess additional squad chip." Macksin nodded vigorously as he saw her type it in. "Standby."

The pads and comm boxes had been designed to be 100 percent non-communicative, as a security measure. It was smart, and a pain in the tail, and it might just save them.

"Yow!" Macksin yelped, and spun.

Vetter smacked at the two jumpers on his ass, stomping them, and then whipped around so Macksin could check her back.

"Clear," he said, wincing and rubbing his butt. "Bishtup bugs. Can we walk?"

She bobbed her head and gestured in the direction they'd been heading in before they heard the box. She handed Macksin the scanner, and they continued on as before, except that they had hope.

Both of them walked faster, in spite of the furnace-like heat, though it was probably pointless. The squad shuttle could collect them almost anywhere, assuming they received orders to get them.

"You think they're coming?" Macksin said. Vetter, still in the lead, shrugged.

Another fifteen minutes in and the comm box bleeped. A message. Vetter leapt to Macksin's side and they read it together: "Standby for pickup. Current coordinates. Six minutes."

They looked at each other, more intently than they probably ever had, and grins spread across their faces. Vetter laughed and Macksin pulled her into a hug, and then a quick, shy kiss.

"This is real, right?" Macksin said, finally. "They're actually coming for us. We're going home."

Vetter nodded and leaned against him, allowing herself to feel safe for just a moment.

And then Macksin smacked at her hip and shuffled her aside, stomping on a jumper. It didn't quite kill the joy, but it brought them down to the dirt.

"Back to back," Vetter said.

They scuffed the ground looking for jumper holes and then pressed against each other's backs so they could keep watch. Given the lack of natural cover, it was the most practical approach. Vetter focused on the scanner again and they waited. Seven minutes in, they heard the squad shuttle's distinctive rumble.

"Where?" Vetter said.

After a moment, Macksin pointed up and to her left. "Coming in steep. Either in a big hurry, or they've been catching fire from the surface."

The comm box bleeped and Macksin pivoted to see it. "Prepare for combat pickup and immediate ascent to orbit for ship departure."

Macksin let out a soft "huh," as the shuttle roared toward them, decelerating hard. "We must have just caught them."

Both of them reseated their goggles and slid dust masks over their mouths.

"Wonder what's really so important about these chips," Vetter said.

He shrugged. "We barely saw anything aside from small groups of lizards. You think there are really minerals here?"

"Scanner didn't report anything. For all I know, they want them because none of the other squads made it."

Macksin grimaced, and he took Vetter's hand and held it gently, rubbing his thumb against her knuckles. "Think we'll still be in the same unit?"

"No idea," Vetter sighed.

As the shuttle came into view, they dropped each other's hands, and stowed the scanner and comm box. The shuttle roared up and smacked hard onto the ground, blasting dust into the air, and they both started running. The doors slid open, they barreled in, and the doors boomed shut again.

A voice called out, "Brace! Brace!" and the shuttle lifted off with tremendous force, throwing Macksin and Vetter both to the deck.

Neither bothered trying to fight the forces pressing them down until they reached low orbit. Finally, the voice came over the speakers again: "Come on forward. Shuttle's nearly empty."

They climbed to their feet, walking through the doors and into the pilot's compartment. There were two people in addition to the pilot: a co-pilot and a very ragged-looking mechanic. He nodded at Macksin, who nodded back, but he ignored Vetter.

They settled into two of the three remaining chairs and strapped in. They could see the transport ship in the distance—aimed for home.

The pilot gave them brief instructions, all of which they already knew, and said they'd arrive at the transport in about a half hour.

"Why so long?" Vetter asked.

"They've already begun moving out of the area, toward the Arrowsmith junction. Going to have to burn rubber to catch them."

"Burn rubber?" Vetter asked. "Hurry," the pilot said.

"Got yer chips handy?" the co-pilot asked. "Command wants them uploaded ASAP."

Vetter moved to pull them out, but stopped as Macksin said, "Why?"

"Hmm?" The co-pilot looked at Macksin.

"Why do they want them now? Why not just upload when we're aboard?"

The co-pilot shrugged. "Because it's command and they asked for it. And they're called command because they give orders, and then we follow them. Right?"

Vetter and Macksin exchanged a look. She said, "We just would hate for them to leave without us."

The other mechanic snorted and the pilot said, "Look, this isn't a discussion. Pull them out and upload them." When she still hesitated, he added, "They aren't going anywhere without us. I guarantee it."

"How can you be sure?" Vetter asked.

"I'm sure," the pilot said.

The co-pilot released his straps, turned in his seat, and held out his hand. "Give. That's an order."

Vetter sighed and slid the data chips from their cases. "Sure hope you're right."

The co-pilot took the chips and plugged them into high-speed data transfer slots, shaking his head and muttering something about crazy damn troops. In less than five minutes, all 487 exabytes of data had been transferred. The system pinged a confirmation, and the co-pilot removed the chips and passed them back to Vetter.

And less than five minutes after that, the pilot let out a string of curses that even the co-pilot seemed shocked by.

The pilot keyed comms. "Transport, you're moving too fast. We won't catch you."

Silence.

"Transport, please respond."

The ship was visibly pulling away, even as the shuttle increased speed to the point that the vessel was shuddering and an alarm siren began squalling.

"Jack?" The co-pilot said. "What? What's happening? They're not...?" He reached out and keyed in a message.

After a moment, a bleep sounded, and all of them could see the response. "Sorry, shuttle. There's no time. Gods be your tailwind."

"Tailwind?" the pilot said, slamming his fist against the panel. "There's no tailwind in the universe that could catch us up with them now, and they know it."

The co-pilot turned and looked at Vetter. "How did you know? *How?*"

She shrugged and sagged in her seat. "I was hoping I was wrong. I just..."

"Are you really that surprised?" Macksin said.

The co-pilot blinked at the question. "Yes! Yes, I'm surprised. Getting us back aboard safely has always been the highest priority."

Macksin shook his head. "It wasn't you, it was the shuttle. The fleet loves their hardware."

The co-pilot said, "But what was the bishtup hurry, anyway? They couldn't wait a few more minutes? It doesn't make any sense."

"Yeah, it does," the pilot said. "Sweet Sarah." He tapped a button on the console, and the port side view came on the main screen. It was one of the lizards' ships—a huge one—heading toward them.

As they watched, tiny glowing dots appeared from the side of the alien ship, racing toward the shuttle.

The other mechanic whistled softly and said, "No wonder those arkots ran for it. Gods be-damned cowards."

Macksin reached out and took Vetter's hand.

She turned and looked at him. "I'm sorry," she said. He squeezed her hand. "At least it's over."

The first missile connected with the shuttle, and they were gone.

The Night of Stars
Jennifer Rachel Bauman

"Dear Moron. Get out."

Kevin rolled his head along the back of the squeaky porch swing and gave her one of *those* looks. Flakes of paint from the metal swing frame already dotted his dark hair; he'd watched her pace before she opened the official foreclosure letter. "It does not say that."

"Might as well," Jessica said. She stood on the rickety wooden porch with the letter warping under her sweating fingers. Dusty sunlight struggled through the particulate cloud that had enveloped the planet after Near Planet Object asteroid Metallica had slammed into the Pacific, annihilating the polar bears and putting an end to the debates about global warming. Earth was now hot, dusty, and dry.

It was also home. Jessica had spent a lot of time out in the stars, sailing between planets, surveying and charting routes and drill sites for mining companies. There were computers and unmanned ships that could do the same job, but mining companies sent geologists, tacked on the name astro-geologist, and then paid them wages that were still cheaper for the corporations than computer ships. It didn't matter—the pay wasn't the point. Conquest was the thing for solar sailors. Tiny, one-body ships, like the universe's smallest interstellar studio apartment. Jessica excelled at it, darting in and out of orbit around dying suns, using their light to propel her close enough to chart the minerals and mineables, dashing away again like a super-powered firefly.

She was good at it, but she'd never relaxed into it. There'd always been that edge of terror for Jessica, the blurred-vision, pounding-heart *How did I get myself into this?* type of panic. Now it had been a year since she'd been out there. Just the idea brought on the edges of panic. Her throat tightened. Her chest seized up. Asthma impaled her lungs.

"Breathe," Kevin said. He stood, the swing creaking behind him in the silent desert air. Not many people had stayed in the western states after the Night of Stars, as an unfortunate number of survivors now called the Decimation.

"How do you always know?"

"I can see it in your face. You go all still. You're never still."

She was still uncomfortable with anyone who understood her. Five years together and she was still uncomfortable knowing he could read her. One year since the Decimation, and she wanted to be brave. Stoic.

She wanted not to wake screaming when she could feel the tail of her ship take the hit, feel the spin start, the heat of free fall through the atmosphere burning her. She'd come to her aunt's house because it seemed safe in the desert. Flat. Uncratered. And at night she could see the stars, when she was brave enough to look up through the constant cloud cover. Out here city lights had never reflected back from the night sky, dimming the stars. And now, there were very few city lights.

Kevin was still watching her. He was going to hug her if she didn't distract him. She was going to cry if he hugged her. Crying would solve nothing. Jessica squinted at the thick paper in her hands. "'Get out. You are no longer entitled to the plot of dirt you thought you bought. We never said it would be easy. We never said it would be fair. We just wanted—'"

"What does it really say?"

"'We just wanted your tax proceeds to finance our galactic hegemony.'"

"Jessica."

"Fine." She wrinkled her nose and drew a breath. The letterhead smelled rich, thick and cardboard-y, of fine offices on some distant planet and of secretaries drenched in perfume. No attorney had ever gone near this letter. It was a form letter, full of spite and venom and greed. On something resembling vellum.

"What's it say?"

"We regret to inform you we are looking into foreclosure proceedings on your property."

Kevin closed his eyes. "And?"

"'You and all your wastrel friends will be thrown off planet—'" But she stopped before he opened his eyes and said, "It's a letter of non-payment. Apparently, they sent a lot of them to my Aunt before she died."

"And she just happened to not mention it when she sold it to you?" He leaned over and took the letter from her. It didn't seem to improve any when he read it.

Jessica thought about the other letter she'd received. The one still in her pocket. The one she hadn't told Kevin about. The "we want you back." The "get out of jail free" letter (or at least get out of debt.) The one from her old employer. Andrews. Not just ex-employer. Ex-lover from many years ago. Ex. The one who said he wasn't going to give up, wasn't going to let her go that easy, and kept reappearing in her life.

"What else does it say?" she asked, distracting herself again.

"We've got until the nineteenth to make payments," Kevin read.

Jessica leaned her forearms on the paint-peeling porch rails and stared at the empty desert. The asteroids, Metallica and its much-smaller, splintered-off friends, had seemed pretty determined about hitting urban areas. Her aunt's property in Very Much Nowhere, Nevada had been spared. Her aunt had owned a lot of acres, a vast spread of empty desert no one had wanted before Metallica.

Almost as vast and desolate as a star field. And everyone wanted it now. Rebuilding the cities would take time. So much devastation. As if bombs had gone off. It was faster, easier, and more financially rewarding for banks and developers to first build in empty, unpopulated and unaffected areas, then take their time moving everyone back to the cities, at least those who were willing to go.

Her aunt's property would make the bank and the developers very happy.

"The nineteenth of what?"

He didn't respond right away, so she already knew what he was going to say. "June."

"That's next week," she said. Overhead rusty-sounding birds circled something unfortunate on the devastated earth. "Listen. They've already sent the vultures."

Kevin moved beside her and leaned one arm over her shoulders. "Those are crows, Jess."

She wasn't so sure.

§

It wasn't like it was a particularly nice house. It was square and squat and small. The paint was peeling everywhere there was paint. It had originally been gray, and had somehow gotten dingier as the gray bleached white over countless desert summers and after the initial radiation blast from Metallica hit.

And it wasn't as if it were an old family homestead. She hadn't spent summers here with her aunt, running barefoot through the sage and catching lizards. She'd only come for single-weekend guilt-visits with her parents, who always seemed to think her aunt was up to something living way out here.

But when Aunt Rose died and Kevin was injured in the initial blasts and Jessica was—her mind veered away—after the Decimation, it became a haven. And when Aunt Rose died, it became Jessica's haven.

A haven mortgaged heavily to galactic banks which were in turn mortgaged heavily after Earth started needing funds to rebuild.

Kevin turned and looked at her and she shuddered. She always did, anymore. That frisson of cold that ran down her back. The familiar features, forever unfamiliar now. Just off. Smooth simulated flesh.

Smooth simulated features. They'd mostly recreated the dark brows, the dark hair. The set of his mouth. The way he usually looked just about to smile.

But they'd missed a scar here, a wrinkle there. And the new body was aging and changing differently. She was never quite able to forget. When the ejecta thrown by the Decimation hit Reno, Kevin had been in one of the buildings that tumbled down. They'd barely gotten him out in time, in the wave of first rescues before the global nature of everything became clear and the authorities stopped actual rescue in favor of triage and recovery. And over the course of that first night, it turned out that *just in time* wasn't.

ReBodies were expensive. They were luxuries, ways to stay with loved ones past what the body said was possible. The new body was a haven for Kevin.

An expensive, heavily mortgaged haven. A haven legally tied to the house.

He put his arm around her in the hot, still afternoon, but his arm felt cold. She thought she could feel him tremble, just a little. Just what he couldn't control.

"We'll figure it out," he said. "I can do some moonlighting, get a second job." There was plenty of rebuilding to do. Survivors were spreading back out from the frightened packs they'd gathered into after the event.

Jessica put her head against his chest and nodded. "I'll contact the bank, the attorneys. Ask for an extension. We'll figure it out," she said. Repeating what he'd said. Hoping to believe it.

Even now that carpenters were in demand, it wouldn't be possible for a carpenter to pay those mortgages back down, not even with a second job. Not a carpenter in a repaired and fabricated body. The banks had them on the run now—high premiums, high penalties for being behind, high pestilence for having been in arrears. High petulance—and resistance—to their getting out. There was no way to win with small payments, even if they both got second full-time jobs. It wouldn't be enough fast enough. Not with Jessica safely on Earth.

The mining companies were still expanding. Off-planet minerals for other human-populated planets. Iron for rebuilding. It was all in demand.

Solar sailing astro-geologist surveyors were in demand.

Jessica took the other letter out of her pocket and looked at it. The mining company's insignia stood out sharply on the white envelope. When she looked up, Kevin was looking at the envelope too. His gaze rose to meet hers. Slowly. He didn't look like he was about to smile.

Nights out here were long and dark. Used to be the night wind was cold and smelled of sage and transient desert moisture. Now, the wind smelled burned, the way Earth did.

Among the stars her tiny one-person world would be sterile, clean, and chemical. It was supposed to be safe again in near space. The band of Near Earth Objects had moved on. No more asteroids nearby.

That didn't mean they weren't out there where she ended up. She wasn't mapping mining possibilities on Earth's sun.

§

"You always knew they were out there," Kevin said.

Kevin's shoulder still felt the same. As if his surgeon had recreated the hollow where her head fit out of some blueprint when he remade everything. From where they lay on the bed she could see out a corner of the window where the curtain kept stirring in the night breeze. When it gusted into the room she could see the moon, three-quarters and fading. The same old moon in the newly designed sky—all the dust made it diffuse and uncertain.

The way Jessica felt. "Do you *want* me to go out there?"

"Of course not." He went up on one elbow and looked down at her. "We can figure it out, Jess. We can do something else. I'd rather."

She sat up with her back to him, her feet on the bedroom floor. They'd lose for certain if she stayed. They couldn't fight the bank. The global economy had reduced individual economies to less than trivial matters.

In her mind, the ship closed around her again, the claustrophobic cockpit tapering into "living space" which was more office than anything else. The mining company didn't care about her living. The bank didn't care about Kevin living.

She could come back from the stars.

Kevin couldn't come back from foreclosure.

§

The launch ship was a weapons regrade. It could still be used to shoot asteroids out of space because, of course, that had worked so well last time. But the cruiser made a good carrier.

Jessica moved through the row of solar ships, her heart pounding twice as fast as her unwilling footsteps. Crew filtered in, other surveyors wearing modified spacesuits like Jessica's—small, light, easy to move around in, made of something light and tough like the under-wrapping plastic used under siding on Earth houses.

She'd kissed Kevin goodbye at dawn the day before and joined the crew. They'd headed out of orbit, into space, heading for a nearly dead star. And she'd done everything she could to avoid Andrews.

You read too much into things, Kevin kept saying. *Like that letter. The foreclosure letter.*

The one that had started with her name. Her mortgage account number. Her husband's mortgaged body's account number.

At least Andrews wants you back on his crew.

She didn't tell Kevin that's what bothered her.

So far, so good, though. Not a sign of Andrews. Maybe he didn't want to see her either. Or maybe he just didn't know she was on his crew.

Or maybe he was standing across the bay from her, apparently oblivious to the hustle around him. He only watched her.

Now that she'd seen him, it was pointless to pretend she hadn't. Jessica kept her eyes on him as he slowly oozed down the line of ships toward her. She couldn't figure out what had been wrong with her. What had she seen in him?

Andrews seemed to think the same thing. What had been wrong with her? He asked, and without waiting, added, "Good to have you back."

On board, Jessica finished his sentence. You mean, *Good to have you back on board.*

But she didn't say anything. She smiled, noncommittal, and climbed into her ship. Just before she launched, she heard Andrews over her radio: "I told you I'd get you back. How's that foreclosure coming? Must be just hell on Kevin."

Kevin and the new body. Andrews and the foreclosure he couldn't possibly know about.

That was paranoid thinking. *You read too much into things.*

Andrews smirked at her and patted her arm with proprietary smugness.

Jessica's stomach shuddered. With all her heart she didn't want to go out there. But she could imagine the forms they'd need to fill out, long, filled with legalese. The forms they would fill out after just a couple mapping runs, if she got lucky. Astro-geologists were in demand now. A couple of trips, and she and Kevin could fill out those forms, stating the mortgage was paid up. The foreclosure was called off. Long legal forms. Badly written instructions to go with. She'd make fun of the language. They'd make fun of it, together, and there'd be a together for them to be.

She set her sights on the stars and headed away from home in order to save it.

The Game

James Dorr

*C*lick!

That was the fourth ball. Two more in play—the fifth one spinning, right up on the edge.

Michael Warren felt his palms sweating.

Steady now...easy now, he told himself. His nerve mustn't falter. He pulled his left hand back—the guillotine blade thunked down, right where his thumb had lain—then thrust it forward. The button. Wobble it.

Change the wheel's pitch so the fifth ball...

"Earthie!"

The fifth ball clicked in place. Gears whirred and rumbled. He pulled his hand out again—the right one this time—then snaked it back onto the game's control surface at a different angle. The sixth ball—he'd never gone this far before.

"You! Earthie! Yes, Warren!"

He tried to ignore the voice. That was a part of the game as well—to try to distract him.

Why "Earthie?" he wondered. He'd never been to Old Earth himself. Had never known anyone...

No! Concentrate instead. The sixth ball. Higher. Pull out his hand—thrust it back. Higher. Up the rim.

Wobble it. Let it circle...

CLICK!

It was over.

The croupier caught him as he collapsed, straining under the weight of his human frame. Guided him to a chair.

"You, Michael Warren."

He looked at the croupier. Looked up now into faceted bees' eyes, at spindly legs supporting a vee-shaped, chitinous body.

"That's my name," he muttered. As if the Aztairan didn't know him. As if he hadn't come in each month to gamble the pay he got from odd jobs around the spaceport.

To play games he couldn't win…except *this* time.

"I want to congratulate you, Spaceman Michael Warren. Your friends will be proud of you. Shall I call Fleet Central?"

Warren shook his head. "You know I'm not FleetCen. I'm merchant space corps. Except—"

The Aztairan croupier held a chit out to him, folding it neatly in one of its pincers before he could take it. "Yes, I know, Spaceman Michael Warren." It thrust the chit out again, letting him have it.

Warren laughed. The croupier had tried its best. Tried to distract him. To rig the game its way. Was even now backing away from him, scanning the neon-lit casino to find a new player in danger of winning.

To cut its losses.

But Warren, in the meantime, had *won*. Won at a game already so stacked against anyone playing it that the payoff it gave was enormous.

It only then sank in—started to sink in. He walked in a daze to the cashier's window wondering—that crack about calling FleetCen—wondering what he would do with his winnings.

"Shall I just transfer it?" the cashier asked him. He looked up, recognizing the voice, and saw it was Angela. Someone he'd known once.

He shook his head. "No." If he *had* been connected with FleetCen, humankind's military arm as well as its government on a mixed-race planet like this one, he could have had his winnings transferred to a base account automatically. Not that gambling was strictly legal, but FleetCen took care of its own against natives, so no one would complain. But—

He looked up, suddenly, seeing the croupier reflected in the cashier's window, talking to someone. Another human, and not a player. He shrugged, then thrust his chit through the slot in the fake marble counter.

"Sir?" the blonde cashier, Angela, prompted. He shrugged again, wondering if she remembered him. Years ago, when she'd first come to this planet, with him an "old hand" of scarcely more than six months' stay himself, already falling into the routine of those that were grounded.

He'd been surprised then that she'd stayed on herself—she hadn't had to, but people settled on off-the-beat planets like this one for all kinds of reasons. They—

"Sir?" she asked again.

"Oh, sorry," he muttered, then added more loudly, "I'll take it in credits."

"It's a lot of money," the woman said, thrusting a bundle of paper through to his side of the window. "Be careful getting home."

"Yeah," he said, shoving the bills in his jumper pocket. Feeling their weight in the slightly less than Fleet-standard gravity.

It sank in further.

People didn't win. They weren't supposed to.

§

It continued to sink in after he'd left the gaming house. What was he going to *do* with the money? It had never occurred to him that he might win something, other than the small pots the house let go now and again just to keep people playing.

The point was the game itself. Playing the game had up to now been just for entertainment—something he did, like eating and sleeping, to keep himself going. Like scrounging odd jobs at the spaceport's perimeter, neither entirely accepted by the planet's natives nor willing, himself, to accept his own people. Not since he'd been—

Been what? Cashiered from the space service? That's what the FleetCen officer told him—even though he had been in the merchant corps. Grounded for loss of nerve?

But now he had more money than even an off-world tourist. He could go to the best human bars, if that was his pleasure. Buy women at an officers' joy house. Drugs or implants, whatever he wanted. Whatever he asked for.

Except people didn't win.

Except he didn't know what he *would* ask for.

A memory. *His* memory…

He shook his head, clearing it, breathing in the planet's warm, thick air. He smelled incense, perfume, musk, sweating women. Both human and native. The smells of meat cooking in human-trade restaurants, the fish-like odors of native cuisine.

Ahead, neon flashed—to his right, five blocks west, was the steadier silver-flecked purple glow that curtained off the native quarter, warning off-worlders like him to stay outside.

"Hey! Earthie!"

He looked up. A person approaching from his left side, a half block away from him. A human person.

"Earthie, yourself," he grumbled back. He didn't want company. Not tonight. He just wanted to get home to the room he rented, to count his winnings, then stash them somewhere. To sleep on the question of what to do with them. But the man who had called out to him was closing fast.

"Hey, Earthie," the new person said again. "Word's out on the street that you've come into some money. You know, around here a guy's gotta be careful."

"So?" Warren said. He stopped to face the man, looking him over. Tall, but thinly built, like a person who had been raised in gravity even lower than this planet's. If it came to it, Warren could take him.

Except—to his right, he saw a shadow. A bulkier shadow.

"You got friends, mister?" he asked his assailant. This time the man laughed. "Like I say, a man with money ain't always safe walking in this district. Now, me and my buddy, we could escort you wherever you want to go. Maybe for only a ten percent cut—that is, for each of us—'less, of course, you want special services."

Which, no doubt, he would, Warren thought. After they'd let him lead them to where he lived, no doubt the word would get out about *that*, too. Or maybe they themselves would rob him then—FleetCen wouldn't mind. The port police might investigate, sure, but when it came back that neither natives nor people in uniform had been involved—just on-the-dock space scum like him who scarcely, officially, even existed—FleetCen's Colonial Service would wash its hands. It wouldn't matter.

But FleetCen's indifference worked both ways. Warren lashed out with his foot as he spun, pulling his work knife out of his belt. He heard the first man go down, moaning as if his kneecap was broken, then turned to the second.

The second man backed away. "Hey, Earthie, no reason to be unfriendly. But, like my associate said, these streets are dangerous. You ought to think twice about—"

"See to your friend's health," Warren replied. He backed to let the second man pass him, then put his knife away. Once, as he continued on, he turned to make sure he wasn't being followed. But, as he walked, he found himself deviating from the route he had intended.

Even if these men had been scared off, he thought, others were watching. They *had* to be watching. His thoughts went back to the croupier's reflection in the hard, plastic, payout window, spreading the word itself, offering anyone a percentage to get it its money back.

And so, it wouldn't be safe to go home. At least not until daytime—and maybe not even then. But in the meantime, he had to think.

He passed a smoke house and, glancing inside, he saw a flash of familiar blonde hair. *Why not?* he thought. He still just wanted to be by himself, but if that weren't possible. And if she did remember from back then?

They *had* loved each other.

He went inside.

The place was hardly filled to its capacity, having most likely just opened, but haze from the customers smoking was already making vision difficult. Still, he steered himself to the back booth, elbowing past the approaching attendant, and plopped himself down across from Angela.

"Off duty?" he asked.

"Huh?" she said. Her speech was slightly slurred.

"From the casino. Remember? A half hour or so ago? The one who won the Game."

Blue eyes gazed up at him through the thickening, sweet-smelling mist. He waved the native attendant away a second time as it came up with a mouthpiece to offer him. "Don't you remember? We knew each other before once, too. Michael Warren?"

"Oh…Warren," the woman answered between taking puffs of smoke from her own mouthpiece. "Yeah, I, uh, I'm off duty. Just got in here. But you don't smoke, do you."

Then she *did* remember—at least that much. The arguments that had finally led to their separation.

"I need my memory," he'd said then. He said now. The smoke, taken bit by bit, over the weeks and months, made forgetting the past too easy. And it was everywhere on the planet, not just in the houses where one paid to breathe it in its pure form. One couldn't avoid it.

But one could resist it.

"I don't," she'd answered, back when they had argued. "Not all one's life is worth remembering. The smoke helps select things, things that are more pleasant, and, even if it changes them somewhat."

One could *try* to resist the whole planet, and yet he, too, had been trying to blend in. To live with the natives.

"You know they can read minds," Angela said now as they sat across from each other. "The native Aztairans—at least a little. I mean we like to think it's just a rumor, but when you feel one of them like the croupier stare in your eyes, you know they're not just finding out your thoughts, but trying to manipulate them."

He nodded. "Yes." That was why the croupier had shouted out his name while he was playing—not just to distract him, but so he'd look up. It was part of the fix. And the drifters who'd tried to mug him outside…

But what about FleetCen?

He glanced behind him, nervously looking back toward the street door. The haze was thickening—dangerous in some ways, since he had to breathe it, too, but at least shielding him from unwanted eyes.

"The Colonial Government," he said. "You mean you think the natives manipulate them as well?"

She nodded back, then scowled when he took the mouthpiece from her to force her to concentrate. "The natives get what they want, don't they? In return for FleetCen's enclave, they get our money. They get trade goods from us. They even get people, like you and me. And anyway, FleetCen rotates its own people out, before their memories become too affected."

She stopped and reached for the mouthpiece he'd taken, but he held it from her. "Go on," he prompted.

"So FleetCen gets what it wants too. An outpost planet, in case it's needed. Cooperation." She reached out suddenly, twisting the mouthpiece out of his grasp and clamping it back between her teeth. She sucked in its smoke, then released it slowly through her nostrils.

"But sometimes," she finally said, "something breaks down. Like you winning, Michael. But that's not important—at least not right now." She paused again, but this time instead of taking another puff from her mouthpiece, she looked in his eyes. Long and hard.

"Michael?" she asked, after several seconds. "What were you going to do with the money?"

He looked at her, thinking—no, *remembering*—how it had been before with them. Maybe she had been right, he thought. That some memories were ugly. Were best forgotten.

Like losing his nerve, his ship diving through a planet's atmosphere. Him—

Someone accusing him. Passing sentence.

Not just for loss of nerve…

"I—I don't know, Angela. I hadn't thought—I mean—hadn't expected I'd actually win. But—"

He looked in her blue eyes, remembering how they had once loved each other. Wondering if she remembered, too.

"I—I mean, I suppose I *should* make plans for it. Maybe for you and me?" He thought she smiled then, at least a little, though with the haze and the tube in her mouth he couldn't be sure.

What did he want to do? Open up his own place, maybe? Now that he could afford to do so. A human-style bar, with a back room for card games—not heavy gambling, though. Just a place where spacers could have fun before shipping out again. Like he used to.

The memory slipped away—he forced himself to look at her again, gazing into the depth of her eyes. Perhaps with her helping him, owning it with him...

He saw a shadow. Some sort of thickening in the haze, to the left where the booth opened out to the narrow aisle.

Two thickening, approaching, spindle-legged forms.

"You know they won't let you," Angela said when Warren launched himself off his bench. He kept his head low, feeling more than hearing sharp pincers clash shut just above him.

He heard a woman's scream—Angela screaming. He tried to ignore it. Knowing they wouldn't dare hurt her.

If natives caused any harm to a human, he knew that would cause FleetCen's intervention. Because it would be a Colonial matter, FleetCen's justice would have to take measures. And that meant killings. Retaliation. Closing down houses like the croupier's, if a connection could be proven. Or even if FleetCen just *said* it was proven.

He scrambled away from both booth and shadows, swimming through smoke to the door to the street.

By the same token, natives would not dare cause any physical harm to him either, not that he couldn't defend himself easily given their spindly frames and weak muscles, compared to his own higher-gravity muscles. But with their brittle external shells, he could cause harm to them far, far too easily—which he would not do unless he was willing to give in to FleetCen. To be just like FleetCen.

Why had he thought that?

While, on the other hand, human assailants, like out on the street before...

He realized then that that was the idea. It made sense in one way to send natives in for him. They at least could see through the smoke. And, even if they couldn't kill him themselves, if there happened to be humans waiting, perhaps just outside the smoke house door...

He kept his head down, half running, half crawling, finding paths where the roiling, sweet-scented smoke seemed the thinnest. He had an idea, *if* he could get outside. He found a table that wasn't filled and grabbed an empty chair, launching himself up and swinging it with him. He pushed it through the smoke house window, then followed it outside, grabbing it up once more to throw it into the knot of just-now-turning men at the door.

He ran across the street, dodging traffic, up the roads he had come down before, heading for the shimmering curtain he'd passed when he'd been attacked by the first two men. The one that marked off the native quarter.

Humans, as a rule, did not go through it. Dared not go through it. But—shreds of a memory crashed back to him, just for a moment—Spaceman Michael Warren had been known to break rules before.

§

He'd made it. He lay on the other side, a dome-like, seemingly solid light curving up and over him. Except it curved so high that when he blinked and looked again, suddenly the dome seemed to shatter, giving way to trackless black, while fragments crashed over his head like fireworks.

He flinched—he knew it was only illusion. It made sense to native eyes, just not to humans.

Except he could *see* it. The fragments crashed over him, doubling and tripling, more like a meteor shower now as they glowed and smoked from the heat of their passage. Except—

He nearly rolled back to the other side, even though he knew his attackers would still be waiting. Single-surfaced human eyes weren't meant to cope with the sights manufactured for native enjoyment.

Except when he had first come to the planet, wanting not to forget but to blend in—to learn to *think* like the planet's natives—he'd entered their sector on two occasions.

Before he had given up.

He'd learned to squint—he remembered it now—to block out the most intense of the illusions. To look out the corners of his eyes, never looking directly.

To see only shadows, and what lay beyond them.

Like now—three moving shapes. Native-sized shadows. A larger one also. And more just beyond them. Hovering. Circling. Waiting for him to move.

It didn't matter. FleetCen's justice could reach even here, in the native sector, if it had cause to. The natives would know that.

He got to his feet, looking, at first, only down to the pavement— even it shimmered and shifted beneath him—and elbowed his way slowly through the first shadows. He felt more than saw them ripple like water out of his way, then fill in behind him as he moved onward, holding his arms out in front like a swimmer, parting the darkness. The light. The bright silver.

The darkness again, this time purple and indigo. Then blue, like Angela. Blue, and shattering, like Angela's eyes, broken up into facets.

"You! Fleetie!"

He heard a voice—that of the croupier.

"I'm *not* with Fleet Central. You know that, damn it."

A sound. High-pitched laughter. Aztairan laughter, rocking around him, as all-encompassing as space itself.

"You! Fleetie! You hear me? I have your friend."

This time he looked straight at where the sound came from. Saw a blinding screen of yellow. The lights of the spaceport.

He'd walked clear through the native sector—at least the curving, octopus arm of the part he had entered—and come out the other side. Here, though, the only humans he saw at first were silhouetted behind the wire barrier that marked the boundary of FleetCen's enclave.

"I have your friend, Fleetie." The croupier again.

His eyes adjusted. He saw her now. Between the croupier and two other natives, Angela stood, her eyes blindfolded, taken with them from the smoke house and dragged through the native sector behind him.

"If you've harmed her," he started to threaten.

"We haven't harmed her, Fleetie," the croupier said. "She volunteered. To make you see reason."

"I'm *not* a member of Fleet Central. I—"

"Yes, it's true, Michael," Angela broke in. She took off her blindfold. "The croupier told me. About your past—the things you've forgotten. The things you've *wanted* to have forgotten. Like Wexford's Planet."

The memory came back then. He had been a civilian spacer, but he and his freighter had been conscripted. He'd been assigned to bomb a city, because there had been a native uprising. They'd needed a lesson.

But he had been in the city before, back when the planet had first been discovered. He'd known its beauty. He'd known that the natives of that planet were peaceful in nature. That any rebellion had been provoked.

And so he'd refused...

"You know what it's like, Michael. FleetCen, the natives here, they get along. They have a system. Except, every once in a while, something goes wrong. Like you winning, Michael, when people like you and me aren't supposed to."

They hadn't known he'd been to Wexford's before and had known its people. And so, when his ship screamed out of space, and only then he'd realized where the coordinates FleetCen had locked in his ship had taken him to, he'd over-ridden the ship's computer. He'd pulled the ship up and back into space, signaling FleetCen he wanted a transfer. As was his right, since they hadn't told him.

"You know what will happen," the croupier broke in, "if you refuse to surrender your winnings? Oh, no, we won't harm you. But word will get out not to have anything else to do with you either. No native will speak to you. No one will touch you. No one will let you in their establishments. Not even humans, if *they* want to get along, except maybe the ones in Fleet Central."

"The ones you hate, Michael."

But he had been a member of FleetCen, at least on a temporary basis, and on active duty. And when he'd arrived at his new command, the story was out that he'd frozen in action—that his refusal had cost men's lives—and so he had been pressured, first from the service, and later, as more stories grew around him, he found himself blacklisted from civilian employment as well.

He'd been accused—of what? It didn't matter anymore—and he'd been grounded on Aztair, his last port of call. This planet.

Begging for jobs outside FleetCen's spaceport. Gambling his money.

"You can't win, you know that. Not in the long run." The croupier again. "Tell him, Earth-female."

"He's telling the truth, Michael. It's not the money—not only the money. It's the example." Warren made up his mind then.

"Excuse me," he muttered. He shouldered past them and waved to a guard at the spaceport's perimeter. He nodded toward the gate.

"Wait!" the croupier yelled. "Look at me, Earthie. You hate your own kind—do you think they'll take you back? Give you a berth and let you back into space?"

Warren turned and faced the croupier one final time. He looked in the native's eyes.

"It's not my fellow humans I hate," he said. "It's just the system. Granted they're part of it—maybe the biggest part. And I may be part of it too since, after all, I *was* part of FleetCen. But now, they don't have to give me anything. I have your money to *buy* my passage."

"Where? To Old Earth? Back to Wexford's Planet?" The croupier waved its pincers in his face. "You don't understand yet, do you, Earthie? No matter where you go, it's the same system."

Warren shrugged. He looked at Angela, motioning toward the spaceport entrance.

She shook her head slowly. "You still can't win, Michael. People like you and me—all of our lives are a kind of game. It's rigged against us."

He shrugged again, then turned back to the spaceport. Yes, the system was rigged, he thought, as he strode through the gate alone, not looking back. Except for one thing.

He touched the bulge in his jumper pocket—the croupier's credits.

He had won at the game once already.

Tower Farm

Vonnie Winslow Crist

The buzz of the tower farm's perimeter alarm woke Crowe. He fumbled for his pistol, then sat up, flung his legs over the side of the bed, rubbed his eyes, and studied the status console. Jax already stood in front of the flashing screens and monitors. She glanced over her shoulder at him and gave a slight wag of her tail.

"What have we got, girl?"

Crowe laid his handgun on the desktop in front of the console, leaned forward, and scanned the displays. Something had disrupted the current which electrified the security fence surrounding Demon's Spine Tower Farm. Since no sentient, human or otherwise, had tried to enter the facility since Jax and he had been stationed there, Crowe figured it was a nocturnal animal.

It hardly seemed worth starting the rover up to check it out. All they would find was a fried critter of one sort or another, cooked and ready for the morning scavengers. What was he thinking? The carcass would likely be consumed before the first moon set. Still, he and Jax were duty-bound to identify what had tried to breach the facility's perimeter.

"Duty-bound," he grumbled. His fingers drummed the desktop in frustration. Guarding a tower farm, no matter how vital to planet-wide operations, was a far cry from the battlefields, heli-drops, and rescue missions of the past. Jax and he had been one of the elite teams called into action when a situation looked dire. They had been the best of the best, but that was before The Explosion.

He pulled on his pants, laced up his boots, slipped on a combat vest, and filled its various sheaths and holsters with weapons, including the pistol from the console. Granted, the gun was old tech and only good for up close encounters, but he had slept with that pistol ever since a band of deserters murdered his parents and younger sister. Crowe was visiting with his uncle when the attack occurred, otherwise he would have been killed, too. Afterward, he never went anywhere without a gun—even to bed.

Jax sat by the door to the rover's bay patiently waiting for him to dress her for the night-time outing.

"Probably nothing," Crowe told her as he Velcro-ed on her burn vest.

The Explosion had burned both of them severely. People rarely noticed Crowe's repaired face and back, but cosmetic surgery was not approved for military dogs. Instead, Jax had been issued a specially designed vest that shielded her scarred and nearly hairless right shoulder and side from sunburn and chilly temperatures.

"And we had better put this on, too. Just in case," he said as he lashed a heavier combat jacket over her burn vest.

Jax barked three times. One of her signals for "Yes."

"Let's go, partner." Crowe could not keep the eagerness out of his voice as he unbolted the steel door between the rover's bay and the living compound, pushed open the heavy barrier, and stepped into the bay. He also couldn't help but hope they saw some real action, as they had done little more than busy-work since...The Explosion. Maybe there really were enemy combatants trying to knock out communications, or scrappers, after the copper used to ground the towers. Or something, anything, that would require the skills of an experienced K-9 and her handler to neutralize the threat.

"Not likely," he muttered. "Everyone thinks we are *has beens* assigned to a babysitting post."

Jax looked at him, tilted her head, and seemed to understand his longing to engage in battle one more time.

The bay was much colder than the living compound, but they would not be staying there long. He punched the unlock code into a panel embedded in the wall, unplugged the power charger, then manually lowered the door in the belly of the rover. It formed a ramp, which Jax and he walked up. The inside of the cabin rumbled as Crowe turned on the rover and closed the belly ramp. Once everything was locked secure, the cab swiveled one hundred and eighty degrees until they faced the outer hatch. Crowe flicked the switch and waited impatiently as the door slowly lifted. Finally, the rover quietly rolled from its subterranean lair onto the gravel road that led to the main tower farm area.

With all three moons out, a blanket of stars overhead, and the flickering of the towers' aircraft warning lights, Crowe doubted they would need to turn on the spotlight attached to the rover's roof to determine what had triggered the alarm. Thanks to the rover's electric engine, they traveled in near silence down the road which circled the tower farm just inside the fence searching for the culprit. He rolled the window down, just a crack, until they could hear the wind whoosh across the mountain top and whistle through the towers.

Tonight, the direction and speed of the gusts were just right. The wind seemed to sing as it rushed between mono-poles, lattice towers, guyed-towers and their anchor wires, and all the various antennas that sprung from the metal structures like spindly appendages.

A quick scan and we will be done, and back at the living compound in no time, he thought as Jax and he surveyed the chain-link fencing.

A low growl stopped Crowe's musing. Jax's ears pricked as her lips drew back exposing her teeth. He followed her gaze and saw a breach in the fence about seventy-five feet ahead. Razor wire lay useless on the ground and where it had been cut, the chain-link curled back like torn paper.

"Jeezus. That was no critter." Crowe stopped the rover but decided against using the spotlight. If someone had gone to the trouble of winding their way through the vast network of canyons surrounding Devil's Spine, climbing to the high desert plateau below, then scaling six thousand feet of sheer cliffs to reach the tower farm, he assumed they would still be somewhere on the premises. The quiet approach of the rover might give Jax and him an advantage against whomever had entered the tower farm.

He touched his lips with a forefinger. Jax saw his signal and stopped growling. With the calmness of a seasoned warrior, Crowe picked up his semi-automatic. Antiquated in most battle situations, a semi-automatic fitted with a night-vision scope in the hands of an expert marksman was the weapon of choice on a tower farm where destruction of the towers and their equipment was to be avoided at all costs. A pulse rifle, blaster, or explosive of any sort could not only damage the towers and their antennas, but also blow to bits the satellite dishes scattered among the towers. It had been made clear to Crowe that government accountants frowned upon the cost of replacing such valuable equipment because a soldier would not obey orders. And even on this lonely mountain top, Jax and he were still soldiers.

Before exiting his vehicle, Crowe studied the displays in front of him. According to the rover's instrument panel, the temperature on Demon's Spine was thirty-nine degrees. Taking into account the strong gusts, Crowe figured the wind chill was below freezing. He pulled a pair of zee-foil gloves from one of his pockets and slipped them on. Snug as a second skin and thinner than parachute silk, they wouldn't interfere with his ability to fire the rifle, but would prevent his fingers from going numb if he was outside for a prolonged period of time. After making sure no one was nearby, Crowe lowered the rover's access ramp, then he and Jax slipped outside.

Directing Jax with barely discernible nods and gestures, they moved to the nearest tower complex. Built of thick, steel-reinforced concrete, the shelters at the foot of the towers housed a base transmitter station for each tenant. He checked the door. It was still locked. His jaw clenched in grim realization. Whoever broke in was not after copper. Scrappers would have stripped the shelters closest to their entry point, then made a quick getaway. He hoped this was a second chance to show Jax and he were still real soldiers.

With a tilt of his head, he sent Jax to the next complex. Making little sound, his dog raced through the scrubby grasses, checked around the far side, then turned her head and nodded the *all is clear* signal. Crowe followed Jax's path until he stood by her side. He reached out and tested the shelter's door. Again, everything was secure.

They repeated the process two more times with the same results. He knew the importance of the towers' tenants grew as they moved toward the center of the facility. The towers on the outer edges of the farm were used by mining companies, cell phone firms, and other commercial tenants. The highest towers, located in the center of the farm, were utilized by the military, public safety command, defense contractors, and classified entities.

He considered who would be interested in sabotaging or destroying the base transmitter stations of those tenants. Maybe humans with plans to hold a shelter's worth of transmitters for ransom. Perhaps a radical group with a political agenda wanted publicity. Of course, there was the possibility of non-human sentients, but he was not aware of any recent alien attacks in this quadrant. But then again, the caretakers of Demon's Spine Tower Farm had limited contact with the nearby military and civilian centers where such information might be known.

He was about to send Jax to the next shelter, when she froze in place with her nose pointed in the direction of a tower about a hundred and fifty yards to the west of their location.

Crowe followed her line of sight and spotted a group of bipeds attempting to pry open the tower shelter's metal entrance door. He frowned. Even from this distance, the fluidity of their movements did not seem human. The over-sized shelter the trespassers had chosen, contained the base transmitter stations for two five-hundred foot military guyed-towers and a public safety self-support tower. It was one of the most vital shelters on the farm. Once inside, they could not only disrupt the legal tenants' signals, but alter the programming and use the towers to send their own messages.

His pulse raced as he realized this was no group of amateurs, they knew what they were doing. With his left hand, Crowe slowly reached up and felt for the emergency button built into his vest which activated a distress signal on the rover. Once he located the device, he pulled off the protective cover and pressed the button. As he lowered his hand, he felt himself slip into a calm, clear-headed battle mode. He knew by now the distress signal had reached Fort Destiny. Though they would not arrive for twenty minutes, Special Forces were at this moment being deployed to Demon's Spine. But until they got there, it was up to Jax and him to protect the tower farm.

Using satellite dishes, towers, and shelters for cover, Crowe and Jax crept closer. As they got within Crowe's optimal firing range, he raised his hand slightly, signaling Jax to halt. Jax and he stood still as stone and studied the individuals who had illegally entered the restricted area. Three bipeds whom appeared human were working on the door and nine biped guards carrying some sort of long-barreled weapon formed a semi-circle around them. Three of the guards also looked human. The other six appeared to be four-armed beings with long, oddly shaped fingers.

Crowe pressed his lips together and raised his weapon. Pressing his eye to the scope, he tried to get a better look at the bipeds by using the device. The bipeds' faces appeared slightly furred and their eyes huge. The four hands clutching each weapon seemed to have suckers on the ends of their fingers. Crowe did not recognize these particular aliens from his training manual. Unless their existence was above his clearance level, they were a new threat. A threat Jax and he had to deter.

Studying the bipeds again, he could imagine how handy those finger suckers had been in scaling the cliff up to the top of Demon's Spine. Who knew what else they were capable of?

Though the temperature was near freezing, sweat broke out on Crowe's brow and trickled down the side of his face. He tore his eyes away from the aliens for a second and glanced at Jax. Her eyes shone and the corner of her mouth twitched. He smiled as he realized she, too, felt the thrill of adrenaline again coursing through her veins at the prospect of entering combat once more.

With back-up forces still ten or more minutes away and the bipeds determined to break into a shelter housing high-priority base transmitters stations, there was no choice. Crowe reinforced Jax's stay command, then charged his weapon.

As he took aim, one of the human-appearing guards transformed into a four-armed alien.

Hell's bells, biomorphs! Crowe's gut clenched as he realized how easily they could blend in with the human settlers. For all he knew, the planet was crawling with them. Were they an alien threat intent on invasion, or worse—were they an indigenous species bent on eliminating the human presence on their planet?

Whatever their intent, right now Crowe and Jax were the only obstacle between them and success.

Jax stood next to him, ready to follow his commands. Battle trained, she didn't flinch when he shot the first biomorph. Before the aliens could react, Crowe hit four more. Dead or wounded? It didn't matter so long as they were not able to return fire.

Screeching in rage, the remaining biomorphs assumed their natural form. All of them turned toward Crowe and Jax, eyes intense with what Crowe could only assume was hatred. He ducked behind cover and fired again as the four guards shot burning projectiles from their weapons at Crowe and Jax. Where the fireballs landed around them, the wind-dried vegetation burst into flames.

Crowe's ears pounded and bile climbed his throat as the radiant heat threw him into a flashback. For a moment, he was back on Perseus Three:

Jax and he left the cave where his unit had hunkered down to walk the quarter mile or so back to base camp and get some grub. They had remained on guard duty while others took their turns, so they were the last pair to head for chow. Everyone else, dog and soldier alike, had a full belly and were settling in for the night. He could hear his comrades' muffled voices and laughter as they waited to drift off to sleep. Then, a high-pitched whine cut the night air. Instinctively, he and Jax turned around in horror, but there was nothing they could do as the incoming missile targeted the cave. Their whole squad disappeared in the fireball.

Crowe had spun away and attempted to escape the blast zone, but the fire roared all around him. Jax, who had been clear of the fireball, had rushed head-long into the flames trying to get to his side. Crowe remembered seeing the reflection of the blazing hillside in his dog's eyes before he blacked out. When he had come to hours later, the medics told him Jax had drug him nearly back to camp before collapsing from the burns she had sustained in his rescue. She had lost the tips of her ears and been severely burned, because she came back for him. He owed her his life.

Returning to the present, he clenched his teeth and suppressed the urge to retreat as the flames licked closer and the aliens continued to fire. Sensing his elevated level of anxiety, Jax turned her muzzle up and gazed at him. Just like that day on Perseus Three, he saw blazing brush reflected in her eyes. Hating the necessity, he gave her the signal to send her through the flames toward the biomorphs and their fireball guns.

He pointed at the aliens, nodded, then lifted his weapon and began to shoot at the advancing biomorphs. Without hesitation, Jax rushed forward, her jaws slightly open. With a grim expression on his face and a rapidly pounding heart, Crowe followed his partner. Despite the fire-retardant fabric of his pants, his legs screamed with pain, and higher up on his body, it felt like a swarm of yellow jackets were stinging his jaw. Crowe ignored the pain and the terror licking at his insides. He held his weapon steady and shot again at the advancing biomorphs. Three of them fell beneath his fire as Jax tackled the fourth.

His dog ripped out the biomorph guard's throat, then looked up for orders. Crowe gave her another nod toward the remaining targets. Jax leapt over the body of the guard and raced toward the remaining bipeds.

The biomorphs gained access to the shelter just as Jax and he neared the reinforced concrete building. A pair of the four-armed aliens remained outside the damaged door while their comrade slipped inside. The two biomorphs on guard raised their fireball guns and shot at Jax. Unable to dodge away, the war dog collapsed as the fireball engulfed her.

Crowe screamed. Charging forward, he fired a stream of bullets, and kept firing until he was out of ammo and the biomorphs outside the shelter were dead. After bursting through the shelter's door, he attacked the remaining alien with a serrated blade he kept in a sheath on his belt. He stabbed and slashed the last biomorph until its lifeless body slumped to the floor, then glanced around. Alien blood and tissue matter splattered every surface, but other than the door, it appeared the biomorphs had not had time to damage the base transmission station's equipment.

Ignoring the sensation of thousands of fire-ants biting his legs, he kicked aside the biomorph's body, shoved open the door, and ran to Jax. Moaning, he knelt by his dog. Even with the protection offered to her by the combat jacket and burn-vest, she was badly injured. A quick glance told him she would lose the lower part of her front legs—if she even survived the burns. His brain latched onto that thought. The legs could be replaced, thanks to modern bio-mechanics, but Jax could not.

She raised her charred head, looked Crowe in the eyes, and tried to wag what was left of her tail.

"Easy, girl," he whispered as he ripped the zee-foil glove from his hand. He wanted to touch her, but had to restrain himself from caressing the side of her face.

As his adrenaline drained away, he felt light-headed from the agony of his leg burns. Between the pain and the smells of burnt flesh and dead aliens, his stomach turned. He clenched his jaw and resisted the urge to retch. Looking down at Jax, he told himself that it was the smoke from the scorched grass making his eyes tear.

Stay conscious, Jax needs you, he reminded himself as the wind sang through the towers soaring above him like a chorus of angels.

Suddenly, shouts and gunfire brought his focus back to his surroundings. Through the smoky haze he saw soldiers running toward them while other uniformed men and women finished off the still-breathing biomorphs. A third group of soldiers bagged alien bodies and collected the fireball guns.

Crowe was vaguely aware of soldiers stopping beside him, then kneeling as they laid a stretcher down. Their mouths moved, but he was too numb to make out the words. He recognized the cross emblem on one soldier's uniform, and realized she was a medic. And as she readied an IV, Crowe surrendered to the pain and slumped down beside Jax.

He fought to remain conscious as the medic grasped his wrist and cleaned a spot on his arm for the IV needle.

"No!" he screamed. "Jax first. Treat my dog first."

"Sir, you are injured. We need to stabilize you, and get you back to the base." The medic then looked over at Jax, "To be honest, I don't think the dog is going to make it."

"I am not leaving without her." Crowe struggled against the soldiers who were trying to restrain him so the medic could stabilize his vitals signs before he was loaded onto the waiting 'copter for transport.

The lieutenant commanding the unit walked over to see what the commotion was about.

"Please, my dog," Crowe begged. "Please, try to save her."

The officer shook his head. "She doesn't look good, son."

"She saved my life. Helped save this facility from alien attack. She has served with honor for years..."

The world seemed to stop as he waited for the lieutenant to speak.

The officer knelt down and studied the critically injured Jax. "Do as he asks," he said, a hint of warmth in his gaze.

The medic started to protest, but the officer cut him off, "That is an order. You will treat and transport both soldiers. This war dog deserves a chance."

We got to make a difference again, thought Crowe as he drifted in and out of consciousness. *Maybe now, they won't consider Jax and me has-beens, and they'll give us another opportunity to serve.*

But the future remained hidden as the military helicopter flew through the darkness and murmured words about an alien invasion hung in the air like smoke. The last thing Crowe remembered before he passed out from pain and meds, was looking over at the stretcher next to him and seeing Jax gazing back.

Target Practice
Steven R. Southard

*C*ranial implants carried the guard's voice to all two thousand inmates in the Dome. "Prepare Prisoner 802253 for Training."

806739, known in Camp as 739, clasped the wide handcuff on 802253's right hand. The latter raised her bald head up from where she sat in the skeeter seat and looked 739 in the eyes.

"I remembered; I have two children." She said it without tears, but there may have been a distant spark of spirit in her eyes.

739 broke eye contact and began spot-welding the manacle in place. "TNTTAI," he said, pronouncing it 'tin-tie.' Inmate-talk, it stood for 'try not to think about it.'

His task done, 739 raised his right arm up. The guards closed the miniature submarine's acrylic bubble remotely. Under the direction of signals from Guard Spire, the mini-sub glided along the chute. All the way, 253's eyes burned into 739's, until the skeeter entered the waterlock. 739 stared back emotionlessly, wondering if he should feel something—shame, sadness, dread? In truth, he felt more attachment to the skeeter than to his fellow inmate; there was something so familiar, so right about it.

He turned and made his way to Viewing Chamber #3, where three hundred other prisoners in the Dome already sat watching the screen. Vidcam and sonar views displayed the entire Training arena, an oval barrier-ringed section of the sea with a single narrow outlet to the ocean. Inmates called the outlet Liberty Strait.

On the sonar screen, 253's skeeter appeared as a blue dot emerging from Prison Dome into the arena. Everyone could hear the clanking chains of the protective fence being lifted, without having to see how the green circle around the Dome shimmered and vanished. When the blue dot passed outside where that circle had been, the protective fence lowered again.

"Prisoner 802253 now controls her skeeter," the voice in their heads intoned. A counter appeared, tracking downward from five minutes, all the time 253 would get as a head start.

All the inmates observed 253's skeeter speed up to 100 knots, streaking for the exit to the north. She had chosen a path well to the east of Guard Spire and its own protective fence.

The counter reached zero. From Guard Spire, a red dot winked into life, representing the guard mini-sub. Chains clanked as the Spire's protective fence moved up and back down once the guard was through. The red dot aimed for a spot along 253's path. The attacker fired his first rocketorp. These rocket-propelled torpedoes showed as streaking white lines on the view screen.

253's skeeter entered a tight arc as the rocketorp neared. Watching from Viewing Chamber #3 in the Dome, 739 experienced a pre-Camp memory: knuckle in the water. A fast-turning sub can create a vortex of water, or 'knuckle,' that can fool a homing torpedo. Indeed, the display grew fuzzy around the blue dot as even the sonar grid coped with difficulty. Having lost its acoustic fix, the rocketorp sped through and past the knuckle, well away from 253's skeeter.

The blue dot then maneuvered frantically, while the guard's sub regained it and recommenced the chase. 253's next tactic was to slow, dive to the bottom, and raise a cloud of silt. This, too, confused the display and the blue dot swelled into a fuzzy blob. For a time, it confused the guard as well, but he finally detected the prisoner by noting the silt cloud's leading edge as it formed.

Another white line lanced out, a rocketorp on its way. A bright orange star-burst on the display painted over the blue dot for an instant, then vanished. The weapon had done its job. It had passed within minimum range, veered away from its target at the end, and fired its neutron pulse.

"The Training has ended," the implant voice blared. "All prisoners commence Work Period Number Four."

Inmates filed out in silence from the chamber. A few were deemed too slow and received a brain-stab at level 2. Some repeated the phrase "TNTTAI" to themselves; others were beyond that.

739 had cleanup duty, so he had to stay and wait as 253's skeeter glided back to the Dome under remote control. The victorious guard mini-sub returned to the Spire. Both Spire and Dome protective fences lifted to admit the returning mini-subs and dropped down behind them.

Minutes later, the skeeter containing 253's body emerged from the waterlock and moved along the chute to where 739 stood waiting. Up came the acrylic bubble and 739 set to work. 253's hands still gripped the controls, her eyes still open. The rocketorp's neutron pulse destroyed only living tissue, but left the skeeter fully functional. 739's task was to remove the body and perform maintenance on the skeeter, readying it for the next Training session in three days.

739 worked quickly. Another inmate would arrive shortly to take the body for disposal into the sea. During his first three times extracting bodies, 739 had been brain-stabbed at level 3 for being slow. The procedure required him to break the manacle welds with a sledge hammer. He soon found a faster way. Two well-placed sledge blows to 253's hand broke enough bones that 739 could slip it out from the handcuff. He lugged the limp body from the vehicle and laid it out on the platform where Prisoner 808427 now waited.

739 looked at the corpse. "She came closest to making it through."

"TNTTAI," replied 427 as she dragged the body away.

739 turned to the skeeter and began inspecting, cleaning, replenishing, and testing all its subsystems. If asked why, 739 could not explain why he enjoyed skeeters, especially that familiar feel of sitting in the cockpit. Something deep and primal, that—like sleep— took him away from Camp life if only for a short time.

Survival at Camp, the endless toil of the inmates, and endless cruelty of the guards, was all 739 could recall of his life. He held no distinct pre-Camp memories, yet he'd been there no more than one year. Logic told him that a world existed outside the Camp, and that he had been part of that world.

Shortly after his arrival among the prisoners, 739 received an education from them. Guards imposed level 2 brain-stabs on any inmate caught socializing, so the inmates passed secrets only briefly and only in the few places out of vidcam view.

"We've pieced together this much: The war between the Manihiki Empire and the Allied Aquanations has gone on for three years," 253 had related one day during a private moment. "Surface forces didn't survive the early battles, leaving only the mother subs and their mini-subs to carry on. We're in an underwater POW camp. Besides seabed mining, our Camp is also used to train enemy mini-sub pilots."

"Why," 739 had whispered, "don't they just practice against unmanned drones?"

"We're a better challenge. We're unpredictable. Listen, I don't have much time to talk. When a prisoner arrives here, the guards confiscate all belongings. They give inmates a neural wipe to erase pre-Camp memories, and they keep it up until we forget our own names. A guard surgically embeds a cranial implant in the language and pain centers of each prisoner's brain, so they can talk to us and give us brain-stabs. Then they permanently remove our body hair, make us wear these awful uniforms, and tattoo a number on our right arm."

"Why?" 739 had asked.

"Haven't you figured that out yet? They do it to dehumanize us, to make us labor machines, unfeeling robots to do their bidding."

"We should revolt!"

"Forget it. They can brain-stab us, and we're unarmed."

739 thought for a moment. "If it's hopeless, what keeps you from killing yourself?"

253 looked him in the eye. "Everyone thinks about suicide. Many have done it, and I know they had their reasons, or thought they did.

All I can say is, here in Camp, you'll have to find your own reason for wanting to stay alive."

"What's yours?"

253 looked far away. "The neural-wiping is never complete, because brains store memories in odd places. For each of us, some pre-Camp memories will start coming back. If I can endure long enough, I might remember my family, my home, maybe even my name. Besides, this crazy war has to end sometime." She shook her head. "TNTTAI, man, TNTTAI."

A string of endless days had passed in Camp since then. The inmates labored in unending misery, extracting minerals from the seabed mine, maintaining the machinery, cleaning, and serving the guards. Prisoners died from the Training or exhaustion. New prisoners arrived. Weeks passed after 253's death, and fewer new prisoners arrived to replace the dead. The guards held more frequent Training sessions, until they occurred daily. No inmates survived them.

The guards then selected 739.

He sat in a skeeter while 427 stood by on the platform.

"Prepare Prisoner 806739 for Training," echoed the voice from their implants.

808427 clamped the heavy manacle on 739's right wrist. "I'm sorry about this. I liked you, 739." She began spot-welding the handcuff in place. "TNTTAI."

"I'm beginning to think TNTTAI is our problem," 739 looked away from the bright welding arc. "We tell ourselves not to think about anything or feel anything. We should always be thinking about our freedom."

427 backed away and raised her arm. "Good luck, 739," she said as the acrylic cockpit bubble came down.

A powerful feeling of déjà vu swept over 739 as he sat in the cockpit. He looked at the controls and indicators as his skeeter slid along the chute. Among them, a vidcam watched his every movement, like some unblinking Cyclopean eye. The subsystem status listing displayed Power, Maneuvering, Ballast, Navigation, and Sonar as

ACTIVE. Weapon status, of course, was INACTIVE. His skeeter possessed no rocketorps; his opponent's mini-sub would be loaded with four rocket torpedoes.

His skeeter entered the waterlock, a chamber just large enough to accommodate it. The door shut behind him and water flooded in. He reflected on the term "skeeter" and what 253 had once told him: "They're called that because torpedoing them is like shooting skeet."

The outer door opened and the skeeter, controlled by Guard Spire, propelled itself outside the Dome. At this depth, 175 meters, 739 knew that there would be little to see, even in the glow of his skeeter's exterior lighting. He'd have to trust his sonar display, the same image shown in Viewing Chamber #3, picked up and relayed from the sonar grid covering the bottom of the Training arena.

Chains clanked as the protective fence ascended. With an array of blue-green lights mounted on its surface every ten meters, it appeared like a giant, luminous cylinder rising to the surface. With the fence lowered, no rocketorp could penetrate it, nor could a rocketorp's neutron pulse affect the Dome within.

739's skeeter passed beyond the fence, which clanked back down. "Prisoner 806739 now controls his skeeter," his implant rang with the news. No doubt, all inmates in the Viewing Chambers heard it as well. 739 deduced that a radio transmitter within his skeeter now communicated with his implant, equally able to speak to him or inflict pain. A digital counter lit up on his control console, counting backward from five minutes.

Five minutes until the guard's mini-sub would arrive.

739 knew the layout of the Training arena and had seen various strategies employed by prior inmates. Ovoid in shape and bordered by protective chain fences, the arena contained a single northern outlet to the ocean—Liberty Strait, his goal. Any prisoner who passed through the Strait, so they said, would earn his freedom. No one had succeeded yet. Guard Spire stood like a sentry in front of that outlet, surrounded by its own protective fence. Prison Dome lay behind him, near the arena's southern extremity.

739 had watched many Training sessions while in Camp, and knew that those who passed to the west of Guard Spire generally made it closer to the outlet than those who passed on its right. 739 chose a different tactic altogether. He circled around Prison Dome and hovered on its far south side, waiting while the counter ticked down. 739 fought the panic that welled up inside and mentally reviewed tactics he'd seen before. Hiding behind the Dome would appear to his opponent as a weak ploy, a timid gambit. He hoped so.

On his screen, the counter reached zero and a red dot emerged from Guard Spire. The Spire's protective fence moved to allow it passage and the enemy mini-sub advanced toward the Dome at high speed.

739 remained diagonally opposite, waiting, hovering. He knew it would take at least eight minutes for the guard's craft to reach the Dome, moving at 100 knots. The guard could not fire rocketorps so long as the Dome remained between them.

The skeeter felt so comfortable, so natural. *I've done this before.* A dim memory returned. *I'm a mini-sub pilot. I must've been captured in action and brought to the Camp. Piloting a mini-sub is what I do.* Even in this lop-sided contest, 739 felt comforted by this thought.

He looked around the tiny two-seated cockpit. Fire extinguisher, flashlight, tool kit, auxiliary air tank, each within ready reach of his free left hand. His manacled right hand could touch only the joystick and console controls.

The guard sub finally committed. The red dot swept around Prison Dome's fence in a counter-clockwise direction. 739 sped away to keep on the opposite side of the circle. This continued for ten minutes as the guard accelerated, decelerated, and changed directions, vainly trying to get a clean shot at 739. Every few minutes, 739 glanced at his fuel cell capacity. He could not keep up this game forever. Even if the other sub's power drained first, they would only send out a fully fueled one. When the time was right, he'd have to break away.

He rounded the north side of the Dome, while the guard remained on its south side. 739 floored the throttle and banked away, bearing for the Spire at 100 knots. A surge of adrenaline coursed through him and 739 found himself breathing heavily.

On his screen, the red dot cleared from behind the Dome. A white line shot out from it. The rocketorp closed the distance rapidly, relentlessly closing on 739's blue dot at the center of his screen. 739 pulled back on the control stick and his skeeter clawed for the shallows. The rocketorp had nearly reached him.

739's skeeter broke the surface and launched into the air at top speed. He killed the throttles. His sonar screen blanked, and his skeeter fell and smacked hard on the water.

He shook his head to clear it, then took stock. A subsystem check told him his skeeter was in sad shape, with control planes knocked out and a steady leak from the waterjet intake duct. Cold seawater flowed onto his bare feet. Blood mixed with it, flowing from a cut on his forehead. Still, he had seen the sun for the first time in a year, a brief glimpse of its warm, yellow light shining over a choppy sea.

Blinking back to life, his sonar screen showed no sign of the rocketorp. *Must have shut down after losing contact with me.* But the guard sub was closing fast. It had not fired again, probably waiting for point-blank range to ensure a kill. Incoming water began affecting 739's depth control. Ballast pumps weren't keeping up, so his skeeter plummeted downward. Chilly water continued pouring in up to his calves. Pressure rose in the cockpit, equalizing with the outside, which finally stopped the flooding.

His exterior lights had failed on impact, so 739 relied on the fathometer to show him details of the approaching sea bottom. Rocky, irregular formations jutted from the sea floor beneath him. A trench appeared, 739's first hint of good luck. He guided his skeeter toward it as best he could. Close behind, he heard the whine of the guard sub's waterjet. A rocketorp rocket engine roared to life. The red dot and white line merged with his blue dot on the display.

739 cut power and let his skeeter sink below the edge of the narrow trench just as the rocketorp flashed past above. The weapon sped past, unable to distinguish its target from the bottom.

This trench proved both narrow and shallow, and his sinking skeeter wedged itself between the walls at a depth of 203 meters, 11 meters below the top of the underwater crevasse.

Fighting bitter feelings of despair and fear, 739 considered his options. He opened the locker where the buoyant escape suit should be. *Empty.* Without it, a free ascent from this depth to the surface was impossible. Wrenching the auxiliary air tank from its mount, he cradled it between his legs. He fished the tool kit from under the water and rummaged through it, selecting a length of plastic hose, a flashlight, and a hammer. His skeeter's electrical subsystem finally winked dead, leaving him in the dark silence of the sea.

Above, the guard's mini-sub cruised in a slow search pattern, beaming its exterior lights into the ravine. The guard was likely searching for the prey that had vanished from sonar.

With a sad sigh, 739 beamed the flashlight on his manacled right arm, binding him to the now-useless skeeter. It took three swings of the hammer to fracture his wrist bones. No worse than a level 4 brain-stab, he told himself, except this pain persisted longer. He withdrew his crippled appendage from the handcuff.

Popping the acrylic canopy, 739 watched the released air bubble ascend. In water this cold and deep, he didn't have much time. He gulped from his air bottle and pinned it to his body with his right arm. The noises he'd made and the air bubble he'd released attracted the guard sub. It glided into view, lights blazing.

Clutching the air bottle, the tubing, and the hammer, 739 ignored the cold salt water biting his wounds and pushed clear of his battered skeeter. Remaining hidden in the shadows of the chasm, he waited, breathing from his air bottle. When the guard's craft had moved almost above his position, he swam up to it.

The mini-sub's smooth, polished hull afforded few places to grab. Shaped like an elongated tear-drop, its only appendages included waterjet intake ducts forward, two rocketorp launchers on either side amidships, the cockpit canopy on top, stubby control planes, rudder, and the waterjet itself at the aft end. *And one more.* Mini-subs had been designed to accommodate limited underwater diving operations, so included a lower access hatch behind the side-by-side seats. A mini-sub's small size prohibited including a separate lock-out/lock-in chamber, so the whole interior had to be equalized from sea to exit or enter the lower hatch, which could be opened from either side.

739 cracked the hatch open, allowing a gradual equalization with sea pressure. Too late the guard pilot—a male—must have realized what had caused his hatch-open warning light. The sub sped up as the guard tried to shake 739 loose, but he'd already opened the hatch and climbed in.

In an instant he wrapped the plastic tubing around the guard's neck and pulled with his good hand. Not enough to kill, but enough to hear him gurgle and gasp. 739 tied the tube's other end to his right forearm, away from his mangled wrist. This freed his good left hand for other work. Retaining his grip, he shut the hatch behind him and climbed up into the free left seat. He draped his right arm behind the guard's seat, keeping a firm grip on the plastic hose.

Like the majority of guards, this one was well-fed, clean, dressed in a blue jumpsuit. He sported a nicely trimmed mustache and precision combed hair.

739 glanced at the instrument panel and switched off the open communicator mike so the Spire couldn't hear them. The weapons subsystem was active, two rocketorps remaining. No camera lens stared at them. *Guards don't watch each other.* Plenty of power in the fuel cells; all other subsystems also active. Already ballast pumps had pumped out the water let in by 739's entry and the cockpit was depressurizing slowly back to normal. At least neither of them would die from the bends.

The guard swung a fist at him. 739 parried the blow with his left hand and yanked the plastic tubing hard with his right arm. The guard's eyes bulged and veins stood out on his neck.

739 relaxed his grip slightly. "Don't do that again," he warned.

"Don't kill me. Just let me breathe," the guard sputtered. "What will you do to me?"

"I'll ask the questions. For now, just shut up." 739 accelerated the skeeter and turned toward Guard Spire. On the weapons console he adjusted some weapon settings. In the seat beside him, the guard stiffened and gasped.

"That's right, I've disabled the turn-away feature and neutron pulse on your rocketorps. Now they're true kinetic weapons."

"But, why?"

Another quick jerk on the tubing. "No questions." 739 paused. "Since you asked, a pulse would only kill a few. I mean to destroy the whole Spire." He seethed with hatred. "What's your name?"

The guard cleared his throat as best he could. "D-David Kerr."

"Well, David, I'd introduce myself, but you guard stole my name along with my memories and my freedom. So I'm not in a merciful mood. One thing's for sure," he tapped his arm tattoo. "My name isn't 806739."

Ahead, the Spire's protective fence glistened with thousands of blinking lights. Within that fence loomed Guard Spire itself, a 55-story seastead rising from the sea floor to well above the surface. 739 had been within it many times, serving guards, cleaning, maintaining equipment. No inmates would be there now, he knew, since they were required to watch the Training session from Prison Dome Viewing Chambers.

"Tell them to lift the fence, David."

"Never." The guard's face turned purple as the tubing tightened. "Ugh."

"Suits me. I'll kill you and head for Liberty Strait."

With tongue hanging out and eyes rolling back, the guard held a hand up. 739 loosened the tubing again and let him gasp for air awhile before flipping on the underwater telephone mike. David gave the appropriate password.

"What of the prisoner, over?" a voice from the Spire demanded.

"He, uh, crashed his skeeter in the trench. He's dead, and his skeeter's ruined, over."

"Understood. You'll receive half credit for the Training session. We're raising the fence now. Return and get ready to deploy again. There's a full alert on and we'll be deploying all mini-subs. Spire out."

739 switched off the mike. Loud, metallic clanking accompanied the hoisting of the Spire's protective fence. The green circle shimmered and vanished from the display. He reached for the rocketorp launch buttons.

"Don't do this, I beg you! Hundreds will die," David pleaded.

739's brow furrowed at the sight of a large, yellow blip at the north end of the sonar display. *Yellow?* A new voice boomed from the underwater telephone.

"This is the commander of the submarine Octopus of the Aquanation Alliance. Stand down all operations here at once. The Manihiki Empire formally surrendered five hours ago. The war is over. This prison camp is in violation of the Azores Agreement. Stand down at once."

"See, it's all over," David gasped. "You can go back home. Rejoin your family. Recover your name. It's over."

The words echoed in 739's mind. Could it really be over? If so, the surrender terms couldn't be harsh enough to make up for what the guards had done to him and to his fellow prisoners. Surely he'd be forgiven for strangling Kerr to death and destroying the Guard Spire. Even if he *were* punished, this would be worth it. There was nothing he wanted to do more than to pay the guards back.

The hardest thing ever done by the free man who had been Prisoner 806739 was to release his grip on Kerr and refrain from launching the rocketorps.

Lunar Epithalamion
Calie Voorhis

Nimue *launched herself to the side and tossed a wind of* caution behind her. With a small puff, an elfin figure was illuminated in the smog. A boggart, one of Merlin's creatures. The smell of peat fires clung to it, thick and dense. It stretched a bony hand toward her shoulder.

Nimue concentrated, envisioned an ancient glen. It phased into a shadowy substance. There by the whispering lake, Nimue saw the rowan tree, white flowers blooming in the May sun. She reached into the dream and pulled back two twigs. Her hands shook as she brought them into reality. She dropped the sticks on the chipped linoleum tiles where they landed crossed. "Thou shalt not pass," she whispered.

The boggart's walnut face wrinkled. He howled in silent frustration and capered. No one in line at the spaceport noticed. Mortals hadn't seen the world of Faery for years, and now it was NeverMore.

Nimue whirled away and continued forward, leaving the boggart behind.

She passed her ticket, frayed and battered from sitting in her back pocket, to the frazzled ticket agent.

"One for the moon," he confirmed, stamped it, and handed it back. "Customs over there." He pointed without turning and gestured to the next person in line.

The custom agent waved her through without a glance, impatient to process the long line. Nimue let go the glamour she'd been holding; a small spell, a trinket of forgetfulness to let her pass without a body search.

She stepped into the debarkation port, her luggage clutched tight to her chest. The precious seed of the WillBe rubbed against her thigh in the pocket of her pants. She remembered the last words before her world had shrunk into the NeverMore.

"Take this," Queen Mab had said, "That we may follow." Then Nimue's world had faded into mortality, the purple haze of evening mist over the land of Faery drifting into the orange glow of coruscating light seen through a smoggy evening. The sounds of birds twittering and a phoenix's rising hoot had bleached away, shrunk into themselves, and turned into the honks and beeps of the Upham spaceport.

She spared a quick glance behind her as she walked through the ramp and passed over her lone suitcase to be weighed. No sign of him, her Merlin. She let out a quick sigh. Time to bid this world goodbye, she knew, and damned herself for hoping to see him, one last time.

Nimue stuck her hand in her pocket and caressed the kernel while she followed a flight attendant to her assigned seat. The object, smooth and round, shivered under her touch with the might of all the realms of the fey, from the darkness of the hobgoblins to the high court of the elves, compacted and warped, a seed waiting for her to plant it.

The interior of the shuttle was wide, two aisles of three seats each, a faded purple paisley carpeted every surface. Splotched stains of indeterminate substances marked it at intervals and it smelled like sweat. Her nerves ate at her and caused her feet to sweat inside her black boots.

She leaned back into her seat. The foam settled around her and pressed against her back like the fur of the griffon on a summer's morning a forgotten lifetime ago. Her heart ached at the loss, but she tightened her mouth against tears. She was Nimue, beloved and adversary, and in her pocket she held the hopes of her people.

She closed her eyes when the countdown started, only vaguely noticing the seat next to her had been filled by a slight lurch. Tension coiled in her shoulders. Her neck ached and she twisted her head to the left, then the right.

"Ten."

She'd loved this earth, once. Her hands gripped the armrest and she felt her knuckles ache.

"Nine."

Funny how the same science that had divided them would now bring them once again together, on the bleak fields of the terraforming moon. Her legs trembled and she pressed her feet against the floor to stop them.

"Eight."

"Seven."

She let the seconds tick away. The smells of fresh plastic and carpet surrounded her, along with a slight tinge of fuel. The air nozzle above her head stirred wisps of her shorn hair. The engines of the ferry rumbled her seat.

Nimue clenched her jaws tighter. Underneath her closed eyelids she could see the soft lilac glow of an oak's shadow in the moonlight. Instead of sterile plastic, she forced herself to smell the loam of earth after a soft summer rain. The engines turned into a memory of a dragon's flight.

"One."

The earth dropped away and gravity slammed her chest. She welcomed the pressure, the lassitude in her arms and legs, the pinch of her boots as her feet swelled. Nimue could feel Merlin's weight on her body, his warm kiss, though she knew he would never be hers again, knew the pressure was the weight of science come down upon her while she carried the realm of myth.

She'd made it. The first step had passed and she and the WillBe were safe.

The engines strained. She felt the ship fight against the resistance of air and the earth. It shivered and shook, a trembling pony fighting his way out of a bog filled with kelpies. The sides of her cheeks drew away from her teeth. Nimue's face pulled toward her ears. She let the tension ease out of her under the massage.

The world flopped and her stomach ran away. Nimue gulped heavy swallows full of spit.

"First time to the moon?" a man asked from beside her.

The timbre, the growl of the sound straightened her back. She knew the voice. She'd let it teach her in gravel tones, had heard it plead with her from the walls of a willow. Merlin had followed her, immune to rowan barriers. She opened her eyes and turned her head. The motion sent nausea reeling through her system as her inner ear tried to find down.

She found it hard to believe the lines on his face under this fluorescent light were the same as the ones she'd tracked with her tongue under candle's glow. But the blue eyes blazed the same and the determined set of his mouth had not changed. Once, he'd had the same look before he kissed her, fortitude fading to passion.

"Let us go," Nimue said. Her hand clenched the seed. She marshaled the powers left to her; the faint light of the sun through a thick port window, the remembrance of moonlight, and a white deer running through summer meadows.

"No." He leaned forward. His white beard floated upward, untethered by gravity. "You would bring legends where science should exist. You would let loose the myths of the past into the future."

Nimue bit her tongue on a retort. It was an old argument, ancient as the bitter ashes their love had turned into. The air grew tight around her.

Her blood coursed, she could feel the thrum in her wrist of her heart speeding. But wait. Merlin had turned to logic, to science and intellect, forsaking the world of Faery. She breathed deep in relief. "You won't do anything," she said. "For any harm to me would be harm to the mortals on this flight." Her voice grew bitter. "You'd condemn our world to oblivion, but you won't hurt the mortals."

A flight attendant drifted past, walking on the ceiling in blue Velcro booties. Merlin met her eyes and she turned her head away to check on a passenger dry-heaving in the next row, despite the anti-nausea pills. The smell of bile reached Nimue and she gagged, feeling sympathetic pains rise in her own stomach. A plastic spoon floated by, followed by a small globule of water. She hoped it was water. She swallowed.

After a minute, Merlin replied. "I might. But you're right. I won't." He shrugged his shoulders. "You know me too well."

The lids of his eyes crinkled at her in the old mischievous way. A pulse jumped in longing at the base of her throat. She tightened her hands on the armrest to keep them from straying to him. The hairs on her arm rose at his presence.

"Have you ever considered that Faery has brought them nothing but harm?" he continued.

"We've inspired their legends, their art." She choked back the rest. He always could draw her out into an argument. "How'd you get free?" she asked, changing the subject.

"When the world faded into the NeverMore, your power faded with it."

She should have thought of that. Nimue cursed her stupidity. The boggart had been nothing more than a distraction, and a waste of her fading power. She reached up and pressed the call button. "I'd like to switch seats," she said when the flight attendant responded.

With a harassed snort, the flight attendant gestured her a few rows forward. As Nimue unbuckled, she floated up and sideways. His breath grazed her thigh. A flush of shame and lust flooded her body. Her breath caught in her throat.

She floated her way to the empty seat, pulling herself on the handrails installed on the roof. Muttering an apology to her seat mate, a freckled young man with orange hair and a pale face, she latched the seat buckle. Once strapped in, her hand went to her pocket.

"Damn him," she said under her breath. He'd picked her pocket with his long fingers. Nimue felt another wave of longing rush over her and her breasts tightened. Memory swept back.

The two of them, curled underneath the midday sun on the solstice, her bare leg flung over his long ones. He'd smelled like musk and crushed grass, and a bee buzzed around them, heavy with pollen.

"I have to go," he'd said as he stirred underneath her. "Arthur will be waiting."

"Your passion for mortals and order," she'd responded, unable to keep the bitterness from her voice. "Takes you away from Faery. From me."

He'd pushed her leg away and sat up. She tumbled to the fragrant grass. Without a word, he dressed and walked away from her into the shade of the heavy oak trees. She hadn't called him back, nor had she followed, but she had waited there the rest of the day, hoping for his return.

Those days were gone, she reminded herself. That world was gone. She had to get the WillBe back so there might be an Is, and not just the NeverMore.

Nimue let the memory fan a flicker of anger, unbuckled her strap and made her way back with shaking hands and churning stomach.

"Missed me," he said. A small smile dimpled his cheeks. "Knew you would." Merlin held the WillBe seed in his hand and let it roll across his palm. The nut brown pit gleamed with mahogany accents, stripes of red and brown flickered in its depths like the fur of the hounds of the hunt streaking across a golden sunset. She could almost hear their howls, could almost smell the winter's wind and Herne's fury.

"Give it back." Nimue reached for it.

He closed his hand and opened it, empty.

Nimue sucked in her breath then smiled. "Don't make me search your sleeve," she said. "Oldest trick in the book. Is that all you're capable of these days, old man? Sleight of hand? Give it back."

Merlin shrugged.

Ire rose and she clenched her teeth. She knew if she made a fuss, the flight attendants would notice. It had to be magic, though she was wearing thin from the journey. She let tendrils of her aura quest out, careful not to touch the blaze of his heart. Like vines, they wrapped around him and through the veins she could feel his fatigue. She ignored it. The pulsing heart of the WillBe called.

He blocked her thrust with a brilliant marble wall.

"You're tired, old man," she said.

"So are you," he replied.

Her skin felt stretched and dry. She let tendrils retract, wither slightly as they reached his wall.

He bought her feint.

The ivy dug deep and twisted into the mortar. Merlin hissed and inhaled, his weariness palpable. She sensed his reservoirs drain as he fought against her. The wall collapsed and she drew the WillBe back with a shaking hand.

She weighed it for a moment. The seed trembled at her touch and she longed to dive into it, to be dreaming with her kind. Triumph settled fierce in her stomach. Once he had been stronger than her, now he was nothing more than an old man.

"We need to talk." Merlin arched his back and combed his beard down with his fingers. As soon as he'd finished, the strands began to rise once more. Nimue laced her hands together to keep them from the silken hair.

"There is nothing left for us to say." Nimue looked out the window. The earth shone to her right and she had to twist in her seat to get a glimpse of it. Gray clouds coated the surface and she could make out the spiral of another hurricane building in the gulf, where the mermaids had sung and elves had walked the streets of New Orleans, one of the last ports of Faery in the new world.

Darkness crept over the surface of the earth, or rather, the ferry moved above and she could see the pinpoint lights of cities. The yellow dots covered the earth like mold, no spot left untouched.

Nimue sighed. This is why the Is had become the NeverMore— there was nowhere left for Faery to hide on Earth.

Merlin noticed her reaction. "It is a world for humans now." His voice was gentle. "No room for legends."

She nodded in agreement but made no other response. The flight attendant handed her a bulb of warm soup. She sipped it and made a face. No chicken had ever been involved in its production; the main ingredients seemed to be salt and oil. Ambrosia, now that's what she wanted, ambrosia and mead made out of the freshest strawberry honey, and golden cakes with melted butter from the milk of a pure white cow.

Beside her Merlin continued to talk. It was going to be a long nine hours, she thought.

His voice still had the power to move her, to content her; the slight growl of his raspy throat reminded her of the past.

He spoke earnestly, reasonably, of the need for logic, for rational science. She kept her face calm; her head tilted towards the window and wanted to scream. Nimue ran through what she would do when they reached the moon as he prattled on.

"I'm sorry," he said.

Her head jerked. She looked at him sideways. The beak of his nose jutted out above a broad chin.

He went on. "I left you. But don't you see, I had to? Arthur was my child, the child we could never have in our immortality. Yet, here we are, mortal, forsaken by our world. We could have another chance."

Nimue took a deep breath and stalled for a moment. The words, "I'm sorry," echoed in her head. Like a spiral, they reached down into her chest and bored into her heart. They'd never understood each other at all, she realized.

She rolled the WillBe around in her hand, feeling the power contained within, the dreams of selkies swimming in a new ocean of dust, the white deer free to run again over pale plains, and the goblins' desire for dark caverns. She balanced these against her own hopes, one she'd never spoken.

Beside her, Merlin spread his hands on his thighs. "We were friends once." The words trailed off and hung in the air, like the stray shoe drifting past them.

She remembered visiting him, trapped in his tree. She'd laid her hands on the bark, pressed her forehead against the wood, and stood there in the shade until her legs wouldn't hold her.

Nimue regarded his hands. Perhaps hers gravitated to his, perhaps she moved them herself, but his hand warmed her and his palm turned up to meet hers. His fingers laced with hers and she caught her breath. He traced her palm. The sensation pierced into her groin and she heard his sharp intake of breath at her reaction. He quieted her by placing his palm once more against hers. His fingers moved to her wrist and massaged the pressure point beneath her thumb in smooth, gentle strokes.

The running and the fear of the past week caught up, and with her hand safe in his, she fell asleep, as she had centuries before. After all, she thought dozing, he couldn't go anywhere she could not follow.

Nimue woke when the kiss of gravity pressed her into the seat and settled her stomach. The seat next to her was empty, although her hand still tingled with Merlin's warmth. She thought she could feel the lasting impression of a kiss on her forehead, a benediction perhaps.

He'd fooled her again. She should never have slept. She felt in her pocket for the WillBe and curled her hand around it. Why hadn't he taken it? She marshaled her fading defenses and prepared herself for his next feint.

Outside the darkened window, the white plains of the lunar landing site shone in the sun, sending stark shadows into barren relief. Solar tubes poked from the ground like mushrooms, sending light down to the greenhouses below. Nimue shivered. This was to be her home, this place of desolation, if she survived.

Two flight attendants walked down the aisle towards her with light steps. Nimue unbuckled. When they reached her row, they stopped instead of going on.

"We need you to come with us," the man said. He smiled at her and held out his hand. The woman beside him said nothing, her arms crossed.

An icy prickle traveled across her scalp.

"Is there a problem?" Nimue stood up and stretched. She made sure to arch her back and display the full swell of her breasts as she twisted from side to side. The man's eyes followed her. She'd known they would.

"You need to talk to customs." The woman laid her hand on Nimue's arm to guide her.

Nimue licked her lips and let a frisson of nightmare slide through her shoulder and down. The woman dropped her hand and stepped a pace back.

Nimue gazed around the empty ferry. Merlin had arranged this, worked with mortals to trap her. She kept her hand on the kernel of

Faery and stepped forward. She might as well go with them, perhaps once out of this ship she could do something.

Nimue bounced as she walked and added a little swivel of her hips for the benefit of the flight attendant behind her. The woman stayed in front and shied away from contact.

They entered the airlock. In silence, Nimue waited while the tunnel to the space port and largest building pressurized. When she stepped through, light in the low gravity, she stopped.

Five customs agents waited for her in a line. Red barricades blocked escape to the left. The walls of the cramped docking facility rose to the right and a sealed hatch led down below. The place smelled of dust and the sweat of too many people crowded together with too little water.

Nimue held out her hands. "What's the problem?" Her throat tightened. To be so close. All she needed was a bit of freedom and the chance to sow the WillBe.

"We've reports that you're carrying illegal plants." The agent stepped forward. "I'm going to have to search you."

Nimue damned Merlin, and if she hadn't known it would take much of her faded energy, she would have made it real this time, would have ensnared him in something much stronger than willow's embrace. She waved the thought away along with a sense of shame in herself for being so trapped.

In chagrin's place, she conjured a seeming woven of the smell of apple blossoms and the texture of scales. The smell of spring and musky snake filled the tight room. The agent stepped back. His nose wrinkled. Nimue saw gooseflesh rise on his arm.

She let the enchantment deepen as she looked around, trying to buy time. The taste of venom, thick and acrid, rose in her throat. Reaching deep into depleted reservoirs, she fashioned the snake out of the moondust that littered the floor.

A man gasped, but she paid him no attention. The struggle to build the power out of her own flesh without resort to a land gone into her pocket kept her attention tight. Her body shook as magic drew energy. Her teeth chattered.

The snake swayed before her. Its white scales caught the rays of sun from the tiny port windows and turned opalescent. The mouth opened. The men stepped further back, crowding the far wall. Her mouth stretched in a grim smile. She would pass; she would succeed, by the old gods to make the new.

The airlock leading below puffed. The trapdoor rose. "I cannot let you." Merlin climbed the ladder. Power beat down on her, familiar as his kiss, as his touch, as the sound of his voice. His earlier lassitude was gone.

Nimue tossed his might away, with an effort that left her gasping. The snake hissed.

Another wave crested over her. "I thought you swore not to use magic again," she said and gritted her teeth. The smell of mown grass battled with snake musk. Out of the corner of her eye, she saw the agents disappear down the ladder. Merlin clanged the door shut.

The power swayed and snapped. The release drove her to her knees; the soft gravity bounced her back. With a puff of dust, the snake shivered into a bright cloud. It sparkled, then fell gray. Motes drifted away.

Nimue's eyes clouded with tears of frustration and her hands shook.

"I broke my vow," Merlin said.

Nimue rubbed her eyes and took a deep breath. "I shouldn't be surprised," she said. "You broke your vow to me as well. To our people." To her shame, her voice caught in her throat. She forced herself to meet his eyes.

They were stern and steel blue and she saw no mercy in the set lines of his mouth. Perhaps regret lay in the vertical wrinkles of his forehead, or the way one hand reached towards her then stopped.

Fine then. Her mouth tightened and she felt a small tic start at the corner of her eye. If she wasn't so tired, a small voice inside her head whispered. If she was home in her glen, safe with the voices of dryads singing their song through the scatter of wind playing on willow branches. Home, where creatures deadly and bright roamed in mist from a far sea, half-forgotten eldritch dreams wandering through time.

Damn him. Nimue met his eyes but couldn't hold them. Heat rose in her face, through her body, and center in her loins. After all this time, he impacted her still. Would she had the same effect on him, but her love had always been stronger. If this was to be the end, then let it so be, she thought.

Nimue drew upon her love—the heat of his glance, the memories of them entwined in summer, the smell of acrid sex, the warm wetness of a kiss. Deep inside she reached, reserving nothing, feeling her body tighten with cramps as muscles gave their energy to her power. Her back spasmed and the muscles in her neck clenched. Nimue opened her hands and released.

The power swam in the air, shifted into a cockatrice. The rooster crowed and grinned dripping fangs. It lunged towards Merlin.

He met her with a wall of his own. The magic beat back at her, hot and heavy. Nimue took it in. Her skin split from the heat. Hands seared and blackened. The pain screamed.

The cockatrice shifted under the storm. Warp waves condensed. The red dragon filled the room.

"No!" Nimue forced the word out through a shiver. She would not have Arthur's symbol in her world.

She pushed. Pouring more into the void, she let go of all the nights they'd spent together, the smiles they'd given each other, the secret glances and touches of lovers. With regret, she gave the beast the memory of her virginity, of the golden light filtered through aspen leaves in the fall, the rocky taste of cold mountain spring water, and her love and hate for the man standing before her. The first time they met, the fire of their first touch, the light pressure of his first kiss; with all these she fueled her fire. Then, lasts. The last goodbye, the last scream of the willow's embrace, the last look on his face, which was now.

She gave herself to the NeverMore. Memory met remembrance, fire battled ice.

The world exploded around her. Air escaped with a hiss as the room blew apart. Pieces of the docking station bounced in slow motion. A small shard of steel pierced her arm. Nimue's ears popped.

She stifled a reflex yawn and held her breath, knowing the air was too thin for her to breath. In a few years perhaps, when the terraforming completed, she could inhale, but not now.

Merlin fell in front of her feet. Like the struts of the station, he bounced, and then went still. A shaft protruded from his chest. Blood bubbled from his lips. He turned his head and smiled.

The light left his eyes.

Nimue bent down to touch him one last time. His lips felt warm against her fingers. Her chest tightened—from the lack of oxygen and regret. She knew she had only seconds left, the air in her lungs was her last breath.

With a hand grown swollen, she reached into her pocket and pulled out the seed. Under the depths of the coating, Faery swam, violent and eager for renewal. With the last strength of her arm, she tossed it.

The seed spun in the air and landed, rolling to the lip of the crater in which she stood. It teetered on the edge, then spun forward out onto the vast plain. A wisp of dust covered it, settled down light as a feather.

The WillBe took root, and in doing so, became the Is.

Nimue watched the explosion with her inhuman eyes. The mortals would never see such glory, she thought as her lungs ached and burned. The world dimmed around her, yet she could see. The realm of the Fae grew and spread out, merging on top of the mortal moon.

A harpy took flight against the black eternal night sky, wings flapped and breasts sagged as she flew off. A goblin, wrinkled gray, emerged, sniffed a long snout in the thin air, and scuttled for the shade in the crater's lip. The creatures came forth, one by one, slowly, then in a rush, all the magic of earth fled to here and now, reborn for new legends.

Nimue wondered what the humans would make of it, how the tommyknockers and brownies would adapt to this world, and in doing so, how the mythology would change and alter, as legends did. She gasped for breath. There was none to be had, not for her, she was too far gone and the world of the Is was too new to help.

She laid herself down by Merlin and took his cold hand in her own. A fierce white horse sped off into the distance, running free over the mares of the moon.

Ice Dogs

Kris Austen Radcliffe

The routines keep us alive. The lists, the check offs, the assorted tabs that must be pressed into the assorted slots at their assigned times, in their assigned order, as we mark off the tasks needed to keep us alive here inside our good spaceship *Eternality*. It's these moments of holding an actual honest-to-God Lucite clipboard in your hand—a bit of mundane from any random office supply store back on Earth—and reading the words scrolling over the paper clipped down to the damned thing at each of its corners.

It's these moments, like now, as I run my finger across the smooth surface of the little screen people call "paper" even though I know my history and understand full well that you don't write on the stuff. You type. Because typing is routine, and out here, long past the heliotrope and into the dead blackness of extra-solar space, it's the routines that keep us alive.

The paper pops up its "morning" questions: *What is your name?* I type the same exact thing I type every twenty-four hours: Master Sergeant Karl Kirkpatrick.

What is your function? I stare at the little black letters embedded in the fake texture of the paper. It's been treated to give it some surface impression, and it feels like running your finger over some silk sheet from some expensive hotel. My mind always goes there—it's become part of the routine—and I have my momentary flash of my ex-wife, but then it's gone. Which, sadly, is also part of the routine.

As are the daily checks of our life support recycling system algae and hyacinths. Of the constant quality testing of the thirty feet of fresh water and one hundred of ice in the reservoir between the ship's outer hull and the inner Can, where we "live." We spin in space, but we're really a submarine packed inch-to-inch with circuit boards and exercise equipment and science experiments all suspended in a big drop of fresh water. It's our insulation and our life support. And if we really need it, our fuel.

Its maintenance is the core of our routines.

How long it takes us to answer the questions is also part of the daily test. The ship's systems monitor mental and physical conditions, and I feel as if the damned psych AI has trained every single camera on the ship at me at this very moment, and I have one of those sour tastes in my mouth. That flavor that works its way up from your stomach, not down from a meal of green paste that's supposed to be a spinach salad or red paste that's supposed to be spaghetti in tomato sauce.

I almost hear the little buzz of servos moving lenses and I wonder if the AI gets confused when it looks inward like that, crossing its many, many eyes so it can look at the inside of our flying can, instead of the outside.

Not that there's anything outside to see. Except the target. The blinking, glowing, *Look at me!* target the telescopes picked up out here in the wide open wilds of absolutely nothing. It's a rock. An asteroid-sized hunk of rock with, as the home-based astronomy types said, a big neon sign on it.

And we didn't put it there.

So here I am, Sergeant Master Karl Kirkpatrick, centrifugally forced feet against the hull of a spinning can, with an army of AIs crawling inside the walls and two other humans.

Because there has to be humans.

So that's my function. Me, Milton, and Redclaw are the meat stuffed inside the *Eternality* and sent out here for this little jaunt into the unknown. No one wanted humanity's first contact to be handled by AIs. They'd try to give the bugs how-to instructions for assembling a crappy bookshelf and we'd be invaded, for sure.

Redclaw appears in my field of vision and I blink. She takes the clipboard from my hand. "Sergeant," she says. It's not a question. It's an order. She's watching me closely with her dark, dark eyes—she has the brownest eyes I have ever seen. Her hair, currently half and inch long, like mine and Milton's, the other human onboard the *Eternality*, is so black it gleams with colors that shouldn't be there. Violet, sometimes. Often a hint of green. How the hell a human head could grow such a crop, I can't fathom, but she tells me it's common among her ancestors.

"Karl." She's smaller than me but her bones are strong and she looks it. Her shoulders aren't wide, but they're shaped well, and I know she can run, swim, and fight like the best athlete. And she can out-think even the science eggheads at home.

They picked us for a reason, and her in particular.

She has a pill pinched between her thumb and her index finger. One of the oblong "don't lick me I'm poison" blue neon ones. She doesn't have to say anything. I know what she wants.

"Can't I have the red pill instead?" I flare my nostrils and cock my eyebrow, to be a jerk.

Milton, who's over in the "corner" of our spinning can of spacefaring goodness up to his elbows in wires and parts and experimental this and that, pipes up. "Shut up you ignorant moron and take the pill. No crazy until we get home."

Redclaw's expression hasn't changed. She and I both have our thoughts on "getting home" but we keep them to ourselves, mostly. Except for some late night chats, after Milton is snoring.

I take the pill and swallow it without water. "Tastes like chicken."

A glimmer of a smile filters across Redclaw's round and naturally red lips, and she steps away along the curve of the can, because out here in deep space, where the universe is at its blackest black, no one walks. We flutter kick.

§

We're two weeks out from the target. It's a big rock, just like the astronomers said. Nothing new at all in the visuals. Dark surface. Striated. Not spinning. And it's giving off the same screaming *Look at me!* levels of heat and light, all spilling from six spots of brilliant brightness, at each of its poles.

So far though, it looks like no one is home.

I take my blue pills. Milton takes his green. Seems Milt and I butt up against each other in our little rainbow of issues, with mine being just a bit cooler. He laughs and Redclaw grins but I know he's wondering why we have to take the brain pills and she doesn't.

When the psych AI points out his resentment, she gives him a little white pill, too.

The pills are standard procedure. Part of the routines. So I follow orders and I don't ask questions. Better for us to have calm life in the Can than to be spilling our guts to the universe, like the target.

The navigation AI pings up its diagnostics. I scan them before I run the same checks through the secondary and tertiary systems, happy these AIs don't talk. Civilian AIs can't shut up, but the military long ago realized that until the programs became smart enough to make fine contextual decisions, they were to be quiet and follow orders. In a battle, AIs don't smell the smoke in the air or taste the dust worming its way into your eyes and nose and mouth. They don't hear the barking dogs three hovels down, where there's not supposed to be anyone.

They don't get that uneasy feeling when you need uneasiness the most.

I tap the paper under my finger. No one wants to hear the opinion of a machine without gut instinct.

The secondary system pings back exactly the same diagnostics as the primary. I scan that, too, pushing along the words with one index finger as I hold the clipboard with my other hand. I'm running hand exercises while I'm doing it, tightening one digit at a time, and it feels good. Adds just that little bit of spice to the dull experience of navigation algorithms.

But the tertiary system pops up something new. The AIs highlight it on the paper in bright pink, as if the three of them are a gaggle of school girls. I have this flash of three little girls, all with pink ribbons in their hair, all screaming and pointing at a bug on the wall. *Oh my Gawd!*

But my gut's knotting. In the back of my mind, I hear the bark of distant dogs. The animals who know what's creeping up on us and aren't afraid of it, but want to say "What are you doing in my yard, bub?" anyway.

The little yippy dogs who bark at everything.

There's a blip off our starboard side. It's small. It's been there in two of the three AI readings over the past two days, but never showing up in all three. Never looking like something *close.* Except now. AI Three says it's not a cloud *out there* between us and the star field, it's *right here,* pacing the ship. And it moves up or to the right or to the left every time the AIs blink data off the background stars, like it's trying to hide.

And it's moving closer. Fast.

"Redclaw," I say, not turning around. I want to look outside, to look out a window, but we don't have one. All we'd see is the bottom of Void Lake, anyway. "The AIs found something."

I hear the treadmill grind to a stop. I hear Milton's clanging against the aluminum infrastructure of our little home away from home stop, too.

I'm still staring at the pink highlighting on my clipboard. "Call up visuals. Now," I bark. I'm that yipping dog. I'm the one calling out "Who are you and why are you on my side of the fence?"

Redclaw's tapping at the screen console and the big monitor comes alive.

"God*damn.*" Milton's next to me now, and he's placed one of his wiry hands on my shoulder. He's a small guy, but he's quick. He hides a brilliant mind behind the tool belt he always wears.

What's pacing us is smaller than the *Eternality.* The AIs get a good read on it and estimate that it's only a little larger than the Can we occupy here in the center of Void Lake. It's sleek, too, and so dark it blends into the blackness perfectly. No energy signatures. Nothing. Just a football-shaped blob of smooth pacing us toward the target.

Redclaw stares at the monitor, her face blank and her hands grasped behind her back. We trained for this. For first contact. It's her function, and why she's out here. Milton, he keeps the systems running. Me, I'm back-up.

We're alone out here, and we knew we would be, if we met anyone. Communication to Earth takes six months.

Redclaw is tapping away at the console. She's pinging them, sending out the first pre-recorded human greeting: An example of our mathematical systems in every format and channel in which we can throw out content: radio, light, infrared.

No response.

"Suits," she says. She watches the monitor but she taps away, typing to the AIs. Neither Milton or I have a clue. "Weapons out. Now."

I pull up the weapons AI and instruct it to open the lockers by each of the three airlocks into Void Lake. We carry rifles, handguns, knives, harpoons. An electromagnetic pulse generator. Equipment that would tear the *Eternality* into little shreds if we used them inside. It's onboard anyway, for bad scenarios.

I have another flash: I'm eight, at my grandfather's cabin at the lake. It's early summer but the water is still ice cold. The world is bright and that light green of young foliage. The frogs are singing. There're reeds and I see a hopper and the next thing I know the cold living-and-dead fish smell of the water is in my mouth and up my nose. Mud clouds my eyes. It's dark in the grass and I'm gulping and I can't yell and I'm drowning.

I focus my eyes on the airlock. Void Lake is pitch black and very, very cold. We have no hoppers here on the ship. Nor do we have a big brother to yank us out if these aliens pierce through and the Can floods.

We have each other. I pull on my red suit, helping Milton carry over Redclaw's green one. She pulls it on, but doesn't lock the gloves. Or her helmet.

The other ship veers toward us, as if its pilot pulled hard on the steering wheel, and it's right there, right off our hull, its surface mirror smooth and perfectly reflective, all we see when we look at it is ourselves. The *Eternality* rolls by, her pot marked external hull dull gray and crisscrossed with antenna, cameras, landing equipment, the explorer robots.

The monitor whites-out for a split second—Redclaw set off a string of strobes on the exterior hull. "Why aren't they responding?"

"Maybe they are. Maybe we can't hear them." Milton's blinking rapidly.

They can't hear us. We can't hear them. They're skinny and ugly and they taste with their eyeballs and have sex with their noses. We trained for every scenario. And we assumed any species advanced enough to be out here would train as well, no matter how weird they might end up being.

No response means at least ill-mannered. And ill-mannered, when the other is equipped better than you, means hostile.

I flash on the barking dogs again. There's movement out here in space, things we don't see. The other operates with intelligence we don't have. We're in a bunker, but we're surrounded. And all they have to do is roll in a grenade.

On the monitor, a reflective blob separates from the other ship. The tension climbs from Redclaw's back into her shoulders and neck, and I see it work into her jaw. I hear her teeth grind. But she pulls up her suit and her body language vanishes under the insulation.

The blob hits hard enough we feel it here in the Can. The wave ricochets off the ice on the far side of the *Eternality* and sets up a loud, dissonant vibration. The pressure hits my eardrums and I duck, squinting. Milton does as well, his hands over his ears. A guttural roar rips from his throat and I'm matching it, even though I try to keep my eyes open. But I feel as if every cell in my body is about to shake apart and I'm going to turn into a blob, just like what's on our hull. Except I'll be meat.

On the monitor, it's spreading across our hull like mercury, or glossy wax globs inside a lava lamp, a water droplet in slow motion.

Redclaw is yelling at the AIs to flash every single version of *stop* they can calculate.

No response.

She orders Milton to power up the two explorer bots the blob of mirror is oozing over, but the AIs have lost all contact with the bot systems. Milton is ghostly white, but he's doing his job.

The explorer bot's moorings fail and it twists on the hull. More screeches reverberate down. The Can shakes again. The lights flicker.

On the monitor, the other ship locks to our rotation, suddenly holding still in the cameras instead of moving from one to the next, as we spin under it. The top of the blob on the hull squirts upward, forming a long arm back toward the other oblong mirror, just like a splashing water drop in slow motion.

"If it's machine life, the ship may be solid." Redclaw talks to herself more than us. "If it's a guard dog, it may not be smart enough to respond."

The splash attaches to the ship. We're connected now, the *Eternality* and our attackers. They have a tunnel into which they can roll their grenade.

I'm blinking. I know I'm blinking because my body is telling me it's blinking because it doesn't know what else to do. We trained for first contact, but we didn't train for this. Not for a hostile glob of machine-based mirror alien. Not for something that did not respond at all.

A new vibration ripples the ice and into the Can. The whine hits my ears and I know immediately what they're doing: They're drilling. Like a dentist into a tooth.

Redclaw is in front of me, cutting off my view of the monitor. She grips the shoulder of my suit and she's looking right at my face with her demon-dark eyes and I wonder if she's a shaman. If she's always been a shaman and they didn't tell us because we didn't need to know.

Not that it matters anymore.

"Karl." She's talking to me. "Take the pill." Her fingers hold it out.

This one is red. I grin, wondering if it will taste like dead cow.

I swallow it dry. It leaves a bitter trail down my throat, but I don't care. Redclaw locks on my gloves and clicks my helmet onto its ring before she makes Milton take the red pill, too. I hear only my own breathing—my com isn't on—but I can see he has the balls to argue with her. He's just wasting time. There's a slap and she's forcing it into his mouth.

The last thing I remember is her locking his helmet and gloves to the rings of his suit.

In my head, I hear them click, even though I don't. I can't. I'm drowning.

§

My big brother reached into the brown water of the lake, into the stew of algae and weed bits and bugs. He was thirteen at the time, big for his age, and he hauled me to the surface, all the while he yelled at me for being stupider than the dog and an idiot who deserved what he got. But his face skin was ghost white—as white as Milton's face—and his eyes as big and round as Redclaw's.

The void is colorless. No blue pills. No red. Not even the little white ones to remove resentment. No reflections, so it all looks black.

I hear my own breathing first. I feel my chest bow out, then pull in. Stale air—air full of my own acrid anxiety stench and peppermint mouth rinse procedure has us using every day—moves around in my helmet. Cold seeps through my suit's insulation and I'm shivering.

There's light. Dim light, but enough my eyes adjust. I see blue, a true blue, one without mingling from other wave lengths. It's the blue of glaciers and of ice. The blue humans try to imitate, because we can't help but stare at it.

This blue is smooth, reflective. It shimmers with its own color, but I see myself floating in it. My red suit looks violet and my weapons as black as the void. I'm alive. I'm awake, and I'm skimming along a mirror loaded head to toe with all our options from the weapons locker.

I realize the chill sucking at my suit isn't trying to rip away my heat. It's trying to push in the cold. Moving is difficult, not because I might burst, but because I'm submerged.

The reflection I see isn't the other ship. It's the bottom of the ice layer under the exterior hull of the *Eternality*. And I'm caught in the current set up by the ship's rotation.

I jolt, my body resetting itself and forcing my brain to wake-up. Truly wake-up, not float here in a daze. I may be cold. I may have swallowed some damned pill because a commanding officer told me to, but I'm alive. I have duties.

Redclaw must have loaded me up and pushed me through the airlock. The rifle is useless in the water, but she gave me the harpoon and a knife belt. I pull one, the magnets in my gloves catching the metal hilt, and swing for the ice.

It catches and I swing around, my back slamming hard, but I don't let go.

The Can is under me, thirty feet away in the murky dark. I make out edges, and some of the lines. It glistens in the water of Void Lake, a tube spun out of one piece of steel glass, brilliantly hard and, or so the engineers said, indestructible.

I toggle on my com. The current pulls and my arm fatigues, but I need a moment to listen. Nothing comes over. No words or orders. No sounds of another person panting.

Closing my eyes, knowing I will have to sooner or later, I flick on my suit's head lamp. The crystal clear water lights up. Things float by: Pieces of experiments. Pieces of a suit.

They drilled through the Can.

Movement flits on the edge of my vision, along my faceplate, upstream in the current. It takes effort to turn my head against the pressure, more I think, because I don't want to see what I know it there.

Procedures mean nothing out here. Routines aren't going to keep me alive. The best I can hope for is that one of the communications AIs screamed about what happened makes it back to Earth. I can't warn them, I don't want to look at what I know is there. I don't want my last words beamed back home to be, "This is Master Sergeant Karl Kirkpatrick, dying a slow death. Commander Redclaw and Engineer Mike Milton were sliced by aliens. Say a prayer for us."

We didn't get to the rock. We didn't investigate its six poles of light. We died out here because a liquid dog took a bite out of us.

The movement flickered again. I didn't fight it this time. I look.

The alien, ten feet away and clinging to the ice with very human-like arms and legs, cocks its human-like head, blinking massive green-blue eyes. It looks female, small and delicate. She glimmers like the ice, hazed blue and translucent, and I see her structures pulse under her skin. Hairless, webbed under her arms and gilled along her shoulders and upper arms, she looks like a skinny newt princess. A wide band of jewelry covers her flat nose. She rocks back and forth where her long fingers and toes gouge into what was supposed to protect the *Eternality*—protect *us,* the crew—from the horrors of space.

I felt a push in my head, like a dolphin had just pinged me with sonar.

"Screw you, bitch." It went out over my com and to, I hope to the remaining AIs. If my suit camera still functioned, her image would go with it.

The fatigue in my arm turns to burning. The cold numbs my fingers and I'm wondering if it's numbing my brain. Or if it's the residue of the pill Redclaw gave me.

"Do you have any idea why she did what she did?" I sniff, watching the newt princess. "Did you snatch her?" I saw suit parts, but no body parts. But my gut says I'm alone in this water with this alien.

The alien's hand lifted off the ice. Her digits moved fast, with precision, and she signed what I could only assume was a greeting.

"I don't understand." Nor do I care to, at this point. She might be able to breathe in subzero water, but not me. "Have you realized you murdered a Special Ops unit? You're an idiot. I bet your species doesn't have first contact procedures, do you?"

She cocks her head again, her fingers still moving.

"I should kill you." I have a harpoon. And I'm cold.

I stare at her weird alien face and her weird alien body, remembering the commands about killing civilians. "This will not end well for your people." I *know* I shouldn't kill her. The first contact procedures are in place for a reason.

She scrambles closer, moving fast and against the current, on her delicate but strong hands.

I let go of the knife. My glove fights it, the magnets pulling, but I swing around and slam full body into her. She twists under me, sliding against the ice.

Her face is right against my helmet. Three membranes close over her eyes, one by one by one. We're gliding along, in the cold, my suit light blaring over the top of her head and setting off dancing glimmers in the ice behind her. They refract through her skin, and for a moment, she looks more like a faerie from a story than an alien.

I feel her arms wrap around my chest and her legs around my waist. She cocks her head again. Menace peels off her like she rang a bell. Maybe she blasted me again with her witch-newt dolphin sonar. Or maybe the red glow of the third membrane closing over her eyes did it.

I don't know. I hear only the far off yipping dogs, barking out that someone's here who shouldn't be.

I'm drowning and my big brother isn't here. My commander is dead.

So, I let the crazy have what it wants. I snap the newt princess's neck.

George the Second

Gregory L. Norris

I *heard my old neighbors the Henrys won the lottery. The news* got delivered through a twisting and circuitous grapevine—an h-mail from a friend of a friend, which sent me on a net search to a short article with a buried headline. They don't like to make that stuff too public. Too many religious nut-jobs out there, eager to form protest lines with placards or, worse, strap on a vest packed with explosives.

The Henrys beat the odds and scored. Better chances of being mauled by a live shark or flattened by a chunk of careening space debris, I read in my attempt to corroborate the truth. I suppose it would have been easier just to call. After nineteen years, I remembered their phone number. Couldn't tell you mine, but the Henrys' was branded into my grey matter.

They won the lottery. George Henry was an only child, which, I'm sure, meant they saved clippings from haircuts or banked blood and other genetic samples. I was the fourth of five; my parents stopped paying into the No Child Lost repository after my brother Cal, their third.

There was a new George Curtis Henry living at Number 17 Willow Lane. The first died nineteen years ago in a car wreck that claimed my best friend's life.

I hadn't been back to that town since the year of the accident, when Al Packer hit a patch of wet leaves left over from the winter on Barron Drive and slammed into a stand of maples growing at the inside edge of the sidewalk. Packer was speeding in excess of twenty miles over the posted limit on a twisting slope where ten over was dangerous. The owner of the house where the car came to rest said he kept meaning to take out those trees, and the trees themselves may have been the culprits who shed the leaves that Packer's wheels slipped through. Maybe those maples were thirsty for human blood. Whether by design or accident, George wasn't wearing his seat belt and got ejected through the windshield. Al Packer was charged with vehicular manslaughter—second-degree, speeding, and driving too fast for conditions. He pleaded guilty and was sentenced to three years jail time—suspended. He lost his license for a year, and that was that.

I didn't like Al Packer and, to be honest, I didn't much like George that year for hanging around with him. I knew why George assumed the role of sidekick to Packer, who wore sleeveless muscle shirts and exuded a smell of motor oil. Packer was a gearhead and drove an old sports car slowly being restored over the course of our senior year. Childish on my part, I know, but we started spending less and less time together, and I resented George for it. The drift was inevitable, I'm sure, even if Al Packer had driven slower or taken a different route on a day that now seems impossibly distant, part of some other life.

We lived at Number 19. My parents sold the house and the family scattered to different towns and states. I heard from half at Christmas, got h-cards on my birthday from the rest.

I'm not sure what I went back there looking for. The easy answer was curiosity. The brain trust that regulated the lottery maintained a tighter fist on the tech than practically any other, except nuclear and the new gray weaponry programs. I'm sure the Henrys put together an inspiring and emotionally steeped package, likely endorsed with letters of recommendation from senators and celebrities alike. What was a reborn-person really like, in the flesh? Sure, we'd all seen the tawdrier exposes about human cloning on h-TV when it came to actors and rock stars, which helped pioneer the technology. But a real person? One who was an integral part of my history? A friend I loved? In some ways, George wasn't the only one who'd died in that car crash. None of us who attended his funeral were ever whole again.

Closure, more than anything, I suppose. I wanted to see George, my first and only best friend, again. Didn't matter that more than half a lifetime had passed since the last time he was alive, or that the world had changed so drastically since my years on Willow Lane. I gassed up the car on a full tank of high-test gellets and drove the distance, feeling the weight of years with the miles.

And then I found myself on Barron, motoring over asphalt I hadn't traveled in nearly two decades. The houses had changed. The road reached that place where it dipped down the hill. I drove, fell, spiraled. I didn't speed. The road was dry, free of wet leaves. Still, to part of me—the soul, perhaps—it felt like spilling over Niagara Falls, or reentry into the Earth's atmosphere. The bottom of the world dropped out, leaving me hanging over a black hole. I struggled for breaths that refused to come easily. A tenth of a mile over pavement that might as well have been an Astronomical Unit. Down the road. Time and space inverted. I suddenly felt younger and then, in the next second, much older.

I reached the trees that had claimed the first George Henry's young life. The house's owner hadn't made good on his promise to remove them. The maples were far taller now, the kind of giants that haunt nightmares. I drove past them, eyes wide and unblinking, convinced they were about to reach out and make a grab at me, thirsty for my blood, too.

I made two more turns and entered the back end of my old neighborhood. My family was long gone from Willow Lane, and an odd sense of indifference replaced the eerie emotions unleashed on my cruise down Barron Drive. Two houses later, a sob hitched in my throat. To my right, the split-level ranch was as pristine-white as I remembered, the shutters a crisp black. Right as I passed and the sting of tears invaded my eyes, plunging the world beneath a flood only I could see, I caught a flash of motion from the periphery as a figure moved into the house. A boy dressed in blue jeans, new sneakers, and a checked shirt.

"Oh my God," I gasped. *"George."*

I continued past the Henrys' house, until the tears made it necessary to pull over. Farther up the road, I wept in a way I hadn't since the day of my best friend's funeral.

§

Turn around, I told myself. Park in the driveway—my sad, banged up relic of the past, running on hybrid gas gellets, beside the clean-burning vehicle I saw in that splinter of a second right before gazing upon George. Surely, the Henrys would be happy to see me, an old friend. But would my old-new friend? I wasn't sure, so I drove away after the shakes passed.

I took a room at a hotel one town over—nothing fancy—and ate a decent meal at a nearby restaurant. The sautéed vegetables had taste, and the salad's leafy components were green. There was that to be grateful for.

It stayed lighter longer now that it was spring. I thought about swimming in the hotel's pool or roasting in the sauna. But I hadn't driven all this way, spent a fortune on gellets, to sweat or soak. After splashing water on my face up in my hotel room, I headed out again in my car. This time, I parked in the Henrys' driveway right as it was getting dark and marched up the path of stone pavers leading to their front door. I rang the bell and willed my galloping pulse to calm. Breathing again stopped being easy or even involuntary. It never occurred to me what I would say if a younger version of my friend were to answer the door.

He didn't.

The outside light switched on, bathing me in a burnished yellow glow. An older woman drew the door open. I knew she was Sylvia Henry—short, pretty, a familiar face that had fast-forwarded through time.

"Yes?" she asked, eyes narrowed.

In the spotlight, I realized I was a stranger now, disconnected from Willow Lane by almost two decades. "Mrs. Henry," I said, and flashed a nervous smile. "Not sure if you remember me."

But she did, and spoke my name. She smiled, too, though I could tell the gesture came with hesitation. Mrs. Henry took a heavy swallow, her body language impossible to misread.

"I wanted," I said, "you know, I heard about…" The sentence went unfinished. "If this is a bad time, I can come back."

"You're here to see George," she said. I didn't know how to respond, so I didn't. Right when I decided to turn and leave, she welcomed me into the house.

I remembered Mr. Henry as having neat, dark hair. The man sitting in one of the two patterned, overstuffed easy chairs across from the sofa sported a close-cropped head of silver.

"You have to understand, we need to be cautious," Mr. Henry said.

"Sure," I nodded, aware of the gesture, of the lone word I uttered. But my consciousness had jumped out of my body, and the exchange was made with a disconnected quality.

I hadn't been in this house in years, but it was, I swore, the same—a mirrored curio shelf over the sofa populated by figurines from Europe, bunches of silk flowers, the familiar grandfather clock whose ticks defied time more than tolled it, and large family photographs in frames. Only I wasn't sure if the school snapshot of George Henry belonged to the dead version or the new.

"We heard you got on TV," Mrs. Henry said. "How exciting."

"Me and everybody else out there," I said. "It was that stupid cook-off, *Slice or Dice*. I got diced in the third episode."

"How are your folks?"

I thought about shrugging. Instead, I lied. "They're doing great. Does he know?"

"About what happened?" This, from Mr. Henry.

I nodded.

"We've been upfront with George. The lottery urges you to let them know exactly where they've come from, like in traditional adoptions. Other kids can be cruel, you know. It could come up at school."

"Does he know about me?"

The Henrys exchanged a look that told me George didn't.

"George, he's..." Mrs. Henry started.

My smile crumbled. "It's okay. If I were such a good friend, I wouldn't have let him get in Al Packer's car to begin with. I would have stopped it before it happened."

"You couldn't have. And you *were* a good friend," she said.

I rose from their sofa. The room attempted to spin around me. A deep breath, and the effects of the time warp stopped. My muscles felt whole again. "It was great seeing you, but I should go."

I headed across the living room.

"No, wait," Mister Henry said. "George'll be home soon. He's studying with a friend."

A good friend, I figured. The best. After their loss and winning the lottery, I was sure the Henrys had kept their son on a very short leash. Curfews and routine consultations with the parents of any potential friend. A friend who didn't speed, who obeyed rules to the letter. I wanted to feel jealous, but the most I managed was relief. The Henrys—and especially their second George—deserved a level of certainty. Their family had suffered enough for one lifetime let alone two.

I started to respond—better for me to go before George returned to his happy, safe home because I didn't belong in this paradigm. I was part of a different George's life, and that life had ended. It was for the best that I left, for the Henrys if not for me. I sensed the events of my trip to Willow Lane would haunt the remainder of my life, however short or long.

"I'm so happy for you and for George," I said.

And then the front door opened. My heart attempted to throw itself into my throat. I froze. Time again slipped free of its axis. Footsteps rose up from the landing.

Through the gaps in the wrought iron rail that delineated living room from stairs, I caught flashes of motion. Dark hair.

Blue eyes. A youthful face. The face of a ghost granted to one of the living.

George.

The dead-returned-to-life, a lost friend brought back by the lottery, rounded the rail. I'd forgotten how young George was the last time we were together, and it reminded me how old I was in my present.

"Hey," he said, and flashed a wary smile, a typical reaction from a teenaged boy uncomfortable in his own skin. Nerves, I sensed—not because he recognized me, but because I was an unfamiliar presence in his family's orderly house.

"Hello," I said, suddenly aware that my mouth had gone completely dry.

Our eyes briefly connected. A shiver tripped down my spine, curiously warmer than cold. When it passed, George was pecking a kiss onto his mother's cheek. This young man was also a gentleman, I thought. You get things right the second time around.

"Sweet ride out there," he said, his gaze again on me. "That car yours?"

"Yeah, that old heap's mine."

"*Heap?* She's a classic."

The ice broke somewhat. Mister Henry asked George about his schoolwork. Mrs. Henry introduced me by name. George extended his hand. I shook. My body was tempted to shiver again, but I willed it to steady.

"Honey, you should know…the two of you used to be friends," she said.

George's eyes sought mine. I detected a look, one I'm sure wasn't uncommon. It said I was from that other time, that other life, that previous George.

"Oh, yeah," he said. "Thought you looked familiar. Figured it was because I saw you on TV."

I laughed for what felt the first time in ages.

I remembered the room with the blue wallpaper of sailing ships. Big ones, not mere sailboats. The kind that crossed vast and treacherous oceans. And the chess set with ceramic white and black pieces. It was a boy's dream bedroom, but to me it was also a snapshot frozen in time.

"I don't think it's any different," George said, his hands tucked into the tops of his pockets. He still looked nervous, though didn't struggle with word choices.

I didn't recall the previous version of my friend as being so well put together. "It's just like I remember."

"This must be weird for you," he said.

"Weirder for you, showing your room around to an old friend from high school you've never met. Emphasis on *old*."

"You into h-games? I've got 'Off-road Race' on holobox...but don't tell my folks. They're strange when it comes to anything involving cars. Understandable," George sighed.

"Sure is."

"They won't even let me drive by myself. I have my license."

I tipped a glance at the single bed with its heavy blue comforter, and exhaustion attempted to overwhelm me. My room at the hotel seemed light-years distant.

"Chess, maybe?" George asked.

I blinked myself out of the trance. "You don't remember me?"

He buried his eyes on the chessboard. "I didn't get his memories. That's not how it works, so they tell me. But there's something about you."

Tiny electric pinpricks rippled over my skin. "There is?"

"Yeah, maybe it's *déjà vu*. A feeling like I know you, or that I should."

There was so much I wanted to tell him, a lifetime's worth of apologies over what had happened. Worse, what hadn't. But to burden him with that kind of confession would be unfair. He was the Henrys' son, of that there was no doubt. But the young man was not my friend, my George Henry.

"Or, maybe you'll let me take that sweet ride of yours for a drive," he said. "I've never been up close to a car that classic!"

I caught the glint of mischief from his side of our bottled gaze. The same look, I imagined, that my George had shown whenever Al Packer pulled up to the curb in his Frankenstein assemblage of cobbled-together car parts.

"Your parents would boil me in oil."

"Then we won't tell them," George said.

I shook my head. "No."

He pleaded his case. "You're supposed to be my friend."

"I was—"

"Be my friend now. Let me take your car for a ride. I'll be with you, so it's safe. It won't be like before, with that other guy. *Please.*"

I sat behind the wheel of my car, paralyzed on the outside, fighting a war with myself within. The white split-level with the crisp black shutters hovered at my back, a ghost visible whenever I tipped my eyes toward the rearview mirror.

Drive, the inner voice that had urged me to flee the Henrys' house again chimed in, attempting to get me away, back to the life I knew far from this neighborhood and town. Not much of a life. I worked as a line cook in a restaurant, lived in an apartment, not a real house, drove a third world version of a car most people would be embarrassed to claim as their own—I was. My only claim to fame was a brief run in a lousy second-tier network h-TV show, and I'd fallen seven episodes short of winning the grand prize and bragging rights.

Drive. Forget you were here, that you even saw the second coming of George Henry.

I fell in reverse through time and memory, saw myself bobbing in our pool in the backyard of my family's long-abandoned house and swatting at a shuttlecock with a badminton racket in the Henrys'. And in these time-bytes, a young me and my George discussed the future.

"I'm going to be a famous restaurateur," that silly version of me boasted. "Write a series of best selling cookbooks. Have my own line of specialized cookware. Host TV shows, like all the great chefs."

"Maybe I'll race cars," said George.

Little did we know at the time that neither of us had a future.

Motion stirred in the rearview mirror, ripples of darkness set before the pristine white of the house. Footsteps sounded nearby. George appeared at the driver's side window. My palsy broke.

"I snuck out through the garage," he said, his voice barely above a whisper.

"I don't like this."

George leaned down. Through the open window, the spring breeze stirred his scent of clean skin, toothpaste, a hint of deodorant. "You promised."

"I didn't."

"You want to be free of what happened. How do you think I feel? Imagine being me. How do I get over it when they never even let me behind the wheel of a car?"

Perhaps he was right. I didn't know. I was beyond thinking clearly. "Okay," I said, and slid over to the passenger's seat. "But not far."

"Just around the neighborhood," George said, and got in.

He turned the key in the ignition, adjusted the rearview, and threw my old gellet-guzzler into drive. Then he gunned the gas, and we tore away from the side of Willow Lane, kicking up lawn and gravel and leaving rubber on the pavement.

"Slow down," I said.

"I'm only going five above the limit. Stop being so parental."

I glanced over, saw his smile in the glow of houselights as we passed, and wanted to feel that young again, that hopeful. Only I knew better. I'd already lived through multiple lifetimes with George.

He fiddled with the radio.

"Stop that. Focus," I said.

He dismissed my remark with a sigh. A song by a band I hadn't heard since the first George died poured out of the satellite channel he selected—oldies. Ice chilled my blood. George drummed on the steering wheel in tune to the music. Houses and streetlamps flashed past. The car accelerated over the asphalt.

"You can't know what it's like," he said above the sad beat of the song's refrain. "Being me. Being *him*. I mean, which one of us got the soul?"

I blinked. The car rocketed forward. Beyond the windshield, the unmistakable crest of Barron Drive materialized. We were at the top of the hill, about to plummet down, down.

"George, *no*," I pleaded. "Slow down!"

I'd escaped the malevolent hunger of the maples at the bottom of that slope once earlier in the day, but doubted I would again, especially with George Henry in the car. They'd already sipped of his life force, had grown to monstrous proportions since their last feeding. We couldn't survive this. We wouldn't.

I looked to my left and, for an instant, the man behind the wheel was older. My age. A version of George from parallel time that had survived that ugly day; had lived to make a run at his dreams. Had, maybe, made them manifest.

We slipped out of the glow of one streetlamp and back into darkness. On the other side, the driver was again a teenage boy, traveling too fast over the speed limit, haunted by the specter of his own ghost.

The bottom dropped out of the world, and we spiraled toward the trees, toward death, toward—

George slammed on the brakes. For a terrible instant, gravity seized hold of our bodies and readied to hurl us through the windshield. Only this time, we were wearing our seat belts. Tire treads gripped the dry road, and my old heap came to a complete stop, inches shy of the tree trunks.

I pulled up to the Henrys' place. A light was on in the living room. The rest of the house sat dark. Part of me longed to rest my head inside those walls, knowing I was safe and loved. But that wouldn't be for me. It was, though, his reality, and as he stepped out of the car, a strange emotion rose up from my guts. I felt happier than I could remember.

George leaned an elbow on the open window. "Sorry."

"Don't be. You've slain the demon. Now, you're free."

I scooted behind the wheel. I was free, too.

"Will you come back? We could hang out."

I told him I wasn't sure, but was fairly certain I wouldn't. I had exorcised the bad spirits of my past on Barron Drive.

"George," I said and, reaching up, cupped his chin. "Have the best future possible. Love your life."

He said he would. As I drove away, I believed him.

Off Day
CB Droege

*W*hen the jumper appeared over the horizon, Otis was in his garden, a small red fruit in his hand. A worn reed basket hung from his other arm, with four of the fruits already in it. He stopped and stared at the thing. He had seen jumpers pass over before, but this one was headed directly for him. After a few moments, he looked up to the beacon on top of the two-story house. Still smashed. Still off the grid. The jumper touched down a few meters from his vegetable patch, blowing the dry soil up in puffs around it. He could smell the death of the soil as he looked around for more vehicles. Nothing but rocks and dust all the way to the horizon in every direction, just like every day. This clean, shiny jumper was an intruder, an invasion. It sat crouched on his sand, facing him, waiting for him to make a move, or maybe for the dust to settle around it, before it attacked. The opaque wind-screen offered up no clues, no personality, no indication of purpose. Otis glanced at his roof again. No light or faint buzz. Those had ended thirty years ago when he had climbed up on the roof and smashed the beacon with a wrench.

He finally placed the plant in the basket and set the basket down. He needed to harvest the remainder of this crop before nightfall, but there was not much, and it was only noon. He had time.

By the time the door of the jumper opened, Otis had moved over to his front paved walk, and removed his hat to let the slight breeze blow over his bare scalp. He closed his eyes against the dust, and scratched at his grey, tufted beard while he listened to the jumper power down and the hydraulic hiss of the opening door.

A moment passed before he heard a voice, "Otis Collier?" He found himself surprised at the sound of the voice; there was something different about it, something wrong in the timbre. He opened his eyes to see the speaker. Of course: a woman. He felt silly then. Had it really been so long since he'd heard a woman's voice that he didn't recognize one anymore?

"Mr. Collier?" She was an official of some-kind. Her clothes were like the professional attire he'd seen as a young-man: The vest was cut tighter to her waist, and the blouse was a brighter pattern of colors, so styles hadn't changed much in thirty years. Her hair was pulled back severely, although one rust-colored lock had escaped and fallen into her face. Her expression was one of worried curiosity. He tried a smile, and it only seemed to deepen her worry. She raised her hand to the nearly invisible visor on the side of her face, and then looked around. Otis could barely make out that her eyes were flicking back and forth, as she read something on the tiny screen in front of her left eye. She spotted the beacon on the roof, and frowned, a flick of her finger indicating that she'd made some adjustment to the document appearing on her visor.

"Please," Otis's voice cracked when he spoke, not from lack of use, as he spoke to his plants every day, "Call me Otis."

Relieved, the woman pushed the stray lock behind her ear, and flashed a professional smile. "I'm Jade Oliver of the Office of Off-World Affairs." She stepped forward and extended a hand to him.

He moved to take it, but stopped himself short, "You'll excuse me, Miss Oliver, if I don't take your hand; I've been working in the garden." He gestured behind him to the half-harvested crops.

She nodded, and let her hand drop to her side. Her eyes followed his gesture, and she saw the rows of stalks and leaves. There had once been a fence around the property, and the remnants of the posts could still be seen along the edges of the garden, but no one had maintained the barrier since before there were still rabbits and deer to protect the garden from, "What do you grow here?"

He looked out over his garden, as if he needed to remind himself, "Mostly Soy, of course, but I indulge myself with some strawberries and tomatoes," He gestured to the fruit in the basket on the ground next to the house, "Would you like to try one?"

She made a sour face, and for a moment Otis could see the little girl behind her features, "Too bitter for my palette, I'm afraid. Thank you for offering."

Otis shrugged. "If you didn't come all this way to try my strawberries, Miss Oliver..."

"Yes, of course," she continued to stare at the basket of fruit while she spoke. The stray lock of hair fell back into her face, "Mr. Collier... Otis, do you know what tomorrow is?"

He laughed and put his hat back on. "Of course I know, miss. It's marked out in red on my calendar. I'd wager I've been preparing for Off Day since before you were born."

He expected this to annoy her—he had unconsciously calculated it to do so, but she only continued to stare at the basket. "So, you're ready to go then?"

"I'm ready, Miss Oliver, but not to go anywhere. I've lived in this house all my life, as did my father and grandfather. I'm not leaving this place."

"I've been ordered to take you back to the office in my jumper," she said gesturing to the small craft behind her, "no one is allowed to stay. The last ship leaves in the morning, and the last of the envi plants will be shut down. Nothing will remain living on this planet for long after."

She finally turned away from the basket of strawberries to look at Otis considering, as if she hadn't seen him before now. Then, she took a lecturing tone, "The directives are clear: The colony must move to an orbital station. Living on a planet which cannot naturally support us is archaic, almost anachronistic." Otis let her speak without interruption, though he had heard it all before. He liked listening to her voice. It wasn't sweet or pretty, but it wasn't his own voice either, and as much as he hated to admit it, it was nice to hear someone else's voice. After a few moments, Otis realized that he wasn't even listening to her words anymore, just her voice.

"This is the future," she was saying when he tuned back in. "No more need to waste resources on terraforming, air-cleaning, escape velocities, communicating through atmosphere…" she trailed of when she noticed him smiling at her.

"You're obviously very passionate about this," he said. "It's good to have a job that you can be proud of."

"Yes, well… today is my last day. There won't be any need for the OWA once the entire population is on the orbital base."

"I'm sorry to hear that."

"It's progress."

"So it is."

They both looked back to the garden. Otis took a step over to a wooden bench, and sat, removing his hat again, and scratching his beard. Another breeze blew across the dusty plains, nothing but rocks and dirt for miles and miles around his small patch of green. Twenty years ago, before the first of the envi plants had been shut down, the whole plain was grass and trees. A hundred years before that, before the first of the envi plants had been switched on, before the colonists had arrived, and his great grandfather had staked this plot of land, it had all been porous pink rock. Someday, it would be porous and pink again. Rocks aren't sentimental for the past. "How did you find me?"

"Your Off Day beacon, of course." she said, "While it seems that the light and transmitter have been damaged, it still has a passive ID chip. We wouldn't want to accidentally miss someone at the end." She smiled disarmingly.

For a few moments he stared up at the roof in shock, then he smiled back at Jade, and finally, he couldn't help but laugh. "For thirty years, I thought that no one was coming to see me because I… because my beacon was damaged." he managed to get out between the hoarse guffaws of a person unpracticed at laughter, "and now, I find that it's just that no one had any reason to see me anyway." He laughed for a few more moments, and then let it die abruptly, and with a deep sigh.

She frowned, not seeing the humor. "We would have been out sooner, if your beacon had been fully functional. We've been checking on the progress of such outskirted habitations for months, ensuring that everyone was packing up, and getting ready in plenty of time. We would have missed you entirely if I had not suggested that we do a final high-powered scan for the passive IDs."

"And when they found one, they sent *you* to see if I was still here."

"Yes."

"Well, you found me," he said, "and I apologize that you've wasted your time."

"Is there no one in the main colony whom you wish to see?"

"Nah," he said, without thinking, "I've never had much need for friends, and I found out long ago that I'm not a family man."

For a moment, she looked as if she wanted to say something, but thought better of it. Instead she turned again to look at the garden, then up at the pinkish mountains in the distance. Otis wondered if in all her life she had ever truly been outside. He had heard stories of the main colony, and when his father had told of the metal city, built mostly from the remains of the colony ship, he had always sounded a bit sad, and Otis felt sorry for all those people made to live in a can, while he got to live out here in the beautiful world.

If the initial orders had been followed since he read them so long ago, most of the citizens should be up in the city-station by now. They would only need one. The colony hadn't grown much since the early days, and the directives ordered a suspension of fertility programs until the city-station was ready. Still, Otis had seen at least two ships go up every day for the last two months.

As if reading his thoughts, a faint pop sounded from the northwest, from the direction of the main colony. Otis looked over his shoulder at the tiny upside-down candle in the distant sky which had, for some years been his only evidence that he was not the only man on the whole planet. When he looked back, he saw Jade had also turned around, and was looking over his head at the ship, undisguised excitement on her face. "I've never seen the ships launch from this distance," she said, "It looks so... slow." She watched it until it disappeared into the sky beyond view, then lowered her eyes to Otis. He had been staring at her slack-jawed, and he composed himself quickly, putting his hat on so it blocked his eyes from hers.

"I'm sorry," he said, "for a moment you looked just like... like someone else."

Jade took the few steps to the bench and sat beside him. Her smell was too sweet, and it made Otis want to turn away from her, but instead he turned and peeked out at her from under the straw brim. She gave him a sad smile, "You have to come with me, Otis," she said, "Is there anything you want to get from the house first?"

He pushed himself up from the bench then, and turned to look down at the woman, who pushed the stray lock out of her face once more as she watched his slow deliberate movements. "Would you like to come in, Miss Oliver?" he asked, "You're probably thirsty, and there is something in the house I want you to see." He walked over to where he had laid his basket on the dirt, picked it up and walked around to the front door. Jade was still sitting at the bench, so he motioned for her to follow before stepping inside.

The main part of the house was all one floor with cooking surfaces and tools at one end, and tables and chairs at the other. All of the surfaces were kept meticulously clean. The steel of the kitchen, and the simulated wood dining table were both clean and polished. The plastic floors were swept clean. Several books, none of them fiction, were stacked neatly on a small shelf over a reading chair in one corner. A narrow staircase ran up the back wall to the second floor, and underneath it sat a shining net-node in a tiny alcove. Otis hung his hat on a small hook near the door and set his basket on one of the counters next to a dehydrator which was currently filled with sliced tomatoes. The door opened and Jade came into the dim room, pausing at the threshold to allow her eyes to adjust while Otis washed his hands at the sink.

"Make yourself at home, Miss Oliver," Otis started. "I'm afraid I haven't much to offer guests right now. Would you like a glass of water or a tomato juice?"

"No, thank you," she glanced around the room. Her gaze fell momentarily on the net-node, and she raised an eyebrow quizzically.

"Oh, I never use that thing, of course," he said, "but that's no reason not to take care of it. Do you need to jack in?"

She stared at it for a moment longer and shook her head. She raised one hand to tap her visor with one fingernail, dislodging the lock of hair once more. "I'm always connected," she said.

"We had those in my day, as well, but I'd wager you've never looked at the net the way we would... I've got some NeWorld pills stashed somewhere, but they may be expired if such things do expire," he explained while opening a drawer and moving some things around. "Aha!" He drew out a small, faded plastic box with a decades old version of the NeWorld logo on it.

"Where did you get these?" she asked.

"You look surprised," he said. "I was once a NeWorld user, but after my wife passed, there was no one left to jack-in with, and the games aren't as much fun alone."

"No, I guess not, I'm sorry," she said somberly, then "What happened... to your wife?"

Otis looked at her carefully, trying to read her eyes. They were flat, and unconnected, but at the same-time they held a certain depth that he couldn't place. He watched as she put her hair back into place again, just like her, just like his wife had done over and over, every day. In the half-light of his kitchen, he could almost believe that he was standing right across from her, but did this girl really look like her, or had it just been so long?

"My wife was pregnant with our first child when she fell ill. Illness is not usually trouble, even all the way out here, but this was strange and dire. I tried to take her into the city, but she didn't make it through the journey, it was too difficult for her." He stammered a moment, "If we had had a nice jumper like yours, or if we had been just a bit closer to the city..."

"...or if they had sent someone out to you?" she finished for him.

He gave her a sad smile, "None of the surgeons would come out this far." He said, "This was right about the time of the proclamation from Earth."

"I'm sorry," she said again, obviously not used to such situations.

He held the small box out to her, "You sure you don't want to jack-in, I don't mind."

"No, thank you," she said, "You had something to show me..."

"Yes, of course," he said, "I'm sure you're busy." He dropped the small box of hallucinogenic pills back into the drawer and closed it.

"Actually, coming out here is my last assignment as an OWA officer," she said over her shoulder as she wondered across the kitchen, past the net-node, and over to the reading chair. "I just need to be on the rocket in the morning and..." Her voice trailed off as she read the titles of the books on the shelf, "These are all about gardening."

"Yes. Are you interested in gardening?"

"Erm...no, but I've never seen books that weren't classic collectables," she said. "My father has one shelf of books like this, which he never touches, they're all the ancient classical writers: Shakespeare, Poe, Asimov, you know. These books aren't like that, they have really been used." She reached out and touched the spine of one book, running her finger over an embossed title, "Are they paper?"

He laughed then, "How old do you think I am?"

She looked sheepish, "Sorry, I've just always heard about how wood used to be so common that they made books out of it."

"My grandfather once told me the same, but I've never seen it myself," he said. "He smuggled one paper book with him from Earth when he was drafted into the colonization program, but he sold it long ago, when he realized what it was worth out here."

"He must have had a lot of stories to tell."

"Yes, he did," he said. "What about your family?"

"What?"

"Well, was your great grandfather a conscript or a volunteer?"

"A volunteer," she said. "He piloted one of the sleeper ships."

"Is that still a fine point back in the city?"

"That my great grandfather was a pilot?"

"That he was a volunteer."

"No," she said. Then, "Well, sometimes my parents' generation still makes a comment about some families being from volunteer stock, and others from conscript stock, but my generation doesn't really see it that way anymore. The families are all so mixed up now it's too difficult to tell anyway."

"That's good to hear," he said.

"You see," she said smiling again, "the city's not so bad as it was; you would do fine there, I'm sure of it, even though we'll all be up in the station."

"Here," he said, as if he hadn't heard her. "Let me show you this." He had stepped over to a small rug in the living room, and lifted it aside, revealing a ring in the floor, which he tugged to reveal a spiral stairwell, leading down into the darkness.

He started to descend into the floor, "Just let me go first, so I can get the lights for us."

Jade took a few steps closer and looked down into the darkness. Otis fumbled for a moment, groping for the panel that would activate the lights and brighten the short hallway. "What is all this?" Jade asked from above, once the light was on.

Otis looked up at her. He paused for a moment, seeing her face lit from below, and framed in the relative darkness of his house above. He shook himself internally. "My father passed away a few years before my wife," he explained as she began to descend the stairs, "he had some investments left over, so I sold them all, and used the funds to have this place installed after my... after the proclamation," He took a step through a large, bulkhead door while he spoke. The stainless-steel room beyond was lined with shelves on both sides, a bed and a small counter with a sink were installed in the back, next to a small door that could only be a bathroom. "It's not as big as the house upstairs, but it's big enough, and as you can see, it's stocked with all the things one needs for a long stay."

He gestured around the room at each of the things in turn. "Plenty of dried food, a water recycler, bed and bath facilities, a shelf for my books, and a CO_2 scrubber and oxygen tanks in the ceiling, in case the few live plants I bring with me aren't enough. A man could live fifteen years in this room, which I daresay is more time than I have left to me.

"So, you see, Miss Oliver? I'm prepared for Off Day. When the last envi plant shuts down, and the atmosphere begins to float off into space, I'll be safe and sound in here."

She stared up and down the shelves at thousands of plastic-wrapped packages, "you dried all this yourself?" she asked, "from the garden outside?"

"I did," he said, "I had plenty of warning, so it really wasn't much work at all."

"But why?" she asked, an expression of clear confusion on her face. "Why not just come with us to the new station?"

"This is my home Miss Oliver," he said, "I've lived in this house since the day I was born, and it's part of me now. I would never leave this place. Not for anything."

"But *this* is not your home, it's just a room, and the accommodations are smaller than you would have on the city-station."

Otis considered this for a moment. "Perhaps that's true, but this is *my* place. I'm the captain here, and all the rules and regulations are my own." He picked up a bundle of dried tomatoes and glanced around the room.

"That's what this is all about?" The way she said it didn't sound like a question. "You don't like authority?"

"No, that's not it, really," he started, "maybe it was once, but the reason for all of this has changed so much over the years. Originally, it was a political statement. Now, I don't know... I guess I'm just used to the idea of spending the rest of my life alone in this box. I've put thirty years of work into preparing this room for Off Day. It would be a shame to let all that go to waste."

"Political?" she mused. "You don't agree with the directive?"

"The directive was fine. Made sense even." He looked down at the bundle still in his hand. "But we should have been let to come to those conclusions on our own. We don't need Earth's directives."

"Earth is the seat of *all* governments."

"And why is that, do you think? Is it because we cannot govern ourselves?"

"Well, I don't really..."

"You haven't really thought about it," he said, showing a spark of the passion these conversations once brought out in his own father. "Earth always has been the authority, and it will be forever if we let it, but we don't need them." He slammed the package back on its shelf, almost breaking it. For a moment Jade simply stared at him, clearly at a loss. Otis realized then that his face had twisted with anger, and he had been nearly shouting at the girl. She must think his solitary life has left him a bit mad, and perhaps she would be right.

She glanced nervously at the door of the room and shrank toward the door. He finally took control of himself and allowed his face to soften. He tried to smile again, but knew how unpracticed it must look. "I'm sorry, Miss Oliver," he said, his voice returning to the soft crackle that it had been outside. "I suppose I haven't moved past these ideas as much as I thought I had. It's been so long since I really thought about the politics..." he let his statement trail off, shaking his head.

Jade tucked the stray lock of hair behind her ear and walked out of the room. "I think I will take that glass of water now," she said simply as she walked up the stairs and back into the house above.

Alone in the small room, Otis turned to the small mirror above the sink, and tried his smile on himself. It was overly toothy, and looked a bit mad. He sighed, and turned to follow Jade, grabbing one of the tomato packages on the way. When back up in the house, he saw that she had placed herself on a stool close to the door and was pointedly not looking at him. He turned and closed the floor panel with one hand, holding the plastic package in the other.

He walked back into the kitchen and set the package on the counter next to the basket. He could feel her silently watching him as he pulled a glass from a cupboard and filled it from the tap. He turned and placed the glass before her on the counter.

"Thank you," she said, and took a sip.

"Miss Oliver, I—"

"I don't believe you," she said, cutting him off.

"What?" Otis was surprised. What didn't she believe?

"You say that you want to live in that tiny little hole for the rest of your life, but I don't believe you."

"Then why—"

"I'm sure you meant to when you first built it, in your grief, and your overblown political righteousness, you meant to be making a place for yourself to live," she said, "but that's not what that is. That's a tomb, not a shelter. You know that you would have a better life, be happier, on the station."

"I'm happy here."

"You're a martyr here, Otis." She pushed the lock of hair out of her face, which was now fierce and more angular than he had noticed before, not angry, but fervent. "This isn't a solution. It's not even a statement. It's a penance. You think you don't deserve to live in the stars. Why?"

"The- The Earth has no right to- to-"

"What did you do?" she demanded

"I killed her," he said, softly, resignedly. Then, seeing her shocked expression, "I didn't murder her, but I might as well have. She was fragile, and I made her stay out here with me and my damn garden. She wanted to live in the city, but I wouldn't have it. That's what killed her."

Jade was silent then, once again out of her element, her streak of youthful wisdom brought to a sudden close. She took a long sip of the water, seeming to be thinking about how to respond.

"You're not even going to use that room are you?"

The question surprised him. In years he hadn't given it as much as a single consideration. He was preparing to live in the shelter after Off-day. That had become his whole existence, but now?

"Look," she was saying, softly, "You can come back with me right now. Come to the city, and ride with me up to the new station. I'll make sure you get nice quarters, and even get you a job in a hydroponics lab..."

"It's too late for me now," he said glancing sadly over at the little carpet in the floor of his living room. "It's just too late."

She sighed. "Nothing's ever too late."

"That's an expression for young people, Miss Oliver."

She looked away. "I suppose it is."

"What will you do?" he asked.

She reached up and pushed a button on her visor." I should call in to the director, have him send some police to arrest you," she said. "The directive is clear. There are no exceptions..."

She sighed again, and turned toward the door, reaching for the handle. When he called out to her, she stopped and turned. Perhaps she thought she'd changed his mind; she raised an eyebrow when she saw that he was simply holding out the plastic package of dried tomatoes. He tried another smile, with fewer teeth this time, he hoped.

She looked at the packet for a moment before reaching out to accept it. She thanked him almost silently and held the bundle against her vest with one hand. She nodded to him without smiling back and turned again to leave.

"What will you tell them?" he asked.

She paused with her hand on the door's lever, not turning around, the stray lock of hair falling into her face. "No one was here when I arrived. All the residents of this household died many years ago." She pushed the lever down and stepped out into the sunlight. Otis leaned back against the counter and let the door slam closed behind her. He closed his eyes and ran his hands over his bald pate. Listening for a moment, he heard the hydraulic door of the jumper, then the whine of the small jets. He put his hat back on and pushed the door open. He wanted to finish harvesting those strawberries before nightfall.

Behind the First Years
Stewart C. Baker

*F*ive *short hours to planet-fall, Pete sat watching Magda die.* Her hands were thin and wrinkle-fine, the leathern color of paper five-hundred years old. She had been Archivist sixty years before him, there in the great, silent bulk of the ship.

"But what am I to do when we land?" he asked. "I have only been Transcriber, Magda. I never—"

"You must look behind the shelf of the first years."

"The shelf of the first years is empty."

"Did I say *on*, foolish man?" Magda tsked. "How can you record history if you do not listen?" Her eyes were as sharp as her voice, clear and precise, honed from the long years of watching her duties entailed.

Pete flushed and bowed his head. "Behind the shelf, Magda. I understand."

How can she possibly die? he thought. Yet the grey-white walls of her quarters were hung with fresh-picked jasmine to hide the stink of it.

"You understand nothing, foolish man. Look at me." And again, kinder, when he did not. "Look at me."

"Yes, Magda."

"What lies behind the shelf of the first years is important but does not change your duty. You must record all things, as I have. Record and preserve, Peter. In all these lifetimes under space, that has been our calling."

"Record and preserve. Yes, Magda."

He had first spoken the words fifteen years prior, when he became Transcriber. His parents cried during the ceremony, then left him to go back to Bottom. Magda had been old even then, and Pete used to go to bed terrified of finding her dead when he woke, and him still an untrained youth. Now, she was going at last.

She coughed once, twice, making no move to clean the deep red flecks from her lips. Her eyes had gone dim.

"Peter," she said, "Peter."

She reached out with one frail hand and he took it. "Yes, Magda."

"You will be building the history of a world. Remember...the first years."

Pete did not respond; she was gone. He placed her hand back on her stomach and wiped her lips one last time with the damp cloth the ship's doctor had left him. The man waited outside the door, polite and sympathetic.

"I know it's hard, but it may be for the best. The dispersal would have been hard on her."

Pete nodded, not trusting himself to speak, and left the doctor to his work. It was eighteen floors down to the archives, but instead of the express lift he took the stairs. Something Magda had said didn't sit right, but he could not put his finger on it. Walking helped him think.

'Remember the first years' was a strange directive. The people of that time had been content to track their history in transient digital form, with the result that little was left. Pete thought with regret of the few scraps of paper that *had* come down to them. Scrawled inventories, engineer-neat lists of meaningless names. In his darker moments, Pete felt the first people were mocking him, conspiring to erase all knowledge of why they had been sent away, what calamity had befallen Earth.

But what did it matter? Earth was a planet he would never see, and in just over four hours he would be walking the surface of a world untouched by human hands. A place to start anew. Even Magda's death could not entirely remove the thrill of it. She had died well, clear and alert until the last. And it was true the dispersal would have been hard on her.

Dispersal! Soon they would spread across the surface of the unsullied planet, down amidst the mottled green-and-black they had so far seen only on the vid-screens, where it hung in the middle distance between the ship and the system's star.

He came out on the archives level and picked up his pace. He had set up an interview with Captain McAllister-Xo the night before, the first part of his duty. He would not have long to examine the shelf of the first years. He was reaching for the panel to open the ever-dimmed rooms of the archives when he realized.

Under. Magda had said *under* space.

§

Captaincy was in McAllister-Xo's bones. His family had guided the ship since the time of the first people—or so it was said. He greeted Pete and spoke to him of approach vectors and automated systems, stopping occasionally to check in with an officer or to type arcane sequences of keys into the mem-pad before him.

In one of these pauses, Pete told him of Magda's death.

"That old witch," the captain said. "I always thought she'd live forever." He paused, coughed, scratched his temple with his middle finger. "Sorry. I know you were close."

"It was her time. But there was something she said before she passed that I thought you might be able to explain."

"Shoot."

"She was talking of the Archivists' Code: record and preserve."

"I've heard it."

"Um, yes. But it was how she described it: 'In all these lifetimes under space, that has been our calling.' She said 'under,' not 'in.' What do you make of that?"

The captain shrugged. "She was old. She was dying. A slip of the tongue, some missed connection between her brain and her lips. What's to make of it?"

The explanation made as much sense as any Pete could think of, but McAllister-Xo had not been there. Magda had been too alert, her voice too clear and strong for the word to be delirium or sickness. He remembered the way she had taken him to task for not listening clearly. There was something to what she had said, he was sure of it.

He thanked the captain and made his way to Bottom. Perhaps popular memory could tell him what high command could not.

§

Bottom, so called for its location at the lowest part of the ship, was a vast expanse of inspired agro-engineering which doubled as the ship's food supply and as a living space for most of its population. It was as large as the rest of the ship.

The express lift plunged from the light-specked ceiling and sank past moisture sprays and clouds. The rolling green landscape which sped to meet him was the same as he remembered from before he had been taken above to the archives. He could just make out the pale, blue-tinged metal of the inner bulkhead a kilometer or so away. Then the trees rushed up and overhead, and the lift doors hissed open.

The smell of Bottom was earthy and moist, as different from the paper-dry odors of the archives as possible. He strode past farms and villages he knew from his childhood, passing within meters of the homes where his family and friends still lived. But he did not have time for a visit today.

At last, he reached his destination. Old Jadwiga had been ancient when he was still a child and, unlike Magda, had lived the hard life of a Bottom woman. She walked with a cane, bent over and shuffling, and her hands trembled as she invited him to sit. Her eyes were rheumy, and he had to repeat Magda's dying words several times before she understood him.

"Under space, hmmm?"

She sat quiet for a few minutes after that, but Pete waited patiently. As slow as it was, even Old Jadwiga's memory would be faster than trying to find just the right Bottom lore in the archives' massive collection, which filled kilometers of shelving.

Just as Pete began to doubt his assessment, the old woman spoke again:

"I remember...under the time of Captain Xo, there was a great anger among the people."

"Captain *Xo?*" But that was ridiculous—the last captain of that name had served almost one hundred years ago. Jadwiga couldn't possibly be that old, could she?

"Yes. Yes. People were angry, for the upper deck families took the best crops and we in Bottom had always to make do with their leavings. One year when I was a young girl..."

Jadwiga continued to speak, drawing out story after story of those long-dead and their actions. Pete let her voice fade into the background, half-listening for anything about the ship being 'under' space instead of in it. After an hour, he excused himself and left the old woman to her memories. They were fascinating enough, but of all she had said there were only two things relevant to Magda's words.

First, something he'd forgotten from his childhood: people here took the designation of 'Bottom' with pride. They were liable to refer to any other part of the ship as "above." But Magda had come from an upper deck family, and in any case she had placed the entire ship under space, not just Bottom.

The second was a children's rhyme, cryptic to the point of uselessness:

Under space and over all,
Ship-bound people standing tall;
When they reach their destination,
They will build a new old nation.

He shook his head as he re-entered the lift. Even the stacks, with their information overload, would likely have given him more than that.

There were only two hours left to landing, and Captain McAllister-Xo expected Pete to make a record of the dispersal. He hoped there would still be time to make it to the shelf of the first years and retrieve whatever Magda had hidden there.

§

The stacks were dark, but Pete did not bother with a light. The shelf of the first years was easy enough to find without looking: it was the only one empty.

He ran his hands over the smooth metal surface, then crouched down, feeling around behind the shelf with one awkward, outstretched arm. There was only open space. He wondered if he had, after all, put too much stock in the words of an old, dying woman.

Then, just as he was standing, giving up, something brushed the tips of his fingers. Something hard, with the texture of rough-spun cloth. He leaned his shoulder into the shelf, extending his arm until the muscles burned, and closed his hand around the item. A book.

Back in the lift, on the way to the McAllister-Xo and the ceremony, he brushed dust off the cover and read the title, embossed in the spine: *The Book of the Ship.*

He had expected something grander from the way the book was hidden, and Magda's cryptic promises. He flipped to a random page, hoping it would make the book's purpose clear. It was in one of the old languages: "...extended isolation studies, which have shown the feasibility of interplanetary travel, were first carried out..." Other pages were filled with similar stuff. Exciting as it was from an archival point of view—it was clearly very old—how could any of it be important to him in the days to come?

Perhaps he was misunderstanding the text, he thought. He had never mastered the old languages as Magda had. But he remembered her words as she lay dying. *How can you record if you do not listen?*

The same must be true of reading, of observation in general. He would have to take the time to decipher it, but time was something he did not have—he would have to wait until the dispersal had begun.

§

McCallister-Xo and a half-dozen officers were crammed into the control room with Pete, the captain going through the schedule one last time before the live broadcast began.

"First Officer Seong, you will say the words to set us on our way. I will then inform the ship about the dispersal order, and the dangers that may await them on the planet."

He had rehearsed these briefly already, his voice terse as he rattled off the items of a list apparently long memorized. The possibility of indigenous flora and fauna, dangerous or benign. Likely meteorological phenomena, dangerous or benign. How to handle riots from the people of Bottom, who were unused to change.

"We touched down three hours ago, ahead of schedule," the captain concluded. "All systems show a planet which matches the specifications from the few remaining scientific records of the first people. Oxygen content and purity is similar to Earth's and the ship's, and our exterior sensors show pressure well within comfort range."

Not for the first time, Pete marvelled at the shipbuilding genius of the first people. He had felt nothing whatsoever during the landing: the ship was silent and still as before. His regret for their missing records intensified, but at least he had the book.

The ceremony made up little more than a scant few words directed at the present, not the future. Vague and visionary things Pete did not bother to remember—the first moments of the dispersal would be infinitely more important, and anyway an officer with a vid crew was transmitting it all live to the entire ship.

They filed into the airlock, thick with the dry smell of centuries of stale emptiness. Pete, at the front of the crowd with the captain, watched the dull steel of the outer door. He wished the first people had put in windows—the scenes from the vid display had done little to whet his appetite for the new world. Yet, as the door hissed open, he could not help closing his eyes tight, preparing poetic turns of phrase to use later when he wrote the events of this day, their first on the planet, the fruition of all their long labors.

But there was a black void beyond the ship when he did look, the only light a dim yellow which spilled from the airlock and illuminated little save a narrow, steel ledge jutting up against the ship. The vid-screen had shown hills, rock-strewn but wide and gentle. There was a sudden surge as the officers at the back tried to push forward out into the planet. Pete stumbled back, jostling against the press of bodies. He felt more than saw the newly empty space beside him—McCallister-Xo had fallen over the side of the ledge. His hoarse yells echoed down and away, punctuated in jerking thuds until at last all was silent.

That silenced them all, and one of the officers took out a maintenance flash-light. The stark white beam pulled fragments of horror out of the dark: bloody streaks left by the captain's fall on the side of the ship; the hull stretching endlessly down, juxtaposed not against some outcropping of rock or grass but hard, slick steel. Dust and mildewed greens.

Across the ledge was a vast platform, similar in design to the ship itself. The far wall was rough stone and stretched up into darkness beyond the range of their vision; set into it were two massive steel doors, the words *May God forgive us what we have done* scrawled rust-colored and huge above them in one of the ancient Earth languages. Pete translated for the others, his mind numb.

Captainless and bewildered—were they still on Earth? How? And why?—they wandered the platform in disarray, all thoughts of their grand journey's fated destination fallen away into the dark. Three of the officers joined McCallister-Xo, walking slow, deliberate steps off the ledge, their descent all the more harrowing for its silence. Pete and the others heard only soft thuds and scratches as they tumbled off the hull of the ship they had served.

At last Pete remembered the book, Magda's dying words. She had known—all the archivists had. His head felt loose on his shoulders as he staggered back to the airlock to read by its light.

§

It took a team of six rugged Bottom laborers several hours to shift the doors at the cavern's edge. While they worked, other teams walked its interior, measuring and probing, trying to find some sort of explanation.

Pete read.

The book turned out to hold two separate texts, joined who knew when. The first, older text was the shorter of the two, and so despite the difficulty of its language, Pete tackled it first. It was set on official looking paper and dated in the old style, which had not been used as far as Pete was aware since the second or third generation.

This was the portion of the book he had turned to when he first found it. The terminology seemed wilfully obscure at points, and even when the words were clear the grammar was strange to him, but eventually Pete determined that it was a study on simulated space travel, commissioned by some long-ago Earth government.

He had struggled through half of it before the team breached the door, revealing empty, winding caves which branched and joined in maze-like arrays. The ship's crew abandoned their search of the cavern where the ship sat and spread outward. It was dispersal of a sort, but tethered and impermanent, a ranging into the caves which always returned to the bulk of the ship.

They found none of the promised meadows, no life of any sort save mildew and fungi. There were streams, little trickling spots of damp which were clear and cool as promises on their tongue, filtered by the endless rock. The water tasted bitter in the dankness of their underground prison.

The teams were always careful to mark the way back to the ship, placing fluorescent strips from long-term storage on the walls or floors of the caves. But even so, some did not return. Other teams would come across markings which simply stopped, with no sign of life nearby and nobody to answer their calls.

When he was not ranging, Pete read the book. By now it was clear the ship had never left Earth, although the reason for this eluded them all. Pete skipped the rest of the first text and moved to the second, which was actually harder to read despite its language being more recognizably his own. It was technical in nature, describing systems the ship used to simulate space travel. Even though he didn't understand most of what it said, Pete continued to read.

Then one day Pete's team found the wall. It was at the end of a long passage which wound inexorably upwards, and it was made of brick. Pete watched, glad he had been there when it happened, as two Bottom men scrabbled at the caulking, hammered at the bricks with stalagmites they ripped from the cave floor, breaking down the dirt and rocks and scree beyond with equal fervor. He made no move to participate, caught up in fantasies of what they would find on the other side and readying what he would say when they returned to the ship.

All they found was ruin and stagnation, silence and death—an ash-choked swathe of land which stretched away beyond their new-made exit in the brick. Clouds of the dust blew past what must have once been a town, billowing out grey plumes from shattered buildings and tugging formless bundles of stuff.

The two men who had torn down the wall walked off into the dust, searching for life, supplies, or signs of what had happened. After an hour or two, with weak sunlight ribboning down, the other members of the party went, too. Pete stayed: he would report back to the ship, he told them.

And so he watched and waited until the sun died a fiery red and the cold of evening set in. In the dim emptiness, he seemed to hear sounds in the distance, low sinuous hissings from the depths of history. The clouds of ash seemed to hide shadowy figures, but when they swirled away revealed only a shattered building, a rusting, useless metal hulk, or nothing at all. He shuddered and returned to the ship's resting place, alone.

When he arrived, they questioned him. Why had he returned alone? Where was his team? What of the time they had spent out in the caves? He only shook his head, filled with grief, and passed them by.

§

"The secrets of the ship?"

"Yes, Captain Seong. Nothing of why we're here, who the first people were or what purpose they hoped to achieve. But all the secrets of the ship's systems, everything we need to prolong the illusion."

"And we should do this even though you found a way out?"

"Just come with me, Captain. Come with me and you will understand. Hope, purpose, meaning, happiness of a sort—what we had in the years before was infinitely, unthinkably better than what awaits us without."

§

Captain Seong took little convincing once he had seen the desolation which lay beyond the caves. He and Pete took a few steps out down the hillside until the ash began to choke them, cold acrid fingers down their throats. They heard the sounds, saw things that were not there. Captain Seong swore he felt something brush his shoulder, though Pete was only a few feet away and saw nothing but ash. They turned back lest they lose sight of the entrance: Earth held nothing for them, and if it did they were terrified of it.

Inside the cave mouth, the other officers waited. At a shake of the head from Captain Seong, they began to rebuild the wall, working in silence. On the walk back to the ship, they tore up the guide-strips. Over the next few days, as Bottom teams tore up the other strips, removing all signs which pointed to their ship, Pete and the officers between them got the ship's systems rebooted.

When all was complete, they sealed the cavern doors and closed off the ship once more. The ship's journey was a lie, but it was one with promise—promise they would pass on to later generations.

§

Pete finished transcribing the last of the records from the dispersal and sat back, cracking his knuckles. It was only right, he thought, that he complete his duty as Archivist before betraying it. His generation would keep few records, and preserve none of them.

He lifted the paper from the desk and set it in the book he held, behind the two older sets of papers, then walked with it from the stacks, nodding to the two officers who stood at the ready with vid-cams and torches.

At the door, he stopped to watch. One last time, one last event: the fire-swept cleansing of all they had recorded, all their history and lore. He felt no regret at the destruction of their legends and dreams, their pasts and their futures.

After a while, he set the book firmly under his arm, turned on his heel, and walked to the express lift and the rich, verdant hills of Bottom. Behind him, the tongues of flame licked over everything but the shelf of the first years, already long since empty.

Thanks for reading!

Thanks for reading. If you enjoyed this book, please consider leaving an honest review on your favorite store's website.

§

About the Editors

Kelly A. Harmon is an award-winning journalist and author, and a member of Science Fiction & Fantasy Writers of America. She is a former newspaper reporter and editor, and now edits for Pole to Pole Publishing, a small Baltimore publisher.

A Baltimore native, Ms. Harmon writes the *Charm City Darkness* series, which includes the novels: Stoned in Charm City, A Favor for a Fiend, A Blue Collar Proposition, and In the Eye of the Beholder. A stand-alone novel, Blood Soup, was winner of the Fantasy Gazetteers Award. Her short fiction has been nominated for a Pushcart Award and short-listed for the Aeon. It can be found in The Pale Leaves and Gallery of Curiosities magazines, Beyond Steampunk, Occult Detective Quarterly, The Best Indie Speculative Fiction Volume 1, and more.

She is co-editor with Vonnie Winslow Crist of Pole Publishing's first three Dark Stories anthologies: *Hides the Dark Tower, In a Cat's Eye, and Dark Luminous Wings, and* Pole to Pole's first four anthologies in the Re-Imagined series: Re-Launch, Re-Quest, Re-Terrify, and Re-Enchant.

Visit her website at http://kellyaharmon.com, or connect with her on Facebook.

Vonnie Winslow Crist, MS Professional Writing, has had a life-long interest in reading, writing, art, science fiction, fairy-tales, folklore, and legends. An award-winning author and illustrator, she is a member of the Science Fiction & Fantasy Writers of America, Society of Children's Book Writers & Illustrators, and Pen Women.

Her books include The Enchanted Dagger, Murder on Marawa Prime, Owl Light, The Greener Forest, and Leprechaun Cake & Other Tales. Her speculative stories can be found in Chilling Ghost Short Stories, Faerie Magazine, Killing It Softly 2, Chaos of Hard Clay, Fae Wings & Hidden Things, Amazing Stories, Cast of Wonders, and elsewhere.

Editor of The Gunpowder Review, Ms. Crist co-edited with Kelly A. Harmon Pole to Pole Publishing's first three Dark Stories anthologies: Hides the Dark Tower, In a Cat's Eye, and Dark Luminous Wings, along with the first four anthologies of Pole to Pole Publishing's Re-Imagined series: Re-Launch, Re-Quest, Re-Terrify, and Re-Enchant. For more information, visit her website: http://vonniewinslowcrist.com/, blog: http://vonniewinslowcrist.wordpress.com, Fb page: http://facebook.com/WriterVonnieWinslowCrist, or http://twitter.com/VonnieWCrist

§

Other Books in the Re-Imagined Series:

Coming Soon!

Re-Quest
Dark Fantasy Stories about Magic and the Fae

With Stories by: Jennifer Rachel Baumer, James Dorr, Jeremy Zimmerman, Jonathan Shipley, Lillian Csernica, Gregory L. Norris, Kelly A. Harmon, Robert E. Howard, Douglas Smith, Chris Kuriata, CB Droege, Christine Lucas, Dale Glaser, Doug C. Souza, Dennis Mombauer, and Bradley Sinor.

Read More: http://poletopolepublishing.com/books/re-quest/

Coming Soon!

Re-Terrify
Horrifying Stories of Monsters and More

With Stories by: Nancy Springer, Douglas Smith, James Dorr, Eric Choi, Darrell Schweitzer, Steve Southard, Gregory Norris, Gustavo Bondoni, Jonathan Shipley, Vonnie Winslow Crist, Meriah Crawford, Nicole Kurtz, Phillip Chamberlain, Kelly A. Harmon, Lisa Lepovetsky, Winston Marks, Geoff Gander, and David M. Hoenig.

Read More: http://poletopolepublishing.com/books/re-terrify/

Coming Soon!

Re-Enchant
Dark Fantasy Stories of Magic and Fae

With stories by: Nancy Springer, James Dorr, Darrell Schweitzer, Christine Lucas, Gregory Norris, Alma Alexander, Jude-Marie Green, Vonnie Winslow Crist, Don Webb, Robert Stephenson, Ace Jordyn, E. E. King, Kelly A. Harmon, Mattie Brahen and April Steenburgh.

Read More: http://poletopolepublishing.com/books/re-enchant/

www.ingramcontent.com/pod-product-compliance
Lightning Source LLC
Chambersburg PA
CBHW030304200626
46816CB00002BA/757